A Fierce Wind

This is a work of fiction. Names, characters, places and incidents either are the product of the author's imagination or are used fictitiously. Any resemblance to actual events, locales, business establishments or persons, living or dead, is coincidental.

A FIERCE WIND
Copyright © 2018 Regan Walker

Paperback ISBN: 978-0-9976567-5-6
Print Edition

Praise For Regan Walker's Work

"Ms. Walker has the rare ability to make you forget you are reading a book. The characters become real, the modern world fades away, and all that is left is the intrigue, drama, and romance."

—*Straight from the Library*

"The writing is excellent, the research impeccable, and the love story is epic. You can't ask for more than that."

—*The Book Review*

"Regan Walker is a master of her craft. Her novels instantly draw you in, keep you reading and leave you with a smile on your face."

—*Good Friends, Good Books*

"An example of 'how to' in good story building... a multilayered novel adding depth and yearning."

—*InD'Tale Magazine*

"Spellbinding and Expertly Crafted... The path to true love is never easy, yet Regan Walker leads the reader to an entertaining, realistic and worthy HEA. Walker's characters are complex and well-rounded and, in her hands, real historical figures merge seamlessly with those from her imagination."

—*A Reader's Review*

"Walker stuns with her gift for storytelling, magically entwining historic fact and fiction to create a thought-provoking, sensual romance, one that will stay with you."

—*Chicks, Rogues & Scandals*

"Walker's detailed historical research enhances the time and place of the story without losing sight of what is essential to a romance: chemistry between the leads and hope for the future."

—*Publisher's Weekly*

"An enthralling story."

—*RT Book Reviews*

Acknowledgements

This story, like *Echo in the Wind*, is sprinkled with French and, for its accuracy, I must thank Liette Bougie, my beta reader in Québec whose French, I understand, would be much like that spoken in France at the time of my story. Liette also makes many other valuable suggestions.

I am also indebted to my friend Chari Wessel, a doctor of veterinary medicine who, for many years, was the gunner on the schooner *Californian*, a reproduction ship of the period berthed in San Diego. Chari is an amateur historian, well versed in Georgian era ships and sailing. She makes sure my ship terminology and scenes are correct. Her judgments are always helpful.

Dedication

In memory of the Chouans and the Vendéens who fought for
their king and their faith and for the men, women and children
among them who were hounded, killed, guillotined and
massacred by the Republic of France. May they never
be forgotten.

Characters of Note

(Both real and fictional)

Zoé Ariane Donet, niece to Jean Donet
Frederick West, brother of the Earl of Torrington

On the Isle of Guernsey:
Jean Donet, comte de Saintonge, captain of *la Reine Noire*
Joanna, comtesse de Saintonge, Jean Donet's wife and sister to the Earl of Torrington
Madame de Montconseil, princesse d'Hénin
Éloise, maidservant to Madame de Montconseil
Pierre Bouchet, physician

On *la Reine Noire*:
Émile Bequel, quartermaster
Gabriel Chastain, seaman, formerly Donet's cabin boy

On Jersey:
Captain Philippe d'Auvergne, Senior Officer of Gunboats and British Spymaster

In the Channel and the Atlantic:
Villaret de Joyeuse, French captain of the *Trajan* and, later, Rear Admiral and Commander of the Brest Fleet
Admiral Lord Howe, British Commander of the Channel Fleet

At The Harrows in West Sussex:
Richard, Earl of Torrington, brother to Freddie and Joanna
Anne, Countess of Torrington
William Pitt the Younger, the Prime Minister
Zack and Polly Barlow, friends of Joanna and Freddie

In Normandy, Brittany and Maine:
Erwan, Vendéen fighter
Georges Cadoudal, Chouan chief
Isabeau le Gallou, Breton girl and her brother, Giles
Aimé Picquet, chevalier du Boisguy, general of the Chouans in Fougères
Jean Cottereau, known as Jean Chouan, leader of the Chouans in Maine
Victorine du Rocher du Quengo, a Chouan known as Captain Victor
General Antoine Rossignol, Commander in Chief, the Army of the Coast of Brest

In Paris:
Robespierre, architect of the Terror and leader of the Committee of Public Safety
Flèche, Donet's butler and former gunner aboard *la Reine Noire*
Gaspar, former carpenter aboard *la Reine Noire*
Pascal ("Pax"), boy in the Conciergerie
François de Dordogne, a lawyer

It was the season of Light, it was the season of Darkness, it was the spring of hope, it was the winter of despair.

—Charles Dickens, *A Tale of Two Cities*

Prologue

A light rain fell on the unfolding spectacle, the heavens mocking the gaiety of the occasion that mingled the revolution's victors with the vanquished.

Frederick West shifted his gaze from the thronging crowds to the girl standing beside him, suddenly seized with a desire to protect her from the storm about to unleash its fury on France. She stared straight ahead, her eyes fixed on the long rows of soldiers in blue and white uniforms standing at attention in the center of the arena.

It seemed like only yesterday he was seventeen and giving the precocious ten-year-old French girl a tour of his family's estate in West Sussex. She had insisted on riding their most spirited mare, her reckless streak manifesting itself even then.

At the time, the little minx had fascinated him. Eventually, fascination had turned into attraction. Now, at sixteen, Zoé Ariane Donet promised great beauty, the flower of French womanhood about to bloom.

Long hair the color of dark mahogany framed her delicate features. Her ivory skin reminded him of a painting of Venus he had once seen in Paris. Dove gray eyes spoke of her youthful innocence. Soon, her slim body, today attired in the tricolors of

1

revolutionary France, would possess a woman's curves.

"Freddie, look at all the banners! Aren't you glad we came? *C'est magnifique, non?*" She spoke from beneath her plumed hat never turning her attention from the pageantry before her.

"Glad we came? I cannot say that, Pigeon, but I grant you, 'tis certainly a grand display."

She huffed in frustration. "Somewhere on the field with all those soldiers is my dear Louis-Pierre, but I cannot see him."

Ah yes, the French soldier she was so taken with. The latest of her girlish infatuations. Freddie took comfort in the knowledge that there would be others, none more significant than the last. He need not worry about her innocence, not yet anyway. Not many men would dally with the niece of the infamous Jean Donet, not even the naïve Louis-Pierre.

Donet, a man trusted by both commoners and king, had once been a pirate, then a privateer and, when Freddie first met him, a smuggler. He was ruthless when he needed to be and good with a blade. Six years ago, with the murder of her father and grandfather, Zoé had become his ward.

From where Freddie stood in the grandstands with the Donets, he had an excellent view of the other end of the field and the altar raised several stories into the air. Thousands had flocked to the *Champ de Mars*, their murmurs echoing in waves around the great arena as excitement rose for the celebration about to begin.

Some of the men sported *le bonnet rouge*, the red cap signifying liberty to the revolutionaries. Given the brutal way France's revolution had begun the year before with the storming of the Bastille, Freddie thought the caps might as well signify blood. It was no surprise to him a revolution led by lawyers would have a cruel beginning.

Today's grand show struck him as a ruse. All of Europe was holding its breath, for behind the ruse lurked a seething mass of discontent.

"To what end do you suppose we gather here, Pigeon?"

"Don't be silly, Freddie," said Zoé, shooting him a disapproving look. The stubborn set of her jaw spoke of the defiance he knew lay just below the surface. "You know very well the reason for this *fête*. France will no longer be governed by the whims of the king but by a written constitution." Raising her chin, she added, "*Comme l'Amérique.*"

Freddie bit back the retort forming on his lips. He would allow Zoé the joy of the celebration. She would face reality soon enough. As for him, he did not consider France's new constitution, forced on the French king and already the subject of controversy, to be at all like America's. Two days before, the new *Assemblée nationale* had approved a Civil Constitution of the Clergy, condemned by the Pope for requiring priests to swear allegiance to the state in the strongest of terms.

Today's celebration had little substance beneath the pomp. And Freddie was certain there would be much pomp. First the ceremonies, then oaths and speeches and finally, a grand feast where bread would be plentiful and fireworks would fill the night sky.

The French had a penchant for the spectacular.

"Oh, there he is!" exclaimed Zoé, waving to a soldier who doubtless could not see her in the grandstand. "Isn't he handsome?" A sigh escaped her perfect rosebud lips. "So brave, so gallant..."

Freddie would never have described Louis-Pierre as gallant but perhaps to a girl of sixteen, the sparkling new uniform of the Blues, the name given to the republican soldiers, bestowed upon Louis-Pierre a certain *sang-froid*.

Wishing to hear no more of Zoé's current love interest, Freddie turned his attention to her uncle. Jean Donet, comte de Saintonge, watched the pageantry with worried eyes, occasionally darting glances at the king and his brother, the comte de Provence, whose strained expressions belied their seeming acceptance of the new order of things.

3

On the other side of Donet stood Freddie's eldest sister, Joanna, who had married the comte six years ago. Freddie had accompanied the Donets to their château set amidst the cognac-producing vineyards in Saintonge and to their homes in Lorient and Paris. But it was the spymasters in London who decided he should work alongside Donet in his merchant shipping business. In the wake of the revolution, Donet moved his family and his business to the Isle of Guernsey, an English Crown dependency just off the coast of Normandy.

Donet didn't trust the lawyers either.

At twenty-three, Freddie had gone from an English earl's younger brother to a man of merchant ships and the sea.

And a spy for the British Crown.

At the urging of the French king, Donet had traveled to Paris for this *Fête de la Fédération*. The celebration was the brainchild of Talleyrand, Bishop of Autun. The least reputable of France's bishops and no friend of the clergy, he had supported the measure that nationalized the Church.

Freddie agreed with Zoé on one point, that the event was supposed to draw all levels of French society together—the clergy, the nobility and everyone else—to swear allegiance to the new constitution and to celebrate, in appearance at least, national unity. But, to Freddie's mind, the veneer of unity was a bit thin, like brawling children forced to be friends. Only these were not children and they would never be friends.

The attack on the Bastille had only begun the rip in France's society. A month ago, the *Assemblée* had abolished all titles, liveries and orders of knighthood, destroying the symbols of the *Ancien Régime*, a gesture most nobles received with disdain. Even the address of "Monsieur" was no longer permitted. Not that it bothered Donet, who had never expected to have a title and didn't much want one. But, like Freddie, the former pirate was not unmindful of the effect of such sweeping changes.

A fierce wind had swept France to the end of an era, but did this celebration mark the beginning of something better?

As though answering his unspoken question, cannons at the other end of the field boomed, sending smoke billowing into the air.

Exuberant cheers rose from the crowd.

The rain stopped as if on cue.

Talleyrand, surrounded by hundreds of priests, doubtless ones who had accepted their new roles, mounted the podium above the cannons to say mass.

The liturgy was mercifully short. As it ended, into the arena, on a splendid white horse, rode Lafayette, chief of the new National Guard, hero of the American Revolution and confidant of the king.

The crowd thundered its approval. At Freddie's side, caught up in the fervor, Zoé clasped her hands to her bosom.

Lafayette dismounted and climbed the steps to bow before the king. Then he turned to address the massive crowd. In a loud voice, he proclaimed, "We swear to always remain faithful to the nation, to the law and to the king, to uphold by all our power the constitution decreed by *l'Assemblée nationale...*"

The people erupted in loud applause.

Watching Lafayette's face, Freddie was inclined to think the marquis believed his own words. Freddie exchanged a glance with Donet that spoke loudly of their shared doubt as to where such oaths would lead.

When the cheers died down, King Louis rose from his chair in the royal box not far from where Freddie stood. "I, King of the French, swear to maintain the constitution decreed by *l'Assemblée nationale* and accepted by me."

An awkward silence hung in the air, followed by a few random displays of clapping.

The hairs on the back of Freddie's neck prickled. The veneer of unity had cracked.

Zoé pressed her fingers to her mouth and looked from the

king to the silent crowd.

Marie Antoinette suddenly lifted her son, the dauphin, in her arms. "Look, my son, they're united, just like me, with the same sentiments!"

The people rose to their feet and applauded enthusiastically.

Zoé beamed her pleasure and joined in.

Freddie fought the urge to dampen her enthusiasm, but refrained. It would do no good. For the moment, she had become a supporter of the revolution. Instead, he leaned toward Donet. "King Louis may have pledged his oath to the new constitution and the queen may have joined him, but after the humiliation they have suffered and their virtual imprisonment in the Tuileries Palace, I doubt they are as agreeable as they appear."

Donet's ebony brows drew together above his intense black eyes. "The king's own brother, the comte d'Artois, left France days after the Bastille fell, like a rat quitting a sinking ship. I cannot help but think Louis should have gone with him. Already the nobles clamor to book passage on my ships to carry them away from what they fear is coming."

Freddie shifted his gaze to Zoé, comforted in the knowledge that when the storm broke, she would be safe on Guernsey.

Chapter 1

The port of La Rochelle on the west coast of France four years later, January 1794

One look at the messenger's ashen face and Zoé's heart sank. The news from the Vendée, the region between La Rochelle and Brittany, must be bad. She shrank away from the boy as he approached, not wanting to hear what he had to say.

He pressed toward her and the din of the tavern faded away as she fixed her eyes on his young face. Removing his hat, he said, *"Monsieur Henri est mort, mademoiselle. Je suis désolé."*

Dead? She shook her head, her mind shouting *Non!* It could not be true, but the tragic look on the messenger's face forced the words into her thoughts. Tears filled her eyes and spilled onto her cheeks as she thought of the golden warrior who was her whole world.

At twenty-one, Henri du Vergier, comte de la Rochejaquelein, had become the youngest general of the Vendéen royalist armies fighting against the revolutionary government in Paris. And now he was gone.

Zoé had never considered the possibility one so full of life, the bravest of men, could die. "How? Where?"

The boy's forehead furrowed over his light blue eyes forming an angry frown. "Near Nuaillé, mademoiselle. Shot in the head by a republican pig who feigned surrender."

Nuaillé, less than a hundred miles north. "Then he never made it back from Granville to the Vendée?"

The boy shook his head. *"Non."*

She could not bear to learn Henri had died in agony. "Did he suffer?"

The messenger crushed his hat in his hands, his face stricken yet sincere. She knew he would tell her the truth. "He lived but a short while. His last words were for you, mademoiselle."

Would his last words speak of his love, a declaration she could treasure always?

The boy raised his chin, the tavern's lanterns reflecting the pride on his face. "Monsieur Henri said, 'If I die, tell Zoé to avenge me!'"

Her heart plummeted and she grabbed on to a table to keep from slipping to her knees. She had wanted to hear an avowal of love that would give life to the feelings she had hoped he harbored for her, but it was not to be. In Henri's last words, she recognized his order to his followers. Famous among the soldiers who had chosen him to lead the Vendéen army was his command, "If I advance, follow me! If I retreat, kill me! If I die, avenge me!"

Henri lived for his faith and his king, the words *"Dieu et le Roi"*, God and the King, embroidered on the *Sacré-Cœur*, the sacred heart patch he wore on his chest. Like the other Vendéen officers, his hat boldly displayed the white cockade of the Bourbons. Symbols of the Catholic and Royal Army of which he was a part. But surely he had loved her no matter his call for revenge. At the end it had been her name on his lips.

Zoé brushed the tears from her cheeks, steeling herself for the task ahead. Silently, she vowed she would not fail him. Henri would have his revenge, not just from his soldiers, who would fight on until victory was theirs, but she, too, would do what she could. France must be freed from the tyranny of men like

Maximilien de Robespierre, the lawyer who had a taste for blood, and Georges Danton, yet another lawyer on the Committee of Public Safety that ruled France. Danton, she recalled, had brazenly called for the king's death.

She remembered the murdered king and queen, their daughter confined to the Temple Prison and their nine-year-old son, Louis-Charles, the dauphin the royalists had named Louis XVII. The revolutionaries kept him in a cage in Paris where he suffered horrible treatment.

Could she do what Charlotte Corday had done the year before? The woman from Normandy, a few years older than Zoé, had slain Jean-Paul Marat, the radical journalist who had wanted more heads to roll. For her service to France, Corday had been guillotined.

Zoé shuddered. Surely there was another way she could serve the royalist cause, something other than taking up musket and sword.

A thought occurred, a way she could help. She could venture into the streets and villages to rescue those destined for the guillotine and work with her uncle to ferry the émigrés to freedom.

"*Pour Dieu et le Roi*" would be her motto, too. She would give herself to the royalist cause until the day a Bourbon king again sat on the throne of France and the people could worship freely.

The port of Granville, Normandy, February 1794

Zoé crept along the stone wall of the buildings facing the quay, heading for the place she would meet Erwan, one of the Vendéen fighters remaining in Normandy after the daring assault in Granville had ended in a terrible defeat.

Over the protests of the crew who had rowed her ashore, she had entered Granville alone, knowing the seamen's presence would only draw the attention of the republican soldiers in control of the town.

The port had become a place of secret departure for émigrés fleeing Robespierre's Terror, in which the constitution had been suspended and anyone accused of having less than patriotic fervor for the revolution faced the guillotine. No one was safe, least of all a woman descended from the comtes de Saintonge with an aristocratic lilt to her voice. Zoé had practiced for many hours to be able to blend with the peasants.

Heavy footsteps sounded on the cobblestones behind her. Seized with fear she would be stopped and questioned, Zoé shrank into the shadows, thanking the saints for the fog shrouding Granville this night.

With her heart pounding in her chest and hoping to remain unseen, she pressed against the stone wall, feeling the damp cold through her cloak. A veil of thick mist flowed over her, blurring her image.

A huge man with thick side whiskers and a revolutionary's red cap passed in front of her, swinging a lantern as he weaved his way down the street, sated with drink. In a slurred voice, he sang the last lines of the song penned by the poet Lebrun the year before, commemorating the execution of Louis XVI.

If some want a master,
In a world from King to king
Let them beg for shackles
Unworthy to be called Frenchmen!

She had heard the callous ditty before. The oft-repeated lines only increased her loathing of those who sang them.

The man disappeared around the corner. She let out a breath and peered into the fog. *Where is Erwan? And the woman and her children?*

Out of the misty shadows, a voice whispered, "Zoé, *est-ce toi?*"

Dressed as she was in peasant's clothing, her hair captured under a dark blue cap and her face streaked with dirt, he had reason to ask. "Erwan," she hissed. "You are late! And alone! Where are the ones we are to meet? *La Reine Noire* lies just offshore and the skiff awaits, but 'tis dangerous for it to linger."

"The woman and her children are not far," Erwan whispered, indicating she should follow. His long brown hair, stringy to his shoulders, was lost in the dark shadow beneath his wide-brimmed felt hat. A Breton by birth, he had gone south to the Vendée when the fighting began a year ago. He'd been a loyal follower of Henri de la Rochejaquelein until his death. Then he joined Zoé in her efforts to save those fleeing the Terror. "The two children were fearful and I could not risk them crying out. I have hidden them and their mother a short distance away."

He led her down the darkened streets and stopped in front of a wooden door on which he rapped three times. Slowly, the door opened, allowing a narrow shaft of light to escape. Following him inside, Zoé inhaled a musty smell and glimpsed a sparsely furnished room before seeing a woman, two children and a maidservant huddled in front of a meager fire.

The whites of the mother's eyes, huge in the firelight, shouted her fear.

Zoé had seen the same fear in the eyes of other refugees. "You are Madame de Montconseil, princesse d'Hénin?"

"*Oui*, and these are my two children." She drew the girl and her younger brother close. The boy clutched his mother's skirts, burying his face in the simple brown cloth. The girl stared at Zoé with haunted brown eyes, making her wonder at the things the child had seen. Gesturing to the servant, the mother said, "This is my maidservant, Éloise."

The servant glanced at Zoé before dipping into a proper curtsey. Older than Zoé by several years, the maidservant was attractive even in peasant garb. She had the bluest eyes Zoé had ever seen and her golden hair curled around her face under the plain mobcap to which was attached the obligatory tricolor cockade.

"No need to curtsey, Éloise," she told the maid in the speech of the locals. "As long as we are in France, we must all act as *citoyens* of the Republic, *oui*?"

Madame de Montconseil, her face lined with care, nodded. "We are so grateful."

Zoé gave the little group a smile meant to lift their faltering spirits. "All will be well." She was gratified they wore peasants' clothing, even the princesse. Erwan had done his job well.

"We must go," he urged, his dark eyes intense, his expression anxious.

"I don't like it," hissed Freddie as he joined the quartermaster, standing at the rail of *la Reine Noire*. "When did Zoé leave?" Freddie stared into the heavy mist toward the tavern lights glowing from the quay in an eerie manner. He had gone to his cabin for only a moment to review dispatches from his contact on Jersey. It rankled that Zoé had left the ship without a word.

Émile Bequel shrugged his powerful shoulders beneath his leather coat. His dark eyes were barely visible under his heavy brows and the russet color of his hair hard to discern in the dim light. "The mademoiselle took a skiff to shore a short while ago. I await her return."

When Donet was away, his right-hand-man, Bequel, took temporary command of the ship. The years he had served alongside Donet were etched deep in his face, the bond between the two men forged in the fires of adversity. It was he who had slid the brig-sloop into the foggy Granville harbor to hide among the other ships, as stealthily as a fox slipping in among sleeping chickens.

The only light allowed on deck glowed red from the port

lantern, serving as a guide for the rescue party's return to the ship.

Freddie's frown deepened as a feeling of foreboding gripped him.

Bequel shot him an indulgent look. "Worry not, *l'Anglais*. Some of my best men are with her."

"She was supposed to wait for me. Why did you let her go?"

Émile chuckled under his breath in the manner of a man in his fiftieth year who had seen much. "One does not tell Mademoiselle Donet to wait when she is setting forth to save those the Republic has marked for death. She has the stubborn will of *le capitaine, non?* The rescue of innocents has been her *raison d'être* since the death of de la Rochejaquelein."

At the name, Freddie let out an exasperated sigh. Zoé still carried a torch for the fallen hero of the royalist army, much to Freddie's chagrin. He told himself he was merely concerned for her safety, dismayed at the personal risks she was taking. Inspired by the memory of her martyred hero, she repeatedly defied the revolution's leaders to steal away their victims. At a deeper level, he had to admit to himself he was jealous. *Jealous of a dead man!* It was insane. He couldn't help wishing that lovely Zoé might be as enchanted by the living man beside her as she was by the fantasy of a man gone from her life forever.

In his mind, Freddie heard again her admonishment earlier that day. "Why do you worry so?" she had asked, her beautifully shaped brows drawn together. "How will this night be any different from the other nights when my friends and I have helped those seeking to escape the guillotine?"

If it weren't for the unsettled feeling in his gut, he would have conceded her point. But because of the foreboding, he had insisted on going with her. "If you must venture into Granville tonight, I will go, too."

"*Très bien*," she replied with a flick of her wrist, "come if you must. But do not get in the way and remember to don the clothes of a *citoyen*. Speak only French and be ready to leave the ship with

13

me. The streets grow more dangerous and I dare not tarry."

He hated wearing the tricolor cockade and the shabby trousers of the *sans-culottes*, the revolutionaries who scorned the breeches worn by the nobility, merchants and lawyers. He found it ironic that the staunchest of the revolutionaries had their own uniform, wearing ill-fitting trousers; some even striped red and white in a ridiculous manner. "I hate what the clothing stands for."

"*Oui*, I know. But since the Vendéens' defeat, the republican army controls Granville. If you are going ashore, you must look the part. Your French is quite good for an Englishman but your disguise must also convince."

"Very well," he had told her. "I will do as you say." He rarely went to such lengths when on his own missions, but she knew none of that. "How many émigrés will you be meeting tonight?"

"At least three, possibly four. Madame de Montconseil, princesse d'Hénin, a guillotine widow and former lady-in-waiting to the dead queen, will bring her two children. There was also mention of a maidservant."

"An illustrious refugee."

"Aye. And there's no guessing when *Oncle* Jean might return."

Donet had gone to Paris to rescue two Ursuline nuns from Saint-Denis where they had once led a convent school. Not content with beheading royalty and aristocrats, the leaders of the revolution had become more virulent in their view of the Church, vowing to destroy it. Houses of worship, cloisters and monasteries were gutted and burned, their lands seized. Priests and nuns were attacked, imprisoned and slain.

The two nuns Donet meant to save had been in hiding since the September Massacres two years before when more than a thousand prisoners, including two hundred priests, had been brutally slain by an angry mob. Word had reached Donet on Guernsey that some Ursulines had been sent to the guillotine and he wanted to make sure these two would not face that same fate.

Freddie had considered the plans to retrieve the refugees tonight. "With you, the women and the men to row, the skiff will be nearly full."

Zoé had given him an angelic smile. "*Oui*, the boat will be crowded, but if I am successful, four souls will be saved." He was dismayed at how blithely she dismissed so great a danger. It had made him more determined to accompany her.

The sound of the sails flapping gently as the ship bobbed in the still water drew Freddie back to the present. The damp air carried a chill. He pressed his tricorne down on his head and drew his arms around him, wondering how long he would be venturing into Granville's cold nights. *How long could the Terror continue?*

What had begun as a means to strike fear in the hearts of France's enemies soon became a hunt for anyone accused of disloyalty. Death carts rolled incessantly through the streets on their way to the guillotines erected in every major town. For some revolutionaries, the guillotine was too slow. Hundreds of priests and nuns had been cast into the Loire and drowned. Others had been shot.

After the Vendéens had fled south, retreating back to their own lands, the Committee of Public Safety, now effectively ruling France, had sent General Turreau into the Vendée with orders to "leave nobody and nothing alive".

Turreau's *colonnes infernales*, the "infernal columns", were still crisscrossing the Vendée, killing thousands of men, women and children and burning all they encountered.

With reports of such horrors reaching him each day, Freddie despaired of the Terror ending anytime soon.

Bequel turned to face the crew on deck, interrupting Freddie's thoughts. "Éric, Bastien! Rig a cable to the bow. Stand by to pass it off to the skiff when it arrives. *Silencieusement, c'est entendu?*"

The crew scrambled to comply with the quartermaster's order, minding the command to do so without making a sound.

Turning back to Freddie, Bequel said, "In this fog, ye understand, we do not exist. The skiff will become our little donkey and tow us out of the harbor and into the Channel."

Looking toward shore, Freddie brooded into the fog. He hoped the continued disquiet that roiled his stomach did not mean the woman he vowed to protect with his life, the woman he hoped to one day make his wife, was facing imminent danger.

Why had she gone without him?

"Take *citoyenne* Montconseil to the skiff," Zoé instructed Erwan. "I will be along shortly."

Erwan shook his head, about to protest, but then he looked at the children, their frightened faces anxiously gazing up at their mother. He knew as well as Zoé if they traveled to her uncle's apartment together, the sound of so many feet would attract unwanted attention. Alone, she could move undetected, like a wraith, wending her way through the darkened streets, leaving Erwan to take his charges directly to the skiff.

"Go!" she prodded.

He gave her a last concerned look, then ushered the women and children outside into the foggy street.

Zoé waited until the small group silently moved away before setting off in the opposite direction.

She paused before an inconspicuous wooden door on the narrow street that led to the rooms her uncle had secured a few years ago. Located close to the dockside taverns and supervised by a fierce landlady with royalist sympathies, the location served their purposes well.

Zoé hoped her uncle had arrived, though he would be earlier than expected if he had. Outside the apartment, she looked for the signal that would tell her he was there. Relief flooded her when she glimpsed the small piece of blue ribbon wedged between two stones.

She retrieved the ribbon, knocked twice and the door opened. She slipped in like a shadow to be greeted by her uncle, sword in hand. He was clothed all in black, save for the tricolor cockade pinned to his tricorne.

With a look of recognition, he returned his sword to its sheath and lit a candle, adding to the light from the flames flickering in the stone fireplace. The room had a small area for preparing food along with a table and chairs. Their landlady often left food and wine when she knew to expect them. Two cots were set against the opposite wall, sleeping places for her uncle and Gabe, his former cabin boy and now an experienced seaman, who accompanied him on many of his runs. But this one her uncle had made alone.

Casting her a worried look, he chided, "I was beginning to think you had encountered... difficulty." Difficulty meant republican soldiers that patrolled the streets in pairs.

"*Non.* I have just left Erwan. He is taking the ones we met tonight to the skiff. Saints be praised, you are early. Have you recovered the nuns?"

From the back room, the only bedchamber, two women emerged, one older and one younger. Each wore a shawl over her head, hiding any hint of shorn locks that might betray the vows of their cloistered lives. Their worn female clothing mirrored that of the tradeswomen in Granville. No one would have guessed they were nuns, that is, until the older one gave Zoé an assessing look and spoke in a refined speech that belied her feigned lower station.

"M'sieur Donet, she could be your daughter, Claire, when last I saw her."

Zoé had been told there was a resemblance between her cousin, Claire, who lived in England, and her although Claire was ten years older.

"*Oui*, my niece has the Donet look about her." He gave Zoé a slight smile that hinted at his approval. Her father and her uncle were so alike in appearance they had often been mistaken for each other. Both had bold features, coal-black eyes and hair, her uncle's now liberally threaded with silver.

Addressing the nuns, he said, "Allow me to present my niece, Mademoiselle Zoé Donet." Then to Zoé, "These are Sisters Augustin and Angélique, who are very dear to my daughter and to me. Claire was educated in their convent school."

Zoé inclined her head, but did not curtsey. She never curtsied when she wore the clothing of a *citoyenne* of the Republic. Her fine manners she saved for the Isle of Guernsey where Joanna, her uncle's wife, insisted she act the lady.

Suddenly looking impatient, her uncle turned to the nuns. "We must make haste; my ship awaits and, by now, I fear my quartermaster is cursing me under his breath."

They were nearly to the quay when two soldiers in the blue and white uniforms of the republican army stepped out of the fog and into their path.

Her uncle muttered a curse.

Beneath his bicorne, the fat soldier displayed plump red cheeks and a bushy brown mustache. The cold eyes of his companion matched his thin lips, curved into a cruel smile, as his gaze roved over Zoé and the younger nun. "*Eh bien...* what have we here? One man with three women? That seems hardly fair when, as you can see, we servants of the revolution have none."

The soldier with the mustache laughed, one hand on his ponderous belly, the other on his long musket. "Surely you can share, *citoyen.*"

From their leering eyes, Zoé did not put rape past either of them. Rumors abounded of the soldiers' abuse of the local women. The thought of one of these touching her made Zoé's skin crawl.

The younger nun gasped and was stilled by the hand of the older on her shoulder. Zoé stepped in front of them and slid her hand into the small slit in her full skirt to reach the sharp knife strapped to her thigh.

"Ah, *mes amis*," said her uncle, adopting the common speech, "on another occasion, if these were but stray cats, I would be happy to invite you to join my party but, alas, this is *family* business. These are my sisters and my wife, women under my protection."

His tone hinted of velvet laid over steel and the red-cheeked soldier did not fail to notice. The smile faded from his corpulent face as his fingers nervously played with the end of his mustache.

Seeing his companion falter, the thin-lipped one aimed his musket at her uncle. "You will share, as I have said, or reap the consequences, *mon ami*."

If the republican soldier thought to intimidate Jean Donet, he picked the wrong man. Her uncle had a fierce reputation known to many in France.

Zoé was tempted to inform these idiots, who played at being soldiers, they were dealing with the great *capitaine* of *la Reine Noire*, the *Black Queen*, but she held her tongue, knowing her uncle could swiftly deal them a deathblow if he chose.

"*Je ne pense pas*," he said to the soldiers. "Not tonight." Before they realized what was happening, her uncle slipped his knife from the sheath at his wrist and sent the deadly blade hurtling through the air and into the neck of the thin-lipped one. His eyes bulged and he made a gagging sound as he clutched his throat, spurting blood, and dropped to the ground.

Zoé did not even blink. Behind her, Sister Augustin exclaimed, "*Mon Dieu!*"

The rotund soldier began to back away, apparently forgetting he held a musket.

Her uncle drew a pistol from the pocket of his frock coat and pointed it at the mustached soldier. "Go now and you will live. The streets of Granville are full of enemies and your comrade did not see the blade coming, *d'accord*? Neither did you see the one who killed him."

The soldier nodded slowly and then, as if coming out of a

trance, turned and ran.

"You have killed him!" Sister Augustin scolded, coming around Zoé and bending over the soldier bleeding profusely from his neck.

The young Sister Angélique, apparently more pragmatic, knelt beside the man and swept her hand over his face, closing his eyes as she murmured a prayer for his departed soul.

Zoé's uncle retrieved his knife, wiping the blade clean on the soldier's uniform. "This is war, Sister, and, in war, to hesitate is to accept defeat. That I will never do."

By the time Zoé and her uncle arrived at the quay with the two nuns, Erwan had settled the four refugees into the waiting skiff and slipped back into town where his plain clothing would enable him to blend with the peasants.

Relieved to see their *capitaine* restored to them, the six seamen touched their foreheads in respect, acknowledging his return.

Zoé shook her head at the boat riding low in the water with the added weight. "The boat is full," she said to her uncle. "We had better stay and ask the crew to return for us."

"There is no time," he said with a worried look. "If the fat one talks, the republican soldiers will be fast on our heels. I will stay but you should go."

"That would mean one in the skiff must step out. Our passengers are too dear a cargo to leave even one behind. You and I can maneuver in Granville's streets where they cannot. *Non*, I must stay with you."

Freddie paced the deck, glancing toward shore, wishing the fog would miraculously part to reveal the skiff he awaited. He had tried to convince Zoé of the foolhardy nature of her excursions into the ports to gather the refugees like a mother hen gathers her chicks. Stubborn as always and determined to save as many as she could, she would hear none of it. While he could admire her courage, he feared for her safety.

Standing amidships, Bequel nervously chewed on a bit of broom straw, bespeaking his unease at the vulnerable state of the ship idling in Granville's harbor for so long.

The crew, silently going about their tasks, kept glancing toward shore.

Except for the occasional band of drunken men, loud in their goodbyes as they left the taverns, silence reigned on the quay some fifty yards away.

Freddie's anxiety reached a crescendo. "She should have returned by now. Something must have gone wrong." He faced Bequel. "Spare me a few of the crew. I'm going after her."

That the quartermaster motioned two of the crew forward and ordered them to lower the boat and take Freddie ashore betrayed his worry for the *capitaine*'s niece.

Moments later, the rowing boat moved silently through the fog-shrouded waters. Freddie's stomach churned, his eyes fixed on the wharf emerging from the dense mist.

What could have happened to her?

Zoé recognized the impatience brewing on her uncle's face as he raked his fingers through his black hair, the silver streaks catching the light from the lanterns on the quay.

"I can see you mean to be stubborn," he muttered, "but we cannot stand here and debate this all night." He gazed around him. "We may be attracting unwanted attention as it is. *Alors*, it shall be as you wish; we will both stay." He ordered the men in the skiff, "Take these people to the ship and return for us but only if 'tis safe. We will be watching."

The skiff shoved off, disappearing into the fog that had settled in wisps on the dark waters of Granville Harbor. Zoé and her uncle began to walk down the wharf toward the quay when a small boat carrying three men emerged out of the fog and pulled up alongside them. She recognized the two men at the oars as crew from *la Reine Noire*. Behind them in the stern knelt Freddie, beckoning to her.

"'Tis Freddie!" she said, her spirits lifting at the sight of her friend.

"Get in!" he implored.

"Be quick," said her uncle, directing her to the wooden steps built into the side of the wharf that ran down to the water.

She climbed down to the rowing boat and her uncle followed. He was nearly to the end of the steps when shouts from the wharf drew their attention.

"*Vous, là*! Halt in the name of the Republic!" The musket-bearing soldier strode toward them, his boots loud on the wooden planks. A short distance away, a half-dozen soldiers hurried to join him.

Her uncle ascended the stairs, pulling a pistol from his coat, and fired. The soldier stumbled and fell to the wharf.

Racing down the stairs, her uncle leapt into the boat. "*Vite*, away!"

The two crewmen pulled hard at the oars.

Freddie drew his pistol.

The cluster of republican soldiers knelt at the edge of the wharf, took aim and commenced spewing shot toward their small boat. Zoé crouched low as the balls whizzed over her head and the loud crack of pistols and musket fire exploded around her.

Freddie and her uncle returned fire.

The crew pressed into the oars and the boat slipped into the fog. Her uncle subsided onto the bench in the bow, stuffing his pistols into his coat pockets.

Zoé cast a long look toward the lights on the receding quay. The sound of muskets still firing echoed in the mist.

One of the soldiers shouted, "I told you he was the one! That was *le porc* who cut Pierre."

Her uncle shook his head. "I should have killed him when I had the chance."

Zoé turned her gaze away from the shore. Finally, the shots died, leaving only the rhythmic sound of the oars pulling through the water. *"Dieu merci*, at least 'tis over."

"Oui, for now," said her uncle. "We have West to thank for our lives."

One of the crew pulling at the oars glanced over his shoulder. "The Englishman has been shot, I think."

Zoé looked behind the seamen. In the darkness, it was difficult to see but she could just make out Freddie's form slumped in the stern. "Freddie!"

Chapter 2

The Isle of Guernsey off the coast of Normandy

"Your skin is as soft as a babe's," Freddie muttered in his fevered sleep. "I want... I want to kiss you... everywhere."

Zoé felt her cheeks heat at his laudanum-induced dream. It was not the first. She had sat vigil at his bedside through what remained of the night after her uncle's surgeon, Pierre Bouchet, had removed the ball and treated the wound. For hours, Freddie had burned with fever, murmuring in his sleep. Despairing of his recovery, she had allowed no other to take her place during the dark hours the fever held him in its grip.

Dipping a cloth in lavender water, Zoé brushed one of his auburn locks off his forehead and soothed his fevered brow.

Suddenly, he grabbed hold of her wrist, pulling her hand to the part of his naked chest not covered in bandages. "Take off your shift," he said in a raspy voice.

She pulled back at the shock of his words but he only pressed her hand more tightly to his warm skin, curling her insides. The feel of his warm suntanned chest beneath her palm made her nipples tighten and sent an echoing shudder coursing through her, something she had never experienced before. But how could that be when this was just Freddie?

It wasn't as if she'd had much experience with men and never before had she laid her hand on a man's bare chest. She had never been alone with Louis-Pierre and Henri had only kissed her once and that had been in celebration of his latest victory.

But her friend Freddie…

His hand dropped to his side.

Slowly, she slid her palm over his heated skin, threading her fingers through the short auburn hair sprinkled across his chest. Fascinated by his nipples, she wanted to touch them, but the thought seemed too wicked. Besides, she scolded herself, he was wounded and fighting for his life.

"Thirsty," he mumbled, his eyes still closed.

She brought a glass of water to his dry lips and managed to trickle a few drops into his mouth, all the while wondering if he were recalling some tryst with a tavern wench. Surely he had no idea it was her hand he had grasped, her hand that had been warmed by his burning skin. *Non*, he must be dreaming of a woman he had met in town.

Guernsey had many public houses whose customers included shipmasters, seamen and merchants, both English and French. Her uncle, his quartermaster and Freddie had often patronized them. Not a few had comely serving girls.

Zoé had watched ladies eyeing her friend whenever she accompanied him in St Peter Port on Guernsey, and many smiles were directed his way at the *soirées* they attended. Yet he had no *petite amie* of which she was aware. Would he seek out a tavern wench for his manly needs? Her uncle's crew did. She had heard them at night on deck bragging about their conquests.

The thought of another woman running her hands over Freddie's bare chest unsettled her.

Freddie tossed his head from side to side and raised his right hand as if to grasp something. She dare not think what he was seeing. If he dreamed of a woman and she was down to her shift, it would only be a matter of time before—

He tried to raise himself from the pillows and grimaced, his eyes never opening. She reached out and gently pressed him back to the pillows. He sighed and relaxed into a quiet sleep.

As dawn approached, *Tante* Joanna appeared and urged her to get some rest. "You'll be no good to him if you fall off that chair to the floor."

Zoé reluctantly agreed but returned a few hours later to again take up her vigil, gratified Freddie was still sleeping quietly. Sunlight flowed in through the window and a breeze ruffled the lace curtain.

"Did he say anything in his sleep?" she asked her aunt, hoping he had not.

"No, not a word. He has been as you see him. I applied the lavender water you left. Perhaps it helped. I'll look in on him a bit later."

Relieved to know her aunt had not been exposed to Freddie's erotic dreams, Zoé took up her book, several times glancing over to see Freddie sleeping.

When her aunt bustled in an hour later with tea, Zoé was still attempting to read the manuscript of a new novel one of their friends had given her. It was *The Mysteries of Udolpho* by Ann Radcliffe, to be published later this year.

"A good story, is it?"

Happy for the interruption, Zoé set the manuscript aside. "Tedious, more like."

"Well then you won't mind being amenable to a spot of tea."

"Not at all." She only hoped Freddie did not give out with one of his sensual utterances while his sister was in the room.

Her aunt poured the tea and looked toward Freddie. "How is he?"

"Still fevered but resting peacefully. M'sieur Bouchet peeked his head in a half-hour ago and told me not to worry, that Freddie will come 'round. But his skin is still overwarm and sometimes he spouts… incoherent murmurings."

Zoé would not tell her aunt what he had said or what he had

27

done while the fever ruled him but she remembered his skin beneath her fingers and the feel of his muscled chest against her palm. She looked down at her tea, hoping her aunt did not see the blush she could feel rising in her cheeks.

Freddie's sister went to stand at his bedside, smoothing his hair off his forehead. "I spoke with M'sieur Bouchet as I was on my way here and he was encouraging to me as well, but then he always is." With a catch in her voice, she said, "Let us continue to pray he recovers."

"He was very courageous," said Zoé, wanting her aunt to know how proud she was of her friend.

Returning to her tea, *Tante* Joanna said, "Jean has told me what happened in Granville. I shudder to think you both might have been shot if not for my brother. Freddie was always a brave one, even when we were children. Once he rushed in to save a cottar's child from a raging river. And, when our father was killed in the American war and then our elder brother in his duty with the Coldstream Guards, it was Freddie who was the stalwart one, the one who held us together. He encouraged our eldest brother, Richard, to take up the title and the leadership of the family."

Zoé sipped her tea, thinking of her fevered companion. "I never saw Freddie as a hero until now. He was only my childhood friend. But now... I owe him my life."

Tante Joanna, her auburn hair and brandy-colored eyes much like her brother's, regarded Zoé over her tea. "Very often, the ones we think know best are the ones we know not at all."

Zoé thought for a moment. "I'm beginning to see how true that is. We form impressions of people and even though they change and grow, we do not alter what we first believed about them." She was only beginning to understand the man Freddie had become.

Rising, her aunt picked up the tea tray and smiled. "You have grown into a young woman of character, Zoé. I like to think I had something to do with it but, in fairness, I can hardly take credit."

"You have much to do with who I am, *Tante* Joanna. You are the very model of the woman I hope one day to be."

"Just don't emulate my faults! Now, I will leave you to your tedious book and your patient. If you would like help or someone to relieve you, you have only to ask. I'll send up the housekeeper in a while to look in on you."

Zoé thanked her. The door softly closed and she went to Freddie's side. When she was certain he still slept peacefully, she walked to the window that faced the front of the house. Outside on the green lawn below, a sculpture of two bronze stags, their antlers locked in combat, reminded her of the struggle for France's future. The forces of all things she considered good fought the evil of Robespierre's régime. Surely, in time, good must win. When that happened, would Freddie return to England? The possibility did not please her.

Behind her, Freddie moaned. The effect of the laudanum was wearing off, but she would give him no more if his fever was waning. She returned to his bedside and felt his forehead, thinking it might be cooler than before. With this encouraging sign, her spirits rose.

"At last you are naked and as beautiful as I'd imagined," he murmured.

He might have meant the words for another woman but it was Zoé whose body reacted as she imagined standing before him, not in a gown but naked. The scandalous thought made her wonder, would he be pleased with what he saw?

Freddie woke to the heady scent of flowers wafting on a breeze. The intoxicating smell carried on the balmy Zephyr could only mean he was back on Guernsey.

Still alive then.

"'Tis about time you joined us, sleepy-head."

Pigeon. He opened his eyes to see her sitting in a chair beside his bed, a clouded expression on her lovely face. *Concern for him?* His wound must have been serious then. He remembered a burning in his shoulder just before he lost consciousness. The throbbing ache he now experienced reminded him of his encounter with the republican soldiers. "The prognosis?"

She gave him an indulgent look. "You are fortunate the ancient Pierre Bouchet decided to retire on Guernsey. He no longer practices medicine, but he agreed to tend your wound as a favor to *Oncle* Jean. When I inquired of the good surgeon a short while ago, he pronounced you 'recovering'. I am not so sure. You appear particularly gaunt and pale."

The throbbing pain in his shoulder told him the bespectacled physician from Lorient had dug deep to remove the ball. His left shoulder was swathed in white muslin, his right shoulder bare above the blanket.

There was genuine worry in Zoé's gray eyes.

"How delightful," he said, trying to sound cheery. "And does my ghostly appearance appeal?"

"All Englishmen appear pale to me," she replied pertly, "but I would prefer you returned to your usual good health."

He acknowledged her comment with a small smile, sensing he'd lost track of time. "How long?"

"You burned with fever for more than a day and slept the next." With a shrug of her delicate shoulders now swathed in blue silk, the tender mounds of her breasts just visible beneath her lace fichu, she said, "I'll spare you your ravings. I paid them no mind."

From her blush, he assumed his mutterings had spoken of her. He could only imagine what he had mumbled in his fevered state. He often woke from dreams of Zoé that featured heated kisses.

Avoiding his eyes, she leaned over his bed and plumped his pillow, bringing her slender neck close to his lips. He inhaled her scent of roses and was sorely tempted to close the distance to her ivory skin with his lips.

A stabbing jolt of pain forced him back against the pillow. "I don't suppose Bouchet left me anything for the pain?"

"Laudanum, but he said 'twas best, once you were awake, to eat something and take more only when the pain requires it and you are ready to sleep. Given how long you've been without food, I agree." Thrusting a bowl of something steaming in front of him, she lifted the spoon to his mouth. "On this rare occasion that I offer to feed you, dear Freddie, you'd best submit. Besides, after the soup, there is your favorite truffle omelette."

Suddenly aware of his half-dressed state and her presence in his bedchamber, he said, "I'm hardly dressed to entertain young ladies."

The corner of her mouth rose in a smile. "Since when do we stand on formalities?"

"Since you turned twenty and Donet watches over you like the pirate he once was."

Her only reply was to roll her eyes and press the spoon to his lips.

The thought of her feeding him was not unappealing. "Tyrant," he mumbled as he opened his mouth and swallowed the gingered carrot soup, another of his favorites. "Is Cook complaining of my special treatment?"

"Not a word after I told her you probably saved my life and that of *Oncle* Jean's."

When he finished the soup, she lifted a bite of omelette to his mouth. He took the fork from her hand. "How about you hold the plate and I handle the fork? We'll work together, *n'est-ce pas?*"

She returned him a fetching one-sided smile, seemingly content with her part as long as he continued to eat. Perhaps it was due to having lost her parents so young but, in the years he had known her, he had observed Zoé had a need to cosset those she loved. That he was considered friend enough to qualify for her care was at least something. One day, he hoped she would want

31

him to be more.

The last of the omelette soon disappeared. With a raised brow, she regarded the clean plate. "You appear to have been ravenous."

"Indeed, I was."

She handed him a napkin. "'Tis a good sign." Reaching to the bedside table, she picked up a single sheet of paper. "I brought you the *Gazette*. What fills Guernsey's meager newspaper is taken from the Paris journals we have yet to receive."

"I cannot imagine any news from Paris is good these days unless it's a battle the Republic has lost to England and her allies."

"Normally, I would agree, however, 'tis a good day when Georges Danton meets the guillotine."

Freddie raised a brow. "The architect of the September Massacres is dead?"

"Aye, along with Camille Desmoulins and thirteen others. It seems Robespierre has taken swift vengeance upon his opponents." She glanced down at the newspaper. "According to this, 'tis because Danton and Desmoulins advocated peace with France's enemies."

"Robespierre could not have been happy to learn Desmoulins, his childhood friend, desired peace."

"... with England, Austria and Prussia," she finished. "And, more than that, Desmoulins wanted an end to the Terror Robespierre himself prescribed." She handed him the paper. "Danton's last words were, 'Robespierre will follow me.'"

"Would that it were so." Freddie glanced at the *Gazette* then gazed out the open window next to his bed, past the flowers at the edge of the lawn to the sun shining off the azure blue waters surrounding Guernsey. A world away from the horrors in France yet only a short distance from the coast of Normandy. A wave of fatigue washed over him. He turned back to Zoé. "Meanwhile, Pigeon, did the refugees get safely to the ship?"

"Aye, they did and now they are all here. Not that I'm displeased with your foolishness, Freddie. But why did you do it?"

"Do what?" He hoped his feigned innocence was convincing.

"Take that boat and come after me!" She narrowed her eyes. "It was me you came after, wasn't it? You could not have known my uncle had arrived in Granville."

He summoned his rational self. He would not mention the horrible fear for her that had overcome him that night. "You were late. Moreover, I was perturbed that you left the ship knowing I meant to accompany you." Seeing she remained unconvinced, he added, "You ask too many questions."

A movement at the open door caused Freddie to look up. There stood a striking young woman poised to enter. He did not recognize her as one of the Donets' many servants but her lace-edged mobcap and simple gown marked her as such. "A new member of the household?" he asked Zoé.

Regarding the woman over her shoulder, Zoé said, "'Tis Madame de Montconseil's maidservant. What is it, Éloise?"

The woman grinned at Freddie. "My mistress sent me to see if I may be of assistance."

"Oh, that won't be necessary," said Zoé, "but come and meet my friend, Frederick West." She turned to Freddie and smiled. "The hero of the day."

Éloise padded toward his bed, her blue eyes twinkling as she dropped a brief curtsey. *"Bonjour, M'sieur."*

"Bon matin to you, Éloise."

Her forehead wrinkled in surprise. "You are *Anglais?"*

"He is… well, almost always," Zoé interjected.

Freddie chided her with a frown. "Best not to venture into that, Pigeon, or you will confuse her. Besides, she need not know." Zoé knew little of his work for the Crown, but there were times, and they could both recite the stories, when he had posed as a French merchant to help her retrieve the refugees. His French was that good he had never been detected as the Englishman he was.

"Here," Zoé said, handing him a small vial of liquid she retrieved from the bedside table, "for the pain."

Anxious to end the throbbing in his shoulder, Freddie downed the bitter liquid and returned the bottle to her. "My thanks."

She rose from the chair, her gaze sliding to his bandaged shoulder. Or was it that part of his chest that was bare that had drawn her attention? As she turned toward the door, she said under her breath, "Hopefully, you can get some rest."

Zoé ushered Éloise through the door, closing it behind her. "Freddie is the brother of my *Tante* Joanna."

"*Je suppose* that explains M'sieur West's hair. 'Tis much like Madame Donet's and that of her son, only darker." The maidservant breathed out a sigh. "His eyes are the same enchanting color, like a rich brandy. M'sieur West *est si beau.*"

Zoé didn't much like the pretty honeyed-hair woman sighing over her friend and speaking of his good looks. Why the compliment annoyed her she did not stop to consider. He was, after all, only Freddie, her friend for a decade.

Finding a more suitable topic, she turned to the subject of Joanna's son. "You have met Jack?"

Éloise laughed. "Oh, *oui*, I have. So full of life, that one. And such a charmer. I left him explaining *l'histoire* of Guernsey to madame's children."

"Jack quite enjoys doing that. He sees himself as a guide for all those coming to the island. *Oncle* Jean indulges him terribly."

Seven years ago, after three years of marriage, Joanna had given Zoé's uncle a son. They named Jean-Jacques Henri after his father and uncle, Zoé's father, who had died when she was ten. In deference to his mother's country, the boy insisted everyone call him "Jack" because, he claimed, it sounded more English. As he was quite serious about the whole thing, the family complied.

"You should see Jack wield a knife," Zoé said.

Éloise's eyes widened.

"Oh, it is not what you think. *Oncle* Jean taught us both, notwithstanding *Tante* Joanna's objections. I have some aptitude with a blade but Jack's skill will exceed mine in time."

Éloise nodded. "As a man, that one will be *formidable*. A bit like his cousin, M'sieur West, *non?* The eyes that sparkle, the *séduisant* smile."

Zoé had heard enough of the maidservant's effervescing over Freddie's virtues for one day. She turned and headed down the corridor, the maid following. "I imagine *Tante* Joanna is with your mistress. Does she have plans for today?"

"*Oui.* Madame Donet is taking the princesse into town where she intends to sell some of her jewelry. Then she and the children will visit the modiste. I am to go with them. We came away with only what we were wearing when you met us and those were not even our clothes."

Zoé paused and turned, a wave of pity for the young woman washing over her. "That is often the case for the ones we help. Most are fortunate to flee with their lives. The princesse can be glad she still has her jewels."

"She had me carefully sew them into a pouch she wore beneath her clothing. Your aunt has been gracious to lend us proper attire until my mistress can acquire other clothing for us."

Struck with a pang of guilt for being angered at the maidservant's fondness for Freddie, she thought to make pleasant conversation. "Your speech is that of an educated woman, Éloise. How did you come to work for Madame de Montconseil?"

"My father died unexpectedly some time ago, which meant I had to work. A friend recommended me to the palace, which is how I met the princesse."

"Did you leave family behind?"

"*Oui* and I worry for them. My mother remains in Paris with my brother. She is an excellent seamstress kept busy meeting the needs of the women close to the revolution's leaders. My brother is... how you say... a clerk for the government. For the time being, he and my mother are safe unless a connection is made to my service in Versailles."

Zoé bit back the comment she was about to make about Paris being a very dangerous place. Anyone living there would be well aware of the escalation of the Terror, the prisons full to overflowing and the guillotine's blade dropping in a steady succession of executions. But she thought it best not to remind the woman of the horrors her mother and brother still faced.

They arrived at the end of the corridor and Éloise looked toward the top of the stairs where the nursery was located. *"Peut-être* I should check on the children. I need to make sure they are ready to leave when my mistress calls."

"Very well," replied Zoé.

Éloise turned to climb up the narrow servants' stairs.

Zoé descended the main stairs to the parlor, her favorite room in the house. Decorated in the warm colors of the gardens and filled with sunlight, spending time there always brightened her mood.

"Good morning," she said to her aunt and the princesse as she entered.

"Come join us," said her aunt, looking very pretty in a lemon yellow gown that complemented her auburn hair and reminded Zoé of the flowers blooming just outside the double glass doors. "I was about to pour some tea for Madame de Montconseil."

Joanna was her aunt only by marriage. But to the ten-year-old orphan Zoé had been when she first met her uncle's future wife, Joanna had been more of a mother. They often took tea together in Saintonge when Joanna had first arrived, bringing into Zoé's life a woman to guide her.

"You look very different without the dirt on your face and dressed as the beautiful young lady you are," said Madame de Montconseil.

"Thank you," Zoé said. Taking a seat on the sofa across from the princesse, she accepted a cup of tea from her aunt and a small plate of pastries. She'd been so anxious to see that Freddie had food she'd quite forgotten to eat and the cup of tea her aunt had brought earlier had not been enough to sustain her.

"Is Freddie awake?" asked her aunt. "Jean wants to see him about a message that has just arrived from Jersey."

Zoé thought nothing of the message as Freddie frequently made trips to Jersey, the island that lay closest to Normandy.

"He won't be awake for some time. After he ate, I gave him laudanum for the pain in the hope it would allow him to rest."

"Ah, well, perhaps he will awaken by the time Jean returns. Just now, he is arranging for one of his ships to take the nuns to Jersey where there is a group of Ursulines teaching in the school for the children of the émigrés."

"Is that the one M'sieur d'Auvergne has started?"

"It is."

"That will suit them well," said Zoé. She directed her next question to the princesse. "Do you have in mind a place to settle in England, madame?"

"I have friends in London we can visit. After that, I'm not sure. I rather like the countryside. For many years, I lived in a small country palace in the Bois de Boulogne near Paris."

"Then perhaps you should consider West Sussex," offered Zoé's aunt. "There is plenty of room at The Harrows, my family's estate, and my brother, Richard, the Earl of Torrington, would welcome you and your children. It would be a fine place to recover from all you have been through at least until you decide. But, if you prefer, Richard could arrange for you and your children to travel with him the next time he goes to London."

"That is so very kind of you, Madame Donet."

"Not at all. It is settled. When my husband sails to England, you shall accompany him. Perhaps we'll all go. I have not visited my brother in a while and he worries about me even though I am

37

on Guernsey."

Madame de Montconseil said, "You must fear for your husband and niece going into France to rescue people like me. However do you stand the agony of awaiting their return?"

Zoé recognized the subtle smile that crossed her aunt's face. It was the look of a woman who had long ago conquered her demons. "I knew when I married Jean Donet I was marrying adventure itself. Oh, perhaps not the terrifying kind he now faces, defying the revolution's madmen. For that, I think he and my niece are quite brave. But I have always known such a man would not be content to sit in his parlor and gaze at his vineyard, though he has—or rather, had—an excellent one. No, once he discovered the sea, there was no other life for him."

The princesse gave Zoé a questioning look. "I can see why Monsieur Donet would undertake the rescues, but why you?"

"I made a vow to a friend that I would do all I could for the royalist cause, no matter the peril I must face."

Her aunt smiled. "Anyone who marries my niece will be making the same decision I made when I wed Jean Donet."

Freddie crumpled the message from Philippe d'Auvergne that arrived while he had been sleeping. The British naval officer on Jersey who acted as go-between with their superiors in London had issued a terse summons for Freddie to sail to Jersey. The demand, devoid of information or orders, caught him by surprise. Why hadn't d'Auvergne reduced his orders to coded writing and placed them in the hands of trusted messengers as he had done before?

Donet, sitting in the same chair Zoé had occupied earlier, gave him an assessing look, his eyes pausing as they passed over Freddie's bandaged shoulder. "I'm sailing to Jersey tomorrow. Will you be recovered sufficiently to go with me?"

"Did you know d'Auvergne demands I attend him there?"

Donet leaned back in the chair and crossed his arms over his chest. "I did assume."

Though ten years older than when Freddie had first met him, the sea captain still had a vigorous appearance, his black eyes intense, his features set in firm determination. The silver in his long black hair he confined at his nape only added to his aristocratic bearing.

The laudanum had clouded Freddie's mind for a brief moment after he'd awakened, but now he saw clearly the path before him. His wound notwithstanding, he must get to Jersey. "I'll be ready."

"Good. I want to see the Ursuline sisters established there. After Jersey, I plan to sail to West Sussex. Your sister intends to take Madame de Montconseil to The Harrows. It would save time if I did not have to return you to Guernsey."

"I have not seen my home for a while. If d'Auvergne is not averse, I would be happy to sail to England for a respite."

Donet got to his feet and patted Freddie's shoulder, the one not wrapped in bandages. "You certainly deserve one."

Before Donet reached the door, Freddie asked, "Will your niece be sailing with us?" After what happened in Granville, he didn't want to leave Zoé free to roam the dangerous streets of France without him.

"I will make sure she is included else my wife will not sleep."

Zoé appeared at the door just then. "Are you two discussing business already?" With a look of disapproval aimed at her uncle, she said, "I came to see if Freddie is ready for dinner. He may have shaken the fever but he has yet to heal."

"Which is why," Freddie offered, "I have agreed to a brief rest at The Harrows. It seems my sister wants to take the princesse there."

Zoé nodded, apparently mollified for the moment. "A rest in England might do you good."

"You will accompany us?" asked Donet.

Zoé looked first to her uncle and then to Freddie. "I suppose I must."

Chapter 3

Gorey Harbor, the Isle of Jersey

Zoé watched Freddie descend the gangplank to the Gorey pier, his arm in a sling and his dark blue frock coat draped over his injured shoulder. The sun gleamed in his auburn hair beneath his tricorne. He wore tight-fitting nankeen breeches and polished black Hessian boots, making him appear very much the British aristocrat. Even his neckcloth had been fashionably tied.

He turned to wave, flashing her a wide smile. She raised a hand in reply. They had exchanged similar gestures countless times before but something was different today and it wasn't just his dashing attire or the evidence of his wound.

For a moment, she remained at the rail admiring him, not just as her loyal friend, who he had always been, but as a man. No wonder Éloise had thought him handsome. Indeed, he was. Why had she never noticed before?

He had told her he was going to meet with Captain d'Auvergne, the British commander of the flotilla of small gunboats that protected the islands. In the distance, she glimpsed the two-story buildings set around the crescent harbor. One of them contained d'Auvergne's headquarters where he received visitors when he was in port.

In addition to the island's security, the British captain was the administrator of the French émigrés in the isles. Zoé had dealt with him on behalf of some she'd helped to rescue, but she'd long suspected he did more for England than that, else Freddie would not be meeting with him this morning without her.

In truth, she wondered if Freddie wasn't a British spy. More than once, she had come upon him leaning against the rail of *la Reine Noire*, gazing through a ship's glass toward the coast of Normandy. "Counting ships," he had told her when she'd asked. Aye, he counted—and doubtless reported—the ships to London, but what else did he do? Freddie was a man of few words, a deep well. At times, he could be maddeningly mysterious.

It occurred to her if she had not taken the side of the royalists, she and Freddie would be enemies. But it was England more than any other country that had aided those fleeing the Terror. And it was to England the émigrés flocked by the thousands.

Casting her gaze around the crescent harbor, Zoé's attention was drawn to *lé Vièr Châté*, the old castle set upon a rocky crag, a stone fortress built in the Middle Ages as a defense against an invasion from France. The isles had always been a contentious issue between the two countries, lying so close to Normandy yet dependencies of the English Crown.

Being French, she had some sympathy for her country's claim on the isles, but that fight had been settled some time ago and the castle had been allowed to return to its sleepy state. With the revolution, however, the fortress had awakened from its slumber to become a fortified garrison with cannons facing out to sea.

Seagulls circled above the castle, occasionally swooping down over the oyster boats just leaving the harbor, their single sails billowing out with the wind. This was the height of the season when the oysters were most plentiful, and the fishermen ranged close to France for the richest beds.

People might be starving in Paris, but on Guernsey and Jersey, they ate well. Good weather and good soil produced a rich bounty of fruits and vegetables; healthy cows provided fine milk, butter and cheese. Wine and spirits were plentiful as well and always had been since the isles were home to many privateers. *Oncle* Jean had been one of them and still kept a warehouse on Guernsey to store his merchant goods.

In addition to oysters, fish and lobsters abounded. The boats leaving now would return from the oyster banks with the shellfish her uncle loved to eat. Those same gulls, shrieking at the prospect of dining well, would meet them along with the fishermen's wives and children rushing to the water's edge with baskets ready to receive the day's catch.

Zoé had watched the reunion many times and thought it a charming sight. One day, the war and the Terror would end and she, too, could return to domestic pursuits.

In the meantime, she had work to do. She had agreed to her uncle's request that she accompany him to England, but only for a short while. Once she made sure Freddie had recovered she would return to the streets of Granville.

Freddie studied the man leaning over the large map of France bathed in the morning light from the windows facing the harbor. Behind the desk stood shelves of books bound in leather that Freddie had often admired, as well as instruments the captain had once used in sailing His Majesty's ships.

On Jersey, d'Auvergne had the title of Senior Officer of the Gunboats. But d'Auvergne had other, less well-known duties that involved Freddie, such as maintaining lines of communication with the Continent and monitoring hostile enemy movements, particularly ship movements. Beyond that, Freddie had often delivered supplies and weapons to those resisting the revolution.

Today, d'Auvergne wore his Royal Navy frock coat over a white waistcoat and breeches, smartly proclaiming his rank. At forty, his hair had already turned a pale gray, which Freddie attributed to the captain's many battles in the American war. Yet there was nothing feeble about him. His waist was trim, his posture erect and his hazel eyes bright with excitement beneath his dark brows.

"Good morning, sir."

D'Auvergne shifted his gaze from the map to fix Freddie with an inquiring look. "Good Lord, West. What happened to you?"

"An encounter with a republican musket in Granville a few days ago."

The captain frowned, making Freddie assume whatever the message, it must be important and Freddie's wound did not figure in the assignment. "Have a seat. I'll not require a wounded man to stand. I trust you are on the mend?"

"Aye." Freddie sank into the chair, wincing at the pain as his shoulder encountered the hard wood, and faced the captain across the desk.

Pointing to Brittany and the area just east of it on the map, d'Auvergne said, "I assume you are familiar with the provinces of Brittany and Maine?"

Freddie nodded. He knew well the map of northwestern France. On orders from Evan Nepean, the Undersecretary of War responsible for intelligence, conveyed through d'Auvergne, Freddie had entered France more than once using forged documents. Paying bribes with forged French assignat notes produced in England, he'd gathered information on the movements of the republican army near the coast. That he had chosen as his method of transport an oyster fisherman's boat had been his own idea.

Donet and his niece smuggled émigrés out of France and Freddie smuggled supplies in, sometimes on oyster boats and sometimes, with Donet's permission, aboard *la Reine Noire*.

The captain straightened, his demeanor taking on a serious mien. "Despite General Turreau's wholesale massacre of the Vendéens, some have escaped to join a group of royalist fighters

44

in Brittany and the neighboring province of Maine. They are led by a timber cutter named Jean Cottereau, though he is known more often by the name Jean Chouan. The Chouans, as they are called, fight in small bands, scouring the countryside, ambushing republican soldiers, couriers and coaches carrying government funds. They are well-disciplined marksmen and highly motivated in their desire for revenge after the slaughter in the Vendée."

Freddie found all this interesting but where was it leading?

D'Auvergne dropped into his chair, leaned his elbows on the map and steepled his fingers. "Undersecretary Nepean wants to support these Chouans but requires intelligence to do so. In short, West, we need to know precisely what they need and where they are." He paused, fixing Freddie with an intense regard. "I proposed to Nepean that we should send you and he agreed."

Freddie was puzzled. "I'm not opposed to the assignment, sir, but why me?"

The inscrutable expression that crossed d'Auvergne's face told Freddie the captain had yet to reveal a salient fact.

"It did not go unnoticed by me that you have formed a bond with the oyster fishermen here on Jersey, even traveling with them on occasion when they sail close to Normandy. Am I right?"

Freddie didn't want to reveal all he had done. "Well—"

The captain raised a hand. "I am not asking for details. I am merely recognizing your initiative, which, I might add, gained us vital information. But there is more than initiative required here. You have the confidence of your brother-in-law, the Frenchman Jean Donet, who, in addition to his home on Guernsey, still maintains a home in Lorient on the coast of Brittany. Moreover, he has allowed you to use his ships to transport arms to the royalists. I am hoping he will agree to participate in this venture as well."

"Likely he will," said Freddie, "but I would not presume upon his good graces."

"Given his views, I am confident Donet will agree to help.

After all, he is married to the sister of an English earl and both Donet and his wife support the royalist cause. One of his ships can take you within striking distance of Lorient. From there you will receive help from *La Correspondance*, our network in the region. The Chouans on the coast will direct you to the interior."

D'Auvergne got to his feet and pointed to a spot on the map in the easternmost part of Brittany. "Before you reach Maine, you will pass through the town of Fougères in Brittany. I'm told the leader of the Chouans there is Aimé Picquet, chevalier du Boisguy, not yet twenty, yet he is considered a skilled tactician."

Freddie's expression must have revealed his skepticism.

The captain returned him a sharp look. "Take Boisguy seriously, West. He has held the town against the republican soldiers for more than a year, an astounding feat. He will know of the needs in Brittany."

"Very well, I will seek him out, but how am I to make contact with the Chouans in Maine?"

"It will not be easy, but Boisguy may prove helpful, which is why I ask you to meet with him. Cottereau's followers are a devoted bunch. They live in secrecy in dense forests and must be approached with caution. Their small bands will be difficult to penetrate. 'Chouan' is a reference to the tawny owl whose call they use to identify themselves to each other." At Freddie's raised brow, the captain added, "Gaining that fact nearly cost a man his life."

Freddie let out a huff. A man's life risked for an owl's cry?

As if reading his mind, d'Auvergne said, "The owl's call is important. Before you take your leave, I will see you are instructed by one who is familiar with the bird's call. Oh, and you will take Jean Donet's niece with you when you sail to Lorient."

"Zoé? No." He shook his head. "I will not involve her in this. She already risks much for the cause."

"I recognize involving her in this presents danger for her but she is needed and she may be the key to your success. Remember, you are English and, after Granville, we are currently out of favor with the royalists. Donet's niece is not so hampered. She is trusted by the Vendéens and respected for her loyalty to their fallen leader, de la Rochejaquelein."

Freddie ground his teeth at the name. "I don't like it. Republican soldiers are known to patrol the streets of Lorient and I have to assume they hunt for these Chouans in the woods of Brittany and Maine. This will only expose her to further danger."

D'Auvergne's face took on a stony appearance. It was clear he would not yield, but Freddie had another thought. Perhaps Zoé might decline. After all, her hands were full with the émigrés escaping France, more every day. "And if she does not want to go?" he asked the captain.

D'Auvergne's smile was nearly a smirk. "Why, then you will persuade her, won't you? But from what I have heard, she will not fail to aid those royalists who lament de la Rochejaquelein's loss and seek vengeance in his name."

Freddie heaved a sigh. He knew Zoé well enough to hear the ring of truth in the captain's statement. Hoping to stall for time, he said, "You should know, her uncle plans to sail from here to West Sussex to visit his wife's relations and he is taking his niece with him."

The captain waved a hand. "No matter. As long as the visit is but a few weeks, we can adjust. Besides, your wound must be healed and I'll need a bit of time to prepare." He rose. "On your way out, arrange for my man Ozanne to teach you the owl's call."

The captain picked up an item of correspondence and, after reading a few lines, glanced up. "Anything else?"

Freddie heard the proverbial door slam in his face. He shook his head and turned to go. Donet was his last hope. As a French citizen, he had authority over his ward. Perhaps he could order Zoé to remain on Guernsey.

While her uncle and young Jack were up on deck, Zoé went below to join her aunt for a breakfast of eggs and brioches.

"We sail for England in two days," *Tante* Joanna reminded her, "which leaves us little time to have any clothes made." She gave Zoé's attire a studying perusal. "If you're to visit the English branch of the family, you will require some new clothing. What you have is terribly out of fashion, dear. The waist on gowns is rising, you know."

Impeccably attired in a round gown of mauve and silver striped silk with a higher waist than the dress Zoé wore, her aunt knew well of what she spoke. Zoé's clothing was woefully out of date. Her last *ensemble* had been made for the *Fête de la Fédération*, an event she regretted ever attending. The gown, its military style in the blue, red and white of the revolution and its matching hat, had been dismissed from her wardrobe with the September Massacres. The terrible events that resulted in the murder of many clergy, including the bishop of Saintes, once her family's bishop.

Her aunt gave Zoé an indulgent smile. "Beyond that, 'tis time you dressed as befits your station. How will you ever find a husband looking like a peasant waif?"

It was a testament to her aunt's commitment to keep their lives as normal as possible that, despite war, revolution and death stalking the streets of France, she could maintain a peaceful oasis for them on Guernsey and concern herself with finding Zoé a husband.

"If I had a husband, *Tante*, he would only tell me to stay home. And you know why I dress the way I do." It wasn't that Zoé objected to her aunt's wish that she wear a lady's clothes, but rescuing people from the revolution's atrocities required the clothes of a peasant, the plain and often soiled attire that allowed her to blend with the townspeople. "My safety depends upon the disguise."

A cloud passed over her aunt's face. "I wish you did not engage in pursuits that require such costumes."

"At least I wear skirts. I'm told the women who fight with the royalist army wear *men's* clothing. Henri used to speak of one named Victorine with great admiration." In her mind, Zoé saw Henri's angelic face framed by blond curls speaking of the valiant woman whose skill with a sword was the envy of his men. "My men call her 'Captain Victor'."

Her aunt shook her head. "Where will it lead? Women fighting with men, young men killed before they're even wed and my own niece traveling the streets at night disguised as a peasant. I know you have taken a courageous path, dear, but I worry so."

"I must do what I can while there is time. Surely you understand."

"I do." Her aunt nervously flicked a thick auburn curl over her shoulder. "Jean and I may not be your parents, but we raised you. Much as I would like it to be otherwise, you take after him more than me." Letting out a sigh, she added, "It is my fate to love you both."

Zoé laughed. "You must remember that *Oncle* Jean and I are both Donets and French. Therefore, we are stubborn, impetuous and given to moments of temper. But be cheered; we could not function without you."

"You two keep me on my knees before God," said her aunt.

"To show you how cooperative I can be, I will go with you and the princesse today for your shopping jaunt but, pray, let us order only the few gowns I will need in England. When I return to France, I must once again don a peasant's skirts."

Freddie endured an hour of instruction in the call of the tawny owl—something the spymasters in London failed to mention would be necessary when they enlisted him—before tromping off to the shore to practice.

The day was fair with a pale blue sky and sun dancing on the water. Shore birds skittered about on the sand in front of the gentle waves. Gathering his resolve and hoping no one could hear him, Freddie began. Though hampered by the sling and the pain in his shoulder, he managed to blow into his cupped hands through his slightly parted thumbs as he had been told to do.

First, he made the shrill "kew-wick" sound of the female owl. When he was satisfied he had mastered that, he moved on to the "hoo... hoo-hoo-hoo" of the male. By then, his shoulder was beginning to ache. Still, he thought he did well enough to rouse a Chouan from the forest if not the owl itself.

"What are you doing?" inquired an amused Jean Donet drawing up beside him with young Jack in tow.

"He's practicing, Papa, though I do not know what."

Freddie smiled his approval at the auburn-haired imp. The lad might only be seven but he was observant. "Just so, young Jack. 'Tis the call of an owl."

"Ah..." Donet pursed his lips. "I recall it now." Whereupon he gave a good imitation of the owl's call but combined the two distinct sounds into one.

"Papa! You can do it, too!" Jack said excitedly as if his adored papa had made some incredible discovery.

Donet lifted his tricorne to his young son at the compliment. "I can at that."

"Well, not exactly," Freddie insisted, feeling obliged to correct Zoé's uncle since, at this point, Freddie had invested more time than he cared to in learning about the owl and its mating habits. "To be precise, 'tis actually a duet. The 'kew-wick' sound is the female calling the male and the quavering 'hoo, hoo-hoo-hoo' is the male answering back and letting other males know the territory is his."

"All the same," put in Donet, "I recognize it from Shakespeare's *Loves Labour's Lost*." He began to quote, "... when blood is nipp'd and ways be foul, then nightly sings the staring owl, tu-who; tu-whit, tu-who a merry note…"

Freddie was tempted to roll his eyes. "Very impressive."

"One has much time to read at sea, Mr. West."

Freddie gave up the fight to stifle a laugh. "Ah, yes. How could I forget? By the bye, I need to speak with you about a matter." He darted a look at Jack, hinting the subject was not for little ears.

"Papa," said Jack, tugging on his father's cuff. "Don't forget you promised me a cup of chocolate at Le Brun's."

"So I did. Here," Donet said, taking a coin from his coat pocket and handing it to the boy. "You run ahead. Freddie and I will join you."

Jack grabbed the coin from Donet's palm and scampered off toward the bakery looking out over the harbor.

Freddie watched the boy for a moment and then began to walk toward the shops. "It concerns Zoé."

Donet paused in his step, his forehead furrowed above his dark brows. "Is she in some trouble?"

"No. At least no more than usual, but I'm concerned she may be if you do not intercede." Freddie took a deep breath, preparing for a conversation he would rather avoid. "Have you heard of the Chouans in Brittany?"

"I have heard of them, *oui*, and not a few times I have sought to aid them."

"D'Auvergne tells me London is committed to helping them and the Vendéens who have joined them. He wants me to make contact with them to gather intelligence on their needs."

Donet made a sound much like a snort. "A bit late, *non*? Where were your English friends when the Vendéens needed their help in Granville? They waited for the English as long as they could, until they had no choice but to flee south, where they faced Turreau's muskets."

Freddie let his attention fall to the pebbles beneath his feet, all too aware of the promised help that had never arrived. "A regrettable chapter, I agree." He looked up, meeting Donet's disquieting dark eyes. "Still, 'tis better the help comes late than it never arrives at all, *n'êtes-vous pas d'accord?*"

Donet gazed toward the bakery they were fast approaching. "I suppose I must agree, but what has my niece to do with that?"

Freddie hoped he could be convincing. "D'Auvergne has ordered me to take Zoé with me. He believes she is essential to the effort, respected as she is by the Vendéens, whereas I, an Englishman, might garner only distrust."

Donet paused, deep in thought. "He is right to think that of Zoé. Her loyalty to the Vendéens is well known. And the Chouans are their brothers-in-arms."

"Notwithstanding her affinity for the Vendéens, I would not put her at risk and was hoping you could help."

Donet's brows lifted in surprise. "You want me to order her not to go?"

"It would help matters greatly if you did."

Donet quietly laughed. "I could, but you know as well as I she is not one to be ordered about and I have not done so since she was a youth. Many times, she has faced danger for the good of others. It was not for nothing I taught her to use a knife. Why, one night in Lorient, she did not hesitate to save a child from a brute who would have killed the boy. With much practice, she has become very good at throwing a blade and does not hesitate to plunge it into warm flesh. Zoé can be fierce, yet she is not stupid when it comes to danger. Her instincts are good."

"Yes, I know, but this will be different. She will be going into the wooded countryside fought over by both revolutionaries and royalists. And 'tis not close to the coast and your ships."

Donet gave Freddie a sympathetic look. "Once she hears she is needed by her friends, she will insist on going. These may be treacherous times but you know Zoé will not be left behind. How can I praise the cause and hold her back from serving where her presence is required? She is well aware women fight with the royalists. It will be safer for her if you plan for her to go with you. Your mission, as I understand it, is to obtain information, not engage in battle. I can send Gabe along to guard her. He has known my niece as long as you have. He is now twenty-two, the same age as most of the Chouans from what I hear. More importantly, he would die to protect her."

Freddie met Donet's dark gaze but the words on his lips he spoke only to himself. *So would I.*

Chapter 4

Aboard la Reine Noire in the English Channel, sailing to England, March 1794

"Sail ho!" cried the lookout from the foredeck.

Standing on the quarterdeck where he could judge how well the sails were drawing wind, Freddie turned from Donet, with whom he'd been conversing, and gazed toward the bow.

The sun glistened off the Channel as *la Reine Noire* cut through the choppy waters, throwing up a fine white bow wave. Until now, he'd been enjoying the crossing but the lookout's cry sent a ripple of foreboding through him. French warships monitored the Channel as well as the coast.

Donet shouted, "Where away?"

"Two points off the starboard bow!" came the reply on the wind.

Freddie shifted his gaze to starboard. In the distance, he glimpsed the top of a mast and a small white cloud he assumed was a sail. Not far from where he stood, Émile Bequel passed a spyglass to Gabe Chastain. The seaman wore the typical blue jacket and loose breeches, or slops, the sailors wore. "Run aloft, lad," said the quartermaster, "and take a look."

Freddie found it amusing that although Gabe was a young man, respected by both captain and crew, Bequel still thought of him as the cabin boy he'd once been. In all the years he'd served Donet, Gabe was still slim enough to climb the rigging faster than an organ grinder's monkey.

Reaching for the spyglass, Gabe stuffed it into his belt and clambered into the rigging. Freddie watched as he reached the yard high above the deck where he perched and extended the brass cylinder to its full length. Clinging to the mast with one arm, he peered through the lens, the wind blowing his curly brown hair around his ruddy-cheeked face.

A moment later, he shouted down, "'Tis a warship, *Capitaine*, a two-decker flying no colors!"

La Reine Noire, disguised as the English merchantman *Gulliver*, likewise flew no flag. 'Twas a stalling tactic considered fair, at least until a ship began firing. But two decks meant many guns, more than the sixteen carried by Donet's brig-sloop.

With the skill of a circus acrobat, Gabe slid down the backstay and landed on the deck with a thump, returning the spyglass to the quartermaster, who promptly delivered it to Donet. "Best take a look, *Capitaine*."

Donet stared into the spyglass.

Freddie asked, "Can you tell if she's French?"

"*Oui*, she is most definitely French. I recognize her. She is the *Trajan* out of Lorient and carries seventy-four guns."

Bequel gave a grunt. "*Merde!*"

Donet lowered the spyglass. "My last report had her patrolling Brittany's coast to prevent the British from aiding the Vendéens. Her captain, Villaret de Joyeuse, is one of the junior officers promoted in the wake of the National Convention's purge of the French Navy last year. Stupid plan," he spat, "to kill off your experienced officers while declaring war."

Extending the spyglass once again, he swept the horizon, then paused, his dark brows drawing together. "Aha! There's *Trajan*'s prey—a little schooner. She flies the British colors... an aviso carrying dispatches, *peut-être?*" He collapsed the glass and handed it to Bequel.

"There is a new packet running mail from Weymouth to Jersey," Freddie offered.

Donet muttered a curse. "We must intervene. A fine time to be without a master gunner!"

With an arched brow, the quartermaster regarded Donet. "*Capitaine*, a man must be present for the arrival of his first-born babe, *non?*"

"Can I be of assistance?" Freddie inquired. "With my arm in a sling, I won't be able to serve the guns, but I can coordinate your fire while you two concentrate on maneuvers."

Donet's deep frown vanished and his white teeth flashed in a grateful smile. "*Très bien*, that will work." Raising his voice to a roar that carried across the ship, Donet yelled, "Run out the guns!"

Preparing for the inevitable clash, Freddie left the quarterdeck to give his attention to the gun crews. Once he was assured the guns were loaded, pricked and primed, ready for the coming action, he rejoined Donet. To Gabe, standing nearby, he said, "M'sieur Chastain, please escort the ladies and children to the orlop deck and tell them to expect action."

The lowest part of the ship, the orlop would be dark, wet and given to ill smells. Zoé would hate it but it was below the water line and the safest place in a battle.

Precisely where he wanted her at the moment.

As Gabe hurried down the aft hatch, Freddie turned to Donet. "Sir, we still have the American colors aboard. Might we raise them as we close on the *Trajan* and only hoist His Majesty's flag as we fire our first round?"

"An excellent idea," said Donet. He gave the orders to Freddie and Bequel. "We will come up to windward of the *Trajan* and rake her port side, then cut around her stern and fire into her as we pass. We may be smaller with fewer guns, but we're faster. Once we pass the *Trajan*'s stern, we'll bear away bound for Chichester."

"That should allow the packet time to escape," put in Bequel. "I'll have Lucien see the colors are ready." Facing the crew, he yelled, "Hands to the braces! Stand by to tack."

Freddie strode to his gun crews and, speaking in French, said, "Double-shot the guns. We'll fire the port side, rolling fire as we pass. Save the last gun, treble-shotted, for the stern as we round up. Then reload on port as fast as you can so we're ready for whatever comes next."

With shouts of *"Oui!"* the crews went to work.

The *Trajan* bore down on the schooner and *la Reine Noire* followed, hoisting her American colors. The French ship hesitated. Perhaps Villaret believed his American ally was coming to assist. Or he might just be confused. But whatever his thinking, the ruse gained them time as Freddie had hoped.

As the gunners poised their linstocks to light the fuses, the French warship hesitated no longer. Hoisting the newly adopted tricolor flag of the Republic, she fired a shot, her gun belching smoke.

A ripping sound pierced the air. Freddie looked up as the shot flew through *la Reine Noire*'s main topsail.

Before the smoke cleared, Donet ordered the British red ensign hoisted and raised his arm meeting Freddie's expectant gaze from amidships.

At the signal, Freddie shouted, "Fire!"

La Reine Noire's guns blazed away, raking the port side of the larger ship. To the French crew, it might have appeared like a cat hissing at a mastiff. But the strategy worked. The rolling broadside passed up through the sides and decks sending pieces of wood from the decks and hull shooting into the smoke-filled air.

Freddie smiled, satisfied. At least some of the *Trajan*'s guns would not be firing again.

Bequel gave the command to bear around the *Trajan*'s stern and the helmsman responded, turning the wheel. The sails luffed, then billowed, as the crew tacked to bring them into position.

La Reine Noire passed in front of the warship's stern and the many windows that gave light to Villaret's cabin. With a shout, Freddie ordered his crews to fire the treble-shotted gun he'd held in reserve.

The shot exploded from the gun, sending glass and pieces of wood flying out in all directions. Doubtless, Villaret was glad he'd been on deck and not in his cabin.

With orders from Donet for a new tack, *la Reine Noire* left the slower warship licking its wounds. Freddie gazed off the port side beyond the *Trajan* to see the small mail packet slip away.

The Harrows, near Chichester, West Sussex, England

Zoé pressed her fingers to her temples, still hearing the guns exploding in her head, still smelling the dank putrid stench in the belly of the ship where the women and children had been confined. The carriage that had brought them from Chichester Harbor dipped into a rut and she lurched sideways, her head throbbing.

"Really, Freddie, was it absolutely necessary to consign us to such a wretched part of the ship? After all, *la Reine Noire* sustained little damage."

"The *Gulliver*," he corrected, "took a ball in the main topsail. Had the *Trajan*'s hull not been so high or the *Gulliver* not so close, their guns could have hit our deck. 'Twas not safe."

"At least I have Franklin, the ship's cat, to thank for removing any rats. We saw none in the dim light afforded by our one lantern." Zoé hated rats.

The carriage slowed as they neared Freddie's family's estate, the home of his brother, Richard, Earl of Torrington, and then stopped in front of the main house behind the two other conveyances.

"The orlop deck is the safest place for precious cargo, Pigeon," Freddie teased, his brandy-colored eyes twinkling with mirth as he handed her down to the gravel drive. "You must recall I had to protect not only you, but my sister and your uncle's heir, along with the princesse d'Hénin and her children."

Zoé found his failure to mention the pretty maid Éloise oddly comforting. "I suppose you are right but, still, 'twas a bleak place even with Jack's wild imaginings to entertain us as to what was happening on deck."

Freddie laughed. "That must have been some tale. Jack hangs on his father's every word when he recounts his adventures as a privateer. Did the boy provide gruesome details?"

"Many, much to the chagrin of *Tante* Joanna and Madame de Montconseil."

Jack had regaled them with vivid descriptions of "the sea battle that was raging on the Channel", as he called it, which had delighted the princesse's children, Cécile and Étienne.

Zoé remembered well the earl's home. It was the place where she'd first met Freddie. She looked up at the rectangular brick edifice, rising three stories into the air. Graced with more than twenty windows, including five dormers set into the roof, it was impressive. Nestled against a forest of beech trees, the architecture was decidedly more English than French and, thus, to Zoé's thinking, more masculine.

The house faced a large round pond, its water a placid green, marking the center of the estate.

Surrounding all was the bucolic countryside of West Sussex. The calm she experienced stood in stark contrast to the war raging across the Channel.

"Come," urged Freddie, offering his arm, "if you hurry, you'll have time for a bath before dinner."

Zoé glanced down at the stained edge of her gown, a souvenir of the orlop deck. She was glad she had not worn one of her new ones for the crossing. The unmistakable odor rising to her nose made her grimace. "I shall try and not be offended by your implication."

Freddie chuckled. "And I shall try not to notice you smell like bilge water."

She glared at him beneath her furrowed brows. Only Freddie could accuse her of that and live. After all, he'd been the cause of the awful smell.

They followed the others up the steps to the entrance where Richard greeted them, his coloring a close rendition of his siblings'. Noble titles might have ended in France, but they were very much in use in England. To the world he was "Lord Torrington", to his colleagues in Parliament, "Torrington", but to his siblings, he remained "Richard", the only member of the West family without a nickname, owing to his rather formal demeanor.

Standing at his side, his attractive wife, Anne, welcomed them with a warm smile and gracious words. "We're so glad you are here. Do come in!"

Owing to her cheerful disposition, everyone called her "Annie". Well, everyone save Richard, who called her "Anne". She was, in all ways, the perfect complement to his staid and serious bearing.

When Zoé's uncle introduced the princesse and her children, Annie's kind face lit up. "Welcome to The Harrows," she said. "We are delighted to have you as our guests. How relieved you must be to be here."

"We are surely that," said Madame de Montconseil with a sigh. "Not just to be out of France, mind you, but off the Channel and off the ship."

"'Twas a bit of a rough crossing," admitted Donet to Richard. "We were forced to deal with one of France's warships."

"What *Oncle* Jean means, dear cousin," said Zoé, "is that while the guns were firing above decks, the women and children were relegated to the belly of the ship. I daresay 'tis not the place the princesse would have wanted to be."

Without mentioning their soiled gowns, Annie turned to her

husband. "Richard, I expect the ladies will want to change."

Collecting himself, Richard said, "Yes, well—"

"Nora can show you to your chambers," Annie said to the princesse. Nora, *Tante* Joanna's former lady's maid had, in the past ten years, become the housekeeper for The Harrows.

His impeccable attire undisturbed, The Harrows' ever-proper butler, Carter, bowed. "Very well, my lady. I shall call her." Hearing the respect in his voice, Zoé was reminded that Carter approved of his mistress, happy to have her in exchange for the more rebellious Lady Joanna West who he'd once served. Until she had married Zoé's uncle, Joanna had acted as Richard's hostess.

Freddie leaned in to Zoé. "I shall see you at dinner." Then he traipsed off with her uncle and the earl toward the parlor. She could see no evidence that his shoulder pained him, but his being on deck during the battle had been a source of worry. What was he doing in the middle of guns blazing with one arm in a sling?

"The Prime Minister is coming *here?*" Freddie sputtered, nearly choking on his brandy.

"Tomorrow," said Richard. "Fortuitous, no?" With a glance in Donet's direction, he added, "I suspect he will be very interested to hear of your skirmish with the French warship."

"I will be happy to oblige him," said Donet cordially. "We French who fight a revolution run amok are happy to align with an England that provides shelter and aid to our émigrés. I will tell the Prime Minister whatever he wants to know. As for the *Trajan*, I was surprised myself to see her so far from France's northwestern coast. Her home port is Lorient."

Richard rose and poured another round of brandy for the three of them. "You mentioned the ship usually monitors the French coast, particularly the Vendée. It turns out that due to his frustration with the Prussians and Austrians in the war on the Continent, Pitt has a growing interest in that province."

"He means to aid them?" asked Freddie, recalling d'Auvergne's words but not realizing the interest went so high as the Prime Minister.

"Pitt is desperate to claim some success in France. If sending arms and supplies to the Vendée to equip a ready-made army would give him that, then yes, I expect he does."

Donet, staring into his brandy, turned the glass in his hand. Was he thinking of Freddie's new assignment and of Zoé's part in it? Looking at Richard, Donet said, "The aid, though late in coming, will nevertheless be welcomed. The royalist army in the Vendée, or what is left of it, has sometimes been forced to fight with farming implements for weapons."

"Yet the royalists in London tell me they are worthy fighters," put in Richard. "That would appeal to the Prime Minister."

"What is the occasion for his visit?" asked Donet.

"Now *that* is a bit peculiar," said Richard with a thoughtful expression. "He sent word he would be in the area and wanted to call upon me. Something to do with the war, I expect."

Freddie had met Pitt many years ago when Richard gave a reception in his honor at The Harrows, but he'd not spoken with the Prime Minister since becoming one of the Crown's spies in France.

Richard gave Freddie's sling a pointed look. "Since you have said nothing, I must ask. Was it on the Channel you managed to be wounded, little brother?"

At twenty-seven, Freddie took umbrage at the reference to his junior status but, then, one had to make excuses for Richard. "No. I owe that to a republican soldier in Granville who did not like the cut of my coat."

A deep furrow appeared between Richard's eyes.

"I jest, Richard. 'Tis not worth the telling."

"Freddie acted quite the hero," said Donet. "Kept your sister,

Joanna, from widowhood."

Richard's gaze darted between Freddie and Donet. Neither spoke a word, their countenances suitably devoid of expression. Richard shrugged. "Very well, be mysterious if you must. But if Pitt asks, you must tell him what happened. He likes good stories."

Zoé spent the next morning with *Tante* Joanna and Freddie, visiting their friends in the town of Chichester. Spring in West Sussex, she decided, though not as warm as Guernsey, nevertheless brought with it a bevy of wildflowers dotting the green hillsides, which made for a lovely sight.

In the carriage, they talked of the family they were to call upon, the Barlows. Zack Barlow, a longtime friend of Zoé's aunt, was the brother of The Harrow's housekeeper, Nora.

Tante Joanna explained that the Barlows had five children, the three oldest, Danny, Nate and their sister Briney, were Polly's by her first husband who had died. "After she married Zack, they had twin boys of their own."

"The twins had just been born when I was last here," said Freddie. With a smile for his sister, he added, "Zack seems to have settled down from those days when we engaged in free trade."

Zoé had known Freddie and his sister once led a smuggling ring to help feed the poor in West Sussex, a story she had forced them to divulge when she caught the two of them laughing about some escapade. But it had taken her weeks to wheedle Freddie into telling more about the French tea and brandy they smuggled that had put food in the mouths of English children.

"That's how your uncle came to meet my sister," said Freddie. The details of that meeting were never supplied, though Zoé had first met Joanna in Saintonge where her uncle had brought her. The thought of them all being involved in some nefarious plot for the good of the poor gave Zoé a new respect for her aunt by marriage and her friend who called her "Pigeon", a name she had come to accept but never quite liked.

Just outside of Chichester, they arrived at the Barlows' whitewashed cottage with its well-kept thatched roof and pretty curtains in the windows. Surrounding the small home, interspersed between the oak trees, was a carpet of bluebells covering the floor of the ancient woodland.

Smoke rose from the chimney announcing the family to be home.

The carriage pulled to a stop and a blonde, blue-eyed woman came out the door. "M'lady! How good to see you. And you, Mr. West. Come in, come in."

Freddie introduced Zoé as their cousin by marriage from France.

Polly was an accommodating woman, rosy-cheeked with a kind demeanor and, despite their countries being at war, Zoé was made to feel welcome. "I've just put the kettle on for tea," she said as she beckoned them inside.

In the main room of the cottage, Zoé met Zack and four of the couple's five children.

In his middle years, Zack was a big man with short brown hair and a scar on the left side of his face. He wasn't handsome, but his wife and children seemed to adore him and his hazel eyes sparkled whenever he glanced toward Polly, who bustled about setting out cups for tea.

Nate was the oldest son still at home, sixteen years and a handsome lad. Both he and his sister, Briney, had their mother's fair coloring, but the two twin boys who appeared to Zoé to be five or six, had their father's brown hair.

They all took places around the long wooden table and Polly poured tea.

"What have ye done to yerself, Frederick?" asked Zack.

"Oh this?" said Freddie with a glance at his sling. "'Tis nothing but a scratch. I'm fine."

"If ye say so," said Zack. Then, turning to Zoé's aunt, he said, "Since yer last visit, Jo, yer brother, his lordship, added a few rooms to the cottage to allow fer the twins' coming. The extra space has been a boon."

Zoé's aunt took the gingerbread biscuits from the basket they had brought from The Harrows. "I'm glad he is good to his tenants, especially you and Polly," she said. Still warm from the oven, the gingerbread, formed into the shape of plump little men, sent an aroma of ginger wafting through the air.

Freddie handed a gingerbread man to each of the dark-haired twins. Briney, who had taken one for herself, ushered the two boys out the front door to play.

"How old are the twins now?" asked Zoé's aunt.

Polly grinned. "Six. Briney is a great help with them."

"We named the boys George and Richard," explained Zack, "fer the king and fer the earl who has done so much fer us."

Through the open door, Zoé watched the two boys playing among the bluebells under the watchful eye of their half-sister. She wondered if she would ever have a child of her own. At twenty, it was not too soon for her to marry but the war had delayed much. She couldn't imagine thinking of such things with the present situation in France. Beyond the peace of England, the world lay in turmoil. And there was the memory of Henri and her vow that drove her on.

"Thanks to the earl," said Zack, "our oldest, Danny, has risen in the Royal Navy and is now a young lieutenant on the HMS *Orion*."

Zoé glanced at Freddie and, not for the first time, wondered why he had not chosen that path. Perhaps he had no love for the military life.

"Young Nate here," Zack said, nodding to his stepson, "helps me with the bit of farming we do."

Nate smiled sheepishly. "I prefer to stay on land."

Freddie said, "I'd wager you have become your father's right hand."

"Aye, he is," said Zack giving his adopted son an approving look.

"I tend the home and still do a bit of sewing," said Polly. "That much ain't changed." Zoé had noted the cottage's windows framed with muslin curtains neatly sewn and embroidered with yellow flowers. They were very pretty.

"I brought you some cloth you might be able to use," said Zoé's aunt. "It comes from France via Jersey. It will make you and Briney lovely dresses."

Polly's countenance brightened, a smile forming on her round face. "How generous of you, m'lady. I will surely use it!"

"I thought of you and your skill with a needle and thread the minute I saw it at the dressmaker's."

Freddie said to Zack, "Jo and I have often thought of you and Polly and the children. I'm glad to see you and your family happy and well."

"Aye, we are," said Zack with a fond look at his wife. "The Good Lord has blessed us and we are content, save that we pray Danny will come home from this miserable war. And ye? How do ye like living on Guernsey?"

"It suits me," said Freddie, "though much of the time I'm on one of Donet's ships."

Polly poured them more tea and then came to stand behind her husband, placing her hand on his shoulder. "We live a simple life here but our needs are met and, unlike the people in France, we do not live in fear. 'Tis a comfort to know you are no longer living there."

Zoé exchanged a knowing look with Freddie but neither mentioned they were often in France.

A short while later, *Tante* Joanna thanked their hosts and rose to leave. "It's been too short a visit but we must go. I will keep your growing family in my prayers."

Freddie got to his feet and extended his hand to Zack. "I will inquire about Danny and the ship on which he serves."

"We'd be much obliged," said Zack. "Only remember when you do, Danny is a Barlow now."

"Indeed, I will," said Freddie. "If you need anything, send a message to The Harrows. You are part of our family, as is Nora."

Zoé eyed him curiously as she stood and bid goodbye to the Barlow family. Something about Freddie had changed. The winsome lad of her youth, who had proudly showed her around his family's estate, had become a man, taking on a man's responsibilities and caring for The Harrows' tenants.

Chapter 5

The Prime Minister and his retinue arrived late that afternoon just as Freddie was coming down the stairs in search of a brandy before dinner. Although he had taken off his sling, pleased he no longer appeared the wounded man, the lingering pain in his shoulder was a constant reminder of that night in Granville. The night he feared he might lose Zoé to a republican's musket ball. That she was safe in West Sussex hardly signified since, upon their return, she would be following him into Brittany, a province in open rebellion against the revolutionary government.

Save for his sister and Madame de Montconseil, who had left earlier for a ride around the estate, Zoé and the others had changed for dinner and were now gathered with Richard and Annie in the parlor awaiting the Prime Minister whose carriage had just pulled up in front of the estate.

"That blue brocade silk becomes you, Pigeon."

"You like it?" she asked, her gray eyes glinting with delight. "*Tante* Joanna selected the fabric for me in Jersey."

"I do." With her hair done up with dark ringlets framing her ivory face, she appeared a French temptress.

Carter announced Pitt shortly thereafter and he and two other men he'd brought with him joined the rest of them in the parlor.

A head taller than his companions, who Freddie took to be his secretary and valet, Pitt dressed in modest style, a black frock coat and breeches, white waistcoat and simply tied cravat. His stockinged legs rose above silver-buckled shoes. He wore his brown hair shorter than Freddie's and combed back from his strong features.

"I must apologize for the short notice, Torrington," he said, taking Richard's offered hand, "but the matter about which I must speak to you is of considerable urgency. I'm paying visits to all the peers on the southern coast between Brighton and Southampton."

"Now you have me intrigued," said Richard.

Freddie's interest suddenly piqued. What could the brilliant leader of the British government have in mind? He had come as a friend, surely, for he and Richard had been good friends for years, but Freddie did not expect it would be a social visit. The Prime Minister was always working, particularly in time of war.

"I've brought my secretary who keeps track of my commitments," said Pitt, introducing the member of his staff traveling with him, who promptly faded into the background.

Turning to the matter of his own introductions, Richard said, "You know my wife, Lady Torrington, of course."

Annie offered her smile and her hand to the Prime Minister, who gently shook it. "Lovely as always, my lady."

"And I believe you know Jean Donet, comte de Saintonge. His wife, my older sister, Joanna, should be here soon. She is out just now showing one of our guests the countryside."

Donet extended his hand. "Mr. Pitt."

Pitt shook Donet's hand. "Welcome to England, monsieur."

A small smile crossed Donet's face, making Freddie think there was something in the Prime Minister's greeting that the Frenchman found amusing. As a French privateer during the American war, Donet had surreptitiously entered London many times with no welcome whatsoever. And, as a smuggler, his ship had often lingered off England's southern coast.

Richard motioned to Freddie. "You might not remember my younger brother, Frederick, but you have been introduced before."

"I do remember meeting Frederick," Pitt said, shaking Freddie's hand. "He has that familiar auburn hair and eyes of the West family, though 'tis been some time. Have you remained in West Sussex since I last saw you?"

"No," replied Freddie. "Monsieur Donet asked me to join his business sometime ago and that took me to France and the Caribbean. Most recently, I have settled on Guernsey where Monsieur Donet makes his home now in the wake of the revolution." Though Donet was well aware of Freddie's work for Captain d'Auvergne on Jersey and Evan Nepean in London, they did not openly speak of it to others.

Lastly, Richard introduced Zoé. "I don't believe you have met Monsieur Donet's niece, Mademoiselle Zoé Donet."

"I've not had the pleasure," said the Prime Minister, fixing his dark eyes on Zoé.

From the look the Prime Minister gave her, it was clear he approved of Donet's ward. Pitt was thought by all to be a confirmed bachelor but that didn't stop Freddie from experiencing a pang of jealousy.

A few years younger than Richard, who was all of thirty-seven, Pitt had a remarkably youthful appearance for a man who had governed England for more than a decade, almost all of it during wartime. One would have expected more lines, more wrinkles, a more haggard appearance, yet Pitt's handsome visage was virtually unlined, his eyes brimming with intelligent gleam.

Having been gone from England for several years, most of what Freddie knew of William Pitt's administration came from the newspapers and Jo who followed closely England's politics.

If the Prime Minister admired Zoé, Freddie could hardly fault the man. She had grown into a beauty of great charm and keen wit. But the last thing he wanted was another hero served up for her impressionable heart when he planned to claim it as his own.

Zoé inclined her head to Pitt, her eyes smiling. "Prime Minister."

Pitt bowed. "Mademoiselle."

To Freddie's relief, Richard chose that moment to turn to Pitt. "Some refreshments?"

"Excellent!" said the Prime Minister. "My throat is as dry as the dust on your West Sussex roads. Port would do nicely."

Freddie recalled Pitt drank only port and had from his youth when a doctor prescribed it for his health. It was reported he drank more than a bottle a day.

A footman escorted the Prime Minister's valet above stairs as Freddie looked around the parlor, a room in which he'd spent much of his youth. In those days, his family had been larger with two older brothers, two sisters and both a father and mother. In a few short years, their mother had died. Then their father and eldest brother, Wills, were killed in the course of their duties as soldiers. The walls were graced with their portraits, the small painting of Wills in his Coldstream Guards uniform consigned to a place of honor almost like a shrine. Freddie would never object; he had idolized his brother.

So many deaths.

Freddie tore his gaze away from the portraits and the memories that went with them to see their guests taking seats on the cream-colored brocade chairs and settees. He drew comfort from the fact the room had changed little in the years he'd been gone. It still felt like home.

A footman added a log to the crackling fire, warming the room. The spring days could be chilly.

Two wing chairs in Prussian blue silk had been acquired since he'd last been here, no doubt owing to Annie's good taste. Richard's countess would also have been responsible for the pillows in the same silk placed at each end of the settees. He liked the change, just as he liked Annie.

The brass chandelier hanging from a medallion in the center of the scrolled ceiling was the same one he'd gazed up at during the long evenings when he was forced to act the adult while dreaming of adventures. The adventures had come to him, though not as he had expected, as a soldier. Rather, they began when he joined Jo in the dangerous business of smuggling, then continued when he decided to sail with her husband, Jean Donet, who was no ordinary merchant ship owner. And now he was a spy for England.

With Zoé in his life, he expected to have more adventures, desired or not. Keeping her safe might yet be the death of him, but he had no other choice, for he had loved her for a very long time and could not envision life without her. He had not told her all he had done for the spymasters in London, but in withholding the truth of it, he worried. She might continue to think of him as merely her childhood friend, an English dandy who knew nothing of war and, in cowardly fashion, had chosen not to follow his father and older brother into the British Army. Until she could come to respect him for the man he was and love him as he loved her, he would allow her to think what she would. It might be safer for her were she ever captured.

Freddie strode to the sideboard where decanters filled with brandy, sherry and port sat on a silver tray. He poured a glass of cognac for himself and a glass of sherry for Zoé while Annie directed the footman to serve the others.

He handed Zoé her sherry and took a seat across from her.

Once everyone was settled, Pitt sat back in the wing chair he had claimed and slowly sipped his port as if gathering his thoughts.

"So," began Richard, "tell us what brings you this far south of London. We are all ears."

Pitt turned to fix Donet with an intense look. "Before I speak, I must know, Monsieur Donet, are you with us this time?" The Prime Minister knew of Richard's infamous brother-in-law, of course, who, with France's approval, had served America in the last war. As a privateer, he'd seized a ship belonging to one of

England's privateers.

Donet raised his head, his dark eyes clear and his face without shadow. "You may count upon my full support, Prime Minister. I like not the revolutionary government, nor the Terror that has gripped France. Like you, I considered the execution of King Louis an atrocious act." Lowering his gaze to his cognac, Donet said in a softer voice, "He was my friend."

Raising his head, he let out a heavy sigh. "My estate in Saintonge is in the hands of others for the time being, as is my home in Lorient. I have moved to the Isle of Guernsey to continue my merchant shipping endeavors while serving the royalist cause. My wife, Torrington's sister, should be returning shortly from taking the princesse d'Hénin for a tour of the countryside. The princesse is one of the émigrés we were recently able to help escape."

Glancing at Zoé, Donet added, "My niece is my partner in rescuing those fleeing the Terror."

Pitt gave Zoé an approving glance. "Good. Then you might be interested in my purpose in coming, though 'tis hardly a secret in London." Addressing himself to Richard, Pitt said, "You are no doubt aware that after we seized Toulon, the French National Convention called for an amphibious assault upon England."

Richard nodded. "Why, yes, I knew of France's threat, all in England did. But I hardly thought anyone credited it."

Pitt leaned forward in his chair. "Ridiculous though it might seem, we now believe the French government, or whoever is ruling the country these days, means to invade England."

Richard returned Pitt a look of shock, his glass of brandy paused halfway to his mouth. "Are you telling us the threat is real?"

"I am," replied Pitt. "That is one reason I have made public our commitment to the annihilation of *le gouvernement révolutionnaire*. I have harshly criticized France's abolition of private property, the extinction of religion and the excesses of the Terror.

It is hardly necessary to add that there can be no peace until the invasion of England is abandoned."

Freddie did not put such an assault beyond Robespierre. He had done worse in an effort to persuade the French people they were winning the war. But to think of The Harrows being the subject of an attack by France seemed impossible.

Wide-eyed, Zoé stared at Freddie with a raised brow, her expression asking, *would France do such a thing?*

He gave her a nod.

Donet, who'd been silent until now, said, "A full-scale invasion is, to my way of thinking, inconceivable. France does not have the naval superiority to be successful in such an endeavor. Moreover, the leadership of the French Navy is, at the moment, in a state of disarray."

"From all I hear, monsieur, you are correct," said Pitt, "however, that large an invasion would not be their objective. Rather, they mean to terrify our people and distract the government from the war on the Continent. Recall that France did this in the Hundred Years' War, burning Plymouth to the ground. It seems they plan to do it again but their purpose would not be conquest, as it was then. They mean to sow terror and panic. To do so, they will target small towns and major harbors, or perhaps a combination of both."

"If Robespierre is serious," said Donet in a contemplative manner, "I would think it would be a combination. 'Twould be more effective."

"You are certain of France's plans?" Richard asked Pitt.

The Prime Minister set his glass of port aside. "In addition to Dutch reports, we have information from other sources that suggest such an attack might be timed to coincide with French-inspired radicals rising in Britain. And then there are the troubling Admiralty reports of French naval activity in the Channel."

"Good Lord," said Richard. "Then 'tis true." Annie reached out and patted his hand.

"Lord Moira," continued Pitt, "who has been very helpful in our war with France in his role as major general, has told me he expects an assault on the Isle of Wight."

"Why, that's just west of here," muttered Richard. "As to the reports of French naval activity on the Channel," he said shooting Donet a knowing look, "I believe my brother-in-law can provide a fresh account."

Pitt's gaze shifted to Donet. "You have observed this?"

"More than observed," said Donet. "On our way here, Mr. West and I did battle with the *Trajan*, a seventy-four gun French ship of the line."

Zoé turned to Freddie with curious eyes. He had not told her of his role in the skirmish, content to let her believe he was a mere spectator. "The *Trajan* was pursuing the new packet out of Weymouth," he offered to Pitt. "We intervened to see her safely on her way to Jersey."

"'Twas fortunate your ship was near," said the Prime Minister, glancing at Richard. "We have identified the most likely landing area for a French invasion to be somewhere between Brighton and Southampton. I don't have to remind you that your lands are in the center of that stretch of coast, which brings me to my purpose in coming. It is imperative that we raise a voluntary militia to guard the southern coast."

"A voluntary militia?" Richard inquired.

Picking up his glass of port, Pitt explained, "If every county adds two volunteer companies to its regular militia reserves, thousands could be added to the National Guard. Of course, we will move regular forces into the areas on the southern coast as well.

Richard pursed his lips. "You want me to raise two volunteer companies in West Sussex?"

"I do, indeed, old boy. Only gentlemen of weight and property can fund and equip the men needed to see the job done."

Richard nodded. "Very well, you may count upon me to do

all I can to deliver them."

The rest of their conversation was taken up with news of the war on the Continent.

It wasn't until dinner that the subject of the Vendée came up.

Zoé's aunt and the princesse joined them a bit later. Once they had changed for dinner, Annie and Richard invited everyone into The Harrows' dining room. As Freddie escorted Zoé from the parlor, she leaned in to whisper to him, "You might have told me you were in the thick of it on the Channel!"

Freddie shrugged dismissively, which only added to her irritation. "Your uncle required a master gunner and I know the position well."

"Master gunner!" she said, incredulous. "I can see it now: you pacing the deck, your arm in a sling, shouting orders with guns firing all around you. You dolt! You might have been killed!"

He had the nerve to smirk. "'Might have' are the operative words, Pigeon. As you can see, I stand before you hale and hearty."

Indeed, he did. The sling was gone and his broad shoulders were now encased in a black frock coat of superfine wool. Peeking from under his coat was a waistcoat of crimson velvet he wore over black trousers. His cravat was impeccably tied. Visions of his naked chest rose in her mind making it difficult to argue with him. Try as she might to carry her own, he was too handsome, too charming and, dare she admit it even to herself, too often right.

"As long as you are taking me to task for putting myself in danger," he began, "how about—"

"Oh, very well," she interrupted, not wishing to hear him scold her for the risks she had taken. "Let us hope you remain hale and hearty." When he arrived at her chair, she took a seat and he went around the table to sit across from her.

Candles set in silver branched candlesticks stood in the center of the table over which hung a brilliant crystal chandelier. Gilded porcelain dishes painted with a Chinoiserie scene of flowers in blue and white were set upon the linen tablecloth. Like Guernsey, it all seemed a bit unreal to Zoé and far from the Terror she had witnessed in France.

The meal the Torringtons served the Prime Minister was an elaborate one. It began with turtle soup—thanks to her uncle's gift of the turtle—followed by trout, stuffed partridges and platters of sliced roast veal. Asparagus and peas comprised the side dishes. The rich scent of the stuffed partridges made Zoé's mouth water. She had eaten nothing since the gingerbread at the Barlows' cottage.

Annie, as hostess, sat at one end of the long table, the Prime Minister on her right. Across from him was Madame de Montconseil, looking very much the French aristocrat in her pale peach silk gown with her dark hair drawn back from her face in an elaborate coiffure.

Zoé was only half-listening to their conversation in which Annie recounted for the princesse the activities engaged in by the émigrés in London when the discussion turned to the country the princesse had left behind.

Zoé's ears perked up when the subject of the Vendée intruded into the conversation.

"It seems to me, madame," remarked Pitt, "the royalists in the Vendée serve with more fervor than some of our allies. Prussia is a shaky partner at best and the Dutch and the Austrians contribute less than they might, whereas the Vendéens fight with few weapons. For that, they have my admiration."

The princesse shook her head as if in dismay. "The word in Paris when I left was that Robespierre and his Committee of Public Safety had given orders to destroy the Vendée, even the women and children. A nasty, terrible man with no honor and no pity."

Pitt laid aside his fork. "I grant you the reports from there are troubling. And any success the republicans have in the Vendée will make Paris less likely to yield to Britain and her allies."

"Though I am loathe to speak of it," said Zoé's uncle, "I can confirm that thousands of Vendéens have been slain and the killing goes on."

Across the table, Zoé met Freddie's steady gaze.

With a pointed look at Zoé's uncle, the Prime Minister said, "You could be most helpful in our desire to aid the royalists, Monsieur Donet."

"My ships are at your disposal," her uncle offered without hesitation.

Zoé caught the exchange of glances between her uncle and Freddie. *Something is afoot and, before we sail for Guernsey, I mean to learn the truth of it.*

From the other end of the table, Richard said, "Should the government decide to support the royalists in the northwestern provinces, it will make the Duke of Portland's Whigs happy. The Vendée is ever on their tongues."

Zoé had heard her aunt railing about the Whigs who followed Portland and were late to support Pitt's ministry and the war with France. Zoé cared little for England's politics except those that helped the fighters who wore the sacred heart patch. She tried to call to mind Henri's angelic face framed by his blond curls, but the mental image proved oddly elusive. The passage of time had weakened her memory. The best she could conjure was a portrait surrounded by a glow of gold, like the painting of a saint in a breviary, halo and all. Had her gallant Henri really looked like that? Of course, he had not, but that was how she had begun to remember him.

"I am eager to end party differences," Pitt told Richard, "and as long as Portland's Whigs continue to support the war, we can find agreement on other matters."

"England has exceeded the whole of Europe in extending its

hospitality to the émigrés," put in Madame de Montconseil with a look of gratitude aimed at Pitt. "I am certain they could be persuaded to join the fight in the Vendée, or what is left of it. I would think you have only to make your request known and they will rush to serve."

"I need not ask them to go, dear princesse," said Pitt. "The émigrés hound the ministry daily, clamoring for us to join the fight."

By the time the pudding was served along with cheese and more port for the Prime Minister, Pitt had said he would seriously consider adding to his list of urgent matters support for the fighters in the northwest of France.

Zoé couldn't have been more pleased, which is why she gave scant attention to the frown that appeared on Freddie's face.

Freddie went searching for Zoé the next morning and found her in the garden dressed in an ivory gown over which she wore a peach pelisse against the chill. Dark ringlets framed her delicate face. It was hard to believe she was the same young woman who traveled the streets of Normandy as a soot-covered peasant.

At his approach, she straightened from where she had been bending over a white rose and turned to face him. Her eyes were the color of the overcast sky. "Good morning," she said rather stiffly.

"Pigeon, I must speak with you."

"And I must speak with *you*," she threw back, her eyes growing stormy, which only added to his anxiety about a conversation he suspected would not go well. "What secret is shared between you and my uncle that you have chosen not to share with me?"

He let out a breath. "That is the matter I wanted to discuss." Her forehead furrowed as he plunged in. "I have been asked to travel to Brittany and Maine to learn the needs of a royalist group there called the Chouans. It seems the surviving Vendéens have joined with them."

"Mr. Pitt asked you?"

"Nay, 'twas Captain d'Auvergne while we were still on Jersey. I don't believe Pitt knows the request has been put to me. I rather doubt he knows of my work in France."

A shadow crossed her lovely face. "Oh, Freddie. It will be dangerous."

"I'm relieved you recognize that fact, Pigeon, which is why I don't want you to go."

She returned him a look of surprise. "Why ever did you think I would?"

"Well, I—"

"Although now that I think of it," she interrupted, "you cannot go alone." He could already see her mind spinning with plans. She pursed her lips. "You will need someone to accompany you as a guard." Chewing on her bottom lip, she added, "perhaps two."

"Zoé," he said in a stronger tone, hoping to take the conversation from himself, "D'Auvergne wants *you* to go with me, but I would be pleased to advise him you have declined."

She turned from her planning to stare at him. "Me?"

"He has some notion your presence would be helpful due to the high regard the Vendéens have for you." Freddie refused to admit the reason was her devotion to the Vendéens' fallen hero; he hoped she had forgotten him.

"D'Auvergne believes I am essential to the effort to help the royalist fighters?"

Freddie looked down at the grass beneath his feet not wishing her to see how close she was to d'Auvergne's actual words. "Something like that."

She crossed her arms in front of her and tapped her toe. "Are you worried I might fail, Freddie?"

He raised his gaze to meet hers. "No, I am worried your life will be more at risk than it already is with your efforts to rescue the émigrés, which exploits, I might add, have caused me many sleepless nights."

"I see." She walked a few steps away and then turned to face him. "Does my uncle know of this?"

"He does."

"And? What does he say?"

Freddie took a deep breath, searching for what he could say without telling her Donet had suggested they plan for her to go. "Your uncle will not insist you stay."

"I should hope not," she said emphatically. "He knows me too well for that. If I can help to identify the needs of the Vendéens and these Chouans, I will most certainly go." Then as blithely as if she were suggesting a trip into town, she said, "When do we leave?"

Freddie hung his head in defeat. He could deny her nothing when she looked at him with those pleading dove gray eyes. And, this time, he had not one ally in his desire to refuse her. She might be fearless but he was not, not where she was concerned. "If I cannot persuade you of the folly of tramping into the woods of Brittany, then you will follow my orders, is that clear?"

"Very." She was too pleased with herself.

"We will prepare once we return to Guernsey." Then he tossed in as an aside, "Your uncle suggested Gabe might go with us."

She gave Freddie a look that told him she was not surprised at her uncle's suggestion or his knowledge she would insist on going. "I think it might be well for us to bring Erwan, too. He is a Breton after all."

Freddie shook his head. He did not have a good feeling about any of this.

Chapter 6

The coast of Brittany, France, early April 1794

It had taken several days for Zoé to convince her aunt the mission to Brittany was only to help Freddie gather information required by d'Auvergne. Even then, her aunt's eyes reflected a grave concern for the danger she and Freddie would face once they left the coast and the safety of *la Reine Noire*'s guns. She could still hear the pleading tone of her aunt's voice.

"Zoé, must you go? Is there no other they can send?"

"In this case, no, but *Oncle* Jean is sending Gabe to protect me."

It wasn't the first time Zoé had set out in the face of danger. When she had first begun helping those fleeing the Terror, she had considered the cost and willingly accepted the possibility she might die for the cause. After all, Henri had given his life.

And so it was, early one morning before dawn with only the light of the setting moon, a skiff launched from *la Reine Noire* dropped Zoé, Freddie and their two companions on an unfamiliar shore just south of Lorient in an area of the coast they were told was seldom visited by republican patrols.

As Freddie helped her to the sand and her hand left his, she felt a chill that could not be explained by the cold wind blowing onshore. Her disquiet grew as she scanned the dense stand of trees guarding the beach.

"Freddie, are you quite certain someone will be meeting us?"

Freddie gazed toward the trees, his expression uncertain. "D'Auvergne assured me he sent a message to his contacts in Lorient who are to guide us to the best route into the interior."

Zoé hoped the British captain in Jersey could be counted upon. Except for the coast, neither she nor her companions were conversant with Brittany's terrain. They had been advised the interior consisted of dense woodlands and rough pastures punctuated by an occasional village or a manor house once occupied by a minor nobleman.

Freddie had taken the lead, being several years older than the rest of them and the one whose mission it was to gather information for the British war ministry.

Erwan and Gabe's wary expressions as they climbed from the boat and scanned the crescent of white sand told Zoé the eerie calm and dark woods had also affected them. Undaunted, they shoved the boat back into the water, their faces speaking only determination.

The two oarsmen lifted a hand in farewell before quickly rowing away.

"Since we have no welcome party, how are we to find these Chouans?" she asked Freddie.

"They will find us," he said with a confident tone she doubted reflected his true feelings. "Perhaps they watch us even now."

She stared into the trees but saw no movement. Oddly, no birds tweeted though the sky had grown lighter with the rising sun. "I don't like the idea of being watched, even by those who mean us no harm."

"Come, Pigeon," Freddie said, offering his hand, "let us move from the beach." Over his shoulder, he had slung a satchel into which she'd observed him stashing small bottles of what looked to be ink and paper along with his spare ammunition, food and other possessions.

She placed her hand in his, comforted by the return of his warmth. Since she had first met her uncle and his English bride, Freddie had been a part of her life. Once she had thought of him as a brother but after those days she had kept vigil at his sickbed, she no longer thought of him that way. Though what he was to her she could not say. Still, the possibility of his falling victim to another republican soldier's musket left her disquieted.

Could she protect him from the revolutionary government that had ordered all the British in France arrested? He was more vulnerable than she. And what if the Chouans cared not that she had once held the confidence of Henri de la Rochejaquelein? Would they trust her? As she thought of these things, her spirit became more unsettled.

On Guernsey, they spoke English, French and "Guernsey French", which was sprinkled with Breton words. But only Erwan spoke fluently the Breton language they might need to communicate with the Chouans.

Gabe and Erwan picked up their satchels and joined her and Freddie. The four of them trudged up the beach toward the trees. Zoé was glad she had replaced her peasant skirts with the clothing of the men who lived in this region, enabling her to walk more freely. The dark brown jacket fell to her hips. Under it, she had donned a linen shirt, umber waistcoat and fawn-colored breeches. On her head she wore the brown wide-brimmed felt hat, a characteristic of the Breton men.

They had been told the peasants often went barefoot or wore wooden sabots with leather gaiters protecting their shins. Erwan wore the sabots of his youth and the Breton peasant clothing, the worn cloth bearing signs of much use.

Zoé preferred boots.

Henri had always worn boots, polished black Hessians, but then he was one of the Vendéen officers from the French nobility who, like the other officers, dressed in accord with his station. Zoé had chosen a pair of scuffed boots that did not speak of wealth.

Freddie wore Hessian boots, as was his custom, though she noted he had not polished them. Gabe wore his seaman's shoes, adding the Breton gaiters.

Zoé's blade her uncle had taught her to wield was strapped at her side. Around her waist, she had tied a wide sash into which she thrust a pistol. In between her lessons in the use of a knife, her uncle had taught her to shoot. A pistol could only be used once and then had to be reloaded but that one shot might save her life.

Freddie, Gabe and Erwan carried both pistols and muskets. Freddie alone had sheathed a French small sword at his hip. Most gentlemen wore them as part of their costume, but did Freddie know how to use it? She had never seen him wield a sword.

Each of them had pinned the sacred heart patch to their jackets. They would have to be careful. The same royalist symbol that would be welcomed by the Chouans would condemn them in the eyes of the republican soldiers.

With trepidation for Zoé, Freddie plunged into the woods, never letting go of her hand. Along with his concern for her, he experienced an excitement stirring in his chest. This would be an assignment worthy of the trust the Crown had placed in him, a chance for him, as a younger son forever in the shadow of his father and older brothers, two of them dead war heroes and the other an English peer, to distinguish himself.

And then there was Zoé's infamous uncle, a hero of another sort, known to both England and France for his daring and courage. With an uncle like that, would Zoé ever see Freddie as a man she could respect? A man she could love?

Freddie wished he had prevailed upon her to remain behind though, from the start, he'd doubted his arguments would be successful. She was headstrong in her pursuit of a royalist victory. For that, he admired her, but she could be reckless, too. With her a part of his mission, he must be cautious.

They had walked some distance when he looked up to see a patch of blue sky above the dark treetops of the tall Scots pines around them. Not much light filtered down to the forest floor except in areas where the trees thinned.

Notwithstanding his counsel to his companions to tread lightly, their heavy footfalls snapped twigs and fallen branches, sounding to Freddie like a family of wild boar hoofing it through the woods.

He wondered if he should be sounding the cry of the tawny owl. Perhaps that is what the Chouans expected, why they waited to reveal themselves. He'd not seen any of the birds nor heard their distinctive cry, but that didn't mean they weren't guarding nests hidden among the foliage. He stopped, let go of Zoé's hand and leaned his musket against the tree. Cupping his hands, he gave the cry of the female owl. Retrieving his musket, he proceeded forward, holding his breath.

With a suddenness that made him start, a half-dozen figures clothed in the colors of the forest soundlessly emerged from the trees to stand before him.

Zoé gave out a small gasp and Freddie placed himself in front of her, his hand lifting his musket, poised to fire.

"Are you *le pêcheur, l'Anglais* we were told to expect?" asked a leathery-faced man of great height who took a step toward him. Thankfully, the man had spoken French and not Breton.

Zoé came alongside Freddie, her brows rising as she turned to look at him. *"Le pêcheur?"*

"'The fisherman'," Freddie muttered. "D'Auvergne's attempt at humor. 'Tis a reference to my friendship with the oystermen on Jersey. A code name, if you will."

Freddie returned his attention to the Chouan spokesman. *"Oui,* I am the one you seek and these are my companions."

The tall Chouan casually stood his musket on end and laid his forearm on the muzzle while he examined Freddie. With the bayonet rising above the muzzle, the man and the weapon were of the same height, taller than Freddie's nearly six feet and that before one counted the Chouan's wide-brimmed felt hat.

He cut a striking figure. Long chestnut hair hung to his shoulders encased in a woolen jacket of dark green over a linen shirt and green woolen waistcoat. His breeches were buckskin and around his waist was a white sash into which he had shoved two pistols with wooden handles. Displayed on his chest was the sacred heart patch of the Catholic and Royal Army. But unlike his men, whose shins were encased in gaiters splattered with mud and their feet shod in wooden sabots, the Chouan leader wore fine black boots and pinned to his hat was the white cockade of the Bourbons.

"And you," the Chouan inquired of Zoé, "might you be the friend of Monsieur Henri?"

Freddie was not surprised the man's discerning eye had recognized Zoé as a woman. Though, from a distance, some might judge her a young man, to Freddie's mind, even in breeches, her delicate features and female curves made clear she was no boy.

"I am," Zoé replied, her voice laced with pride, her chin rising slightly. "Mademoiselle Donet. And who might you be?"

Amusement danced in the Chouan's dark eyes. Inclining his head, he said, "Georges Cadoudal, *à votre service*."

Freddie had heard the name for it was one d'Auvergne had mentioned. A Breton politician of some consequence and a royalist who had been rescued from the Vendée. He now fought with the Chouans. Clearly no peasant by his dress, speech and manners.

Gesturing to Erwan and Gabe, Cadoudal asked Freddie, "And these two?"

"Erwan is a Breton. Like yourself, he is a surviving soldier of the Vendéen army."

The Chouan chief's brows rose with Freddie's indication that he understood something of Cadoudal's past.

"And Gabe," Freddie went on, gesturing to the seaman, "is a trusted member of Monsieur Donet's crew on the ship that brought us to Lorient."

"*Eh bien!*" exclaimed the Chouan. "I am aware of M'sieur Donet. Your father, *peut-être?*" he asked Zoé.

"*Mon oncle.*"

Cadoudal smiled. "*Votre oncle* is of one mind with us. A friend of the royalists. *Très bien*, we go." Tossing a glance at his men, but apparently judging it unnecessary to introduce them, the Chouan leader took his musket in hand and set off into the forest, his long legs setting a fast pace.

Freddie followed with Zoé close behind him. Erwan and Gabe guarded their backs and Cadoudal's men brought up the rear.

They wove their way single file through the dense woods of pine, birch, oak and beech. The world around them became a sea of green. At one point, Freddie spotted a tawny owl peeking out between branches of an oak. If the circumstances had been different, with no republican soldiers to worry about, he might have enjoyed the excursion. Frequently, he glanced back at Zoé to see if she was tiring and to offer her a drink from his waterskin. His spirited companion drank the water, never pausing or complaining.

As the trail narrowed, Freddie looked back over his shoulder and saw no trace of their having traveled the path.

After what seemed to Zoé like hours of trudging through the woods, the tall Chouan suddenly stopped. Glad for the pause, however brief, Zoé removed her hat and wiped her forehead. The sun was high overhead but its light was diffused among the oak trees where they stood.

Lifting his cupped hands to his mouth, Cadoudal made a

sharp "kew-wick" sound.

Freddie shot her a glance as if to confirm what he had told her before they left Guernsey, that the Chouans used an owl's call as a signal.

From some distance away, a "hoo-hoo-hoo" answered back on the light breeze stirring the leaves of the trees.

Having apparently received the acknowledgement he sought, Cadoudal resumed his forward march. Soon they came upon a clearing where a makeshift camp had been set up around a fire over which hung a black cauldron, steam rising above its rim. Zoé sniffed the aroma that smelled of stew and experienced a gnawing hunger.

Around the fire, she counted a dozen men dressed in haphazard fashion she assumed reflected their profession as farmers and tradesmen. Some wore waistcoats of rough goatskin and breeches of faded, dirt-splattered cloth. Their shirts, stained with the soil of their travels, were of various shades of white and chalk. Each of their jackets, most of a fawn color, displayed the sacred heart patch. Around the necks of a few were long rosaries in further defiance of their suppressed faith.

None wore boots like their leader but, instead, wooden sabots and gaiters.

They regarded Zoé and the others with suspicious eyes.

At Cadoudal's approach, one man rose to speak to the leader and Cadoudal answered in the Breton tongue.

"He tells them we are the ones expected," said Erwan, lifting his hat to run his fingers through his long dark hair. "They have done business with others sent by d'Auvergne before, but his men are distrusting of English offers of help."

"With good reason," muttered Zoé.

Freddie shot her a quelling look.

She raised her chin defiantly. The English failed the Vendéens in Granville and that failure had led to Henri's death. She would not say otherwise.

"You can rest here," said Cadoudal, coming up to them. He gestured to a log placed alongside the fire. "Sit. I've asked my men to bring you food."

A few of his men rose from the log, making room for them.

Tired from their morning march through the woods and feeling famished, Zoé was happy to take a place on the log in front of the fire. The air had remained cool and she welcomed the heat from the blaze.

Freddie dropped down beside her. Gabe and Erwan found places on either side of them.

"How are you, Pigeon?" Freddie asked.

"Tired, but then I expected to be." She glanced at Freddie, who didn't appear at all fatigued. Rather, he seemed energized. "And you?"

"Only a little. I'm encouraged we made contact with the ones who can help us." Zoé could see the relief on his face. He had the responsibility of not only his mission, but of finding their way through the woods and ensuring the safety of their lives. He hid well his anxiety.

One of the Chouans gave them bowls of something that proved to be a thick vegetable soup. There was no bread but then she had not looked for any. In France, few could afford bread. Since Brittany had been a hotbed of revolt for well over a year and the farmers had been fighting rather than tending their crops, bread would be scarce.

Another man poured a dark liquid into cups he'd handed to them. A taste told her it was coffee sweetened with some kind of syrup.

"'Tis my preferred drink," said Cadoudal. "Picked it up in Paris in better times and now I can't live without it."

"The coffee is quite good," Zoé said, "and sweeter than what *mon oncle* serves aboard his ship."

Cadoudal tipped his hat to her. "If you like, you can take a skin of wine with you. Mind, 'tis not that red wine the revolutionaries drink when they speak of the blood they have spilled and the liberty they would deny us." His chest puffing out with pride, he pronounced, "We drink the fine Muscadet of Brittany, the white wine of the Bourbons."

Freddie said, "We are grateful for your help, the food and your offer of wine. I am curious about one thing. Your men all have muskets, yet I was led to believe many royalists fought with only farm implements."

"We have won enough battles that we have reaped a harvest of muskets from dead Blues. Many Chouans are hunters who can shoot and shoot well. Some had muskets before the war."

Freddie nodded. "I have heard that Chouans are good shots. And do you need more muskets?"

"*Bien sûr*. We do. Our army grows; it is now well into the tens of thousands. As you travel north, you will find men joining us who have no muskets."

"Our intention is to travel first to Fougères to meet with your general there, the young chevalier du Boisguy, to ask what he may know of the Chouans' needs."

"*Le petit général* is well known to us. It is good you will visit with him. We cannot take you all the way to Fougères, but we can see you to Rennes and set you on the right path. The young sister of one of our chiefs has been imprisoned in Rennes due to her relationship with us. We go to free her before it is too late."

Freddie frowned. "Isn't Rennes the headquarters of the republican army?"

"*Oui*, it is," said Cadoudal, "*Mais peu importe*, 'tis of no matter. We must see to our own and Rennes is where the Blues hold their prisoners."

Freddie shook his head. "I've no desire to venture into that nest of vipers."

The Chouan placed a fist on his hip and gestured north with his other hand. "The road to Fougères leads through Rennes. To skirt it from the south would be difficult without a guide and I can spare none. You will be safe with us."

Zoé sensed Freddie's unease and his reticence to go through Rennes. She, too, did not wish to enter the stronghold of republican soldiers, but there were good reasons to do so.

Freddie raised a brow at Erwan. The former Vendéen soldier merely shrugged. Being from Brittany, he would know Rennes better than the rest of them, and he had faced republican troops before and survived.

Likewise, Gabe voiced no protest. "I go where the mistress goes."

"Perhaps we should accept M'sieur Cadoudal's offer," she urged Freddie. "That way, we would not be traveling alone. And we may gain information in Rennes that would prove useful."

Freddie rose, a look of resignation crossing his face. "Very well." He offered his hand to Cadoudal. "It seems my companions agree with you. We accept."

Cadoudal shook his hand. "Rennes is nearly four days' journey north. Every day the child is in the hands of those pigs is a day she is in grave danger. We must leave within the hour."

At his command, the Chouans began to decamp and, before an hour had ended, the fire had been snuffed out, the ashes strewn about and the clearing made to look as if no one had been there for days. Zoé supposed after the last few years of guerilla warfare, they had perfected their ability to disappear quickly.

When their leader gave the command to depart, the Chouans lifted their satchels, picked up their muskets and moved as one in Cadoudal's footsteps.

Freddie looked at her, his brow furrowed with worry.

She ran her finger over his forehead, brushing away the frown. "You made the right decision and I have faith you will see it through."

He caught her fingers against his cheek and pressed them to his warm skin. "I have a good partner."

Drawing a steadying breath, she met his intense gaze. A jolt of emotion surged through her but she couldn't have explained why if she'd been asked. Here was Freddie, possibly her best friend, paying her a compliment. He had done so before, not often but she could recall a few times. So why should this time be different? They were joined in a cause, surrounded by danger but could it be something had changed?

Chapter 7

Rennes, Brittany

After days of tramping through the rain-soaked woods and sleeping in decrepit sheds and deserted cottages, Freddie had cause to wonder if Zoé still had faith in his decision. But he could count among the reasons he had agreed to go with Cadoudal and his men that they were in the company of trained fighters and headed in the right direction.

"I will never again complain of rough seas," said Zoé, looking down at her mud-caked boots.

"At least tonight you will be sleeping in a bed and not in the woods, Pigeon. Though the call of the tawny owl last night was a pleasant inducement to sleep, don't you think?" The owls had been active the night before, some of them, he was certain, were Chouans returning from their night patrols. They were so good at mimicking the bird's call it was difficult to tell which call was real and which the counterfeit.

She tossed him a sardonic smile. "A sound I will always remember."

As they reached the outskirts of the city, Freddie took comfort in what Cadoudal had told him as they traveled north. The city of Rennes, the capital of Brittany, had a population numbering thirty thousand. It was hoped their small number could remain hidden among so many people.

Cadoudal paused and looked ahead to the walled town. "To oppose the Chouans and the Vendéens who fight with us, the republican army has used fortified towns like Rennes, defending them with their territorial guards. Their commander is General Rossignol, a man of military incompetence and violent passions, who has never considered himself constrained by society's morals or his wedding vows. I happened to be in Paris when word came of his promotion to chief commander of the Army of the Coasts of Brest. Much laughter was heard in the city when the tale was told of his wife rushing to the National Convention to argue before the deputies her husband was unfit for the post. She was right, of course, but Robespierre approved the promotion and sent Rossignol back to the army in triumph where he now glories in barbarity and lascivious behavior." He let out a deep sigh. "Alas, Rennes is his headquarters."

One of the Chouans spat in the dust, muttering Rossignol's name and a few words in the Breton tongue.

Erwan translated. "He speaks of 'that bastard and his false Chouans'."

"Another of Rossignol's ideas," put in Cadoudal. "To create fake Chouan outlaws who engage in thievery and worse in order to discredit us." With a stern expression, he said to Freddie, "Be mindful of such when you leave us."

Cadoudal gave orders to his men in Breton. Immediately, they divided into three groups. Turning to Freddie, he said, "We will be less noticed if we separate and take different routes to the place we will stay."

Each of the men removed the royalist patch from his coat and added the tricolor cockade to his hat. Cadoudal, too, altered his attire to change his appearance from a Chouan officer to a supporter of the revolution.

Freddie and his companions unpinned the patches from their own coats and stuffed them into their pockets. On their hats, they now donned the cockade that was the emblem of the revolution.

"You and your companions best stay with me," said Cadoudal. Gesturing two of his men to go with him, Cadoudal nodded to the other two groups that quickly departed. Then he set out, taking the path to the right toward the eastern side of the city.

Freddie, Zoé, Gabe and Erwan followed.

As they drew nearer to the city, republican soldiers became more evident, making Freddie's skin crawl. Congregating in groups, their blue and white uniforms appeared everywhere.

"They are like swarming locusts," he said.

"Do not be concerned," said Cadoudal. "Our numbers are greater than theirs, just unseen until they are needed."

Rennes was a city of contrasts from medieval buildings on narrow cobblestone streets to great stone edifices on wide avenues opening into grand squares rivaling any in Paris.

At the far end of one large square stood an imposing building of two stories, its slanted slate roof reminding Freddie of buildings in Paris. Seventeen tall windows stretched across the façade with a single wooden door leading to its entrance. "What is that?"

Cadoudal frowned. "The *Palais de Justice* where they keep the prisoners. Very convenient for them as the guillotine stands close." He pointed to one side of the square.

Freddie's gaze shifted to where the instrument of death rose fourteen feet in the air above its wooden platform, the mechanical monster's jaws still soaked in the blood of its victims.

Freddie turned away from the hideous sight to see Zoé's expression turn to loathing. Setting her jaw, her eyes burned with anger. She had lost friends to that demon device.

A group of republican soldiers suddenly turned to stare at them.

Freddie moved to block their view of Zoé. He wanted no undue interest in her by soldiers who thought the Breton peasants were available to them. He doubted she could pass for a lad to an observant man who would recognize her for what she was, a beautiful woman. He comforted himself with the thought people rarely stopped to look closely. Most saw only what they expected to see.

"Come, let us go!" Cadoudal whispered, moving from the square and quickly rounding a corner. A few streets away, they encountered buildings four stories high that looked to Freddie to be from the times of the Tudors.

"That one," Cadoudal said, pointing to a smaller building, "once housed priests. Now it is a tavern frequented by the Blues where Rossignol brags to his men of the priests he has killed, a strike against his already black character none of us will forget. Some of the priests were members of Breton families."

At his side, a look of despair crossed Zoé's lovely face. "Erwan and I might have known them."

Erwan shook his head, his eyes downcast. "I knew many."

Freddie fought the urge to pull Zoé into his arms and soothe her grief. Instead, he placed his hand on her shoulder as an older brother might. "Those priests are now in Heaven, Pigeon, a place Rossignol will never see."

Cadoudal led them down a cobblestone street away from the city's center to where there were fewer republican soldiers. As the street widened, they came to a building made of warm golden stone with a tavern opening onto the street. A row of black shutters marched across the front like soldiers at attention. "Ours," said the Chouan leader. "A safe place to pass the night."

From what Freddie could ascertain, the customers of the tavern, if not the inn, were farmers and tradesmen who, at the moment, were sitting around drinking wine. Were they all Chouans, royalist fighters? He wondered. Several men, slouched over their tankards, looked up as Cadoudal entered and nodded in recognition.

The Chouan leader acknowledged them with a dip of his head and strode to the bar. In French, he addressed the proprietor, a rotund man of middle years, a bald head and a large mustache.

"Good sir, I hope this day finds you well. My friends and I have traveled far and require rooms for a night, perhaps two."

The man busied himself wiping down the top of the wooden counter, glancing up at Cadoudal for a brief moment. *"Bien sûr,* I have several chambers on the top floor you can have."

A look passed between the Chouan leader and the proprietor that told Freddie this scene had been enacted many times before, but to one who had just strolled into the tavern, it would appear a first encounter.

The proprietor handed Cadoudal a handful of keys and waved him to the stairs at the back of the tavern.

"But where am I to sleep?" Zoé asked when Freddie followed her into the chamber and closed the door behind them.

Freddie's mouth hitched up in a grin. "Here with me, of course."

"With you!" She surveyed the room, noting the small bed that could accommodate two only if they slept close together, a side table with basin and pitcher, and a table and two chairs. She knew travelers' inns often required guests to share beds but she had never done so, not even with her aunt. Her uncle had sufficient homes so that they rarely frequented inns and, when they did, they were fine establishments.

Freddie shook his head. "Not in the same bed, Zoé, but neither will I leave you alone. 'Tis the floor where I'll make my bed. Erwan and Gabe will guard the door." When she opened her mouth to protest, he said, "Count yourself fortunate not to be sleeping in the woods."

She let out a breath. *"Oui,* I suppose you are right. If it were anyone else but you, Freddie, I would refuse the arrangement." Resigning herself to the awkward accommodations, she asked, "So, when are the Chouans to rescue the child?"

"Tonight when few lanterns light the square and the guards are tired and about to change shifts. Some of the Chouans will appear as their replacements."

"They can do that?" she asked, bewildered. "Transforming a Chouan into a republican guard would take a miracle."

"Apparently they are confident they can. They know the routine of the guards and they have the proper uniforms. I don't wonder they have posed as the guards before."

Zoé removed her brush from her satchel and shedding her hat, took down her hair and began to brush the dust from the long strands, all the while thinking of the danger they would face. Out of the corner of her eye, she caught Freddie watching her. She paused in her brushing. "What?"

"Oh, nothing," he muttered, shaking his head. "Are you hungry?" Then, without waiting for her answer, he took one of the blankets from the bed and set it next to the fireplace, reminding Zoé he intended to sleep on the floor. They would still be sleeping in the same room, of course. Images of his suntanned chest sprinkled with auburn hair rose in her mind. Did he sleep naked?

"You can stay here and rest if you like," he said, walking toward the door. "It might be awhile before the proprietor thinks to send up our dinner. I'll bring food for us."

She thought of the men she had seen in the common room, a hardened lot who would easily see through her disguise. "If you don't mind, it might be best."

"There will be plenty of time before I leave for the rescue for us to eat."

She set down her brush and faced him. "You're going with them?"

He nodded. "How could I not? Besides, Erwan wanted to go as well. You needn't worry. Gabe will stay with you."

"'Tis not myself I am concerned about, Freddie, 'tis you! Such a reckless venture. Why, 'tis fraught with danger. What is your role to be anyway?"

"One of Cadoudal's men will lead the group disguised as guards. The Chouan chief would go himself but he fears recognition. I will go with Cadoudal and the rest of his men to wait on the edges of the square should we be needed."

She chewed her bottom lip, thinking of the planned rescue that would have him facing republican soldiers. "It seems an unnecessary risk with all that lies before us. We have yet to reach even Fougères." The thought of losing him to a skirmish or worse was too horrible to contemplate. She had tended his wounded body once; she could not bear to see him bleeding again.

He left the door, crossing the distance between them. In a soft voice, he said, "Cadoudal has helped us, Pigeon, and he has promised to set us on the path to Fougères. It didn't seem right not to participate now when he may need every man."

She could not let him go alone. "Then I will go as well." She could at least cover his back.

His face turned rigid. "No, you won't. And that's an order."

Zoé could feel her temper rising. She wanted to argue, to plead with him not to go, but she knew Freddie well enough to know when he got that look, he would not budge. Too, this was his mission and she had promised to follow his lead. Resigned but not liking it one bit, she pressed her lips together and crossed her arms. "You will be careful, *oui*?"

"Of course," he said with a nonchalant smile, which only made her fret more.

Freddie shared dinner with Zoé in the room he now thought of as their chamber. The small table set before the fireplace made for an intimate setting as the fire subsided to embers and a single candle illuminated their faces.

Their meal was a humble one but, shared with her, it seemed a feast. He would have called the thick soup "beef stew" if he'd been in one of England's taverns. The rich broth contained pieces of beef, carrots, onions and potatoes, the latter being a vegetable Cadoudal had told him was previously considered unacceptable by the French. But famine, brought on by poor crops and fields abandoned when farmers were conscripted into the republican army, had forced the potato on the country.

The only thing the meal lacked was a slice of thick crusty bread and butter. Still, the wine was good and there were apples for dessert. And the company was all he could hope for, though Zoé spoke little and ate less, occasionally moving her spoon around in her soup.

She did drink her wine, running her tongue over her bottom lip and driving him half-mad with want of her. Even dressed as a Chouan, she raised a longing within him so strong, he had to fight the urge to take her in his arms and make his dreams a reality.

Patience, he reminded himself, was a virtue. "Aren't you hungry?" he inquired. "You've been walking all day."

For a moment, she stared at him over her glass. "I am tired and my feet are protesting my boots, but my appetite has escaped me." A small smile played about her lips. "I promise to save an apple to celebrate your return."

She would never admit it, but he glimpsed fear in the tightness around her eyes and the way she worried her bottom lip between her teeth.

He set down his spoon, leaned his elbows on the table and drew a steadying breath. "Pigeon, rest easy. I am not new to this game of assuming another man's identity." Hoping to bring a smile to her face, he said, "I can curse with the best of the sailors in Guernsey's taverns; I can fish with the oystermen and pass myself off as one of them; and I can speak enough of the local French in the port towns to move easily among the dockside workers." He smirked. "Trust me to blend with the peasants tonight and to be quick in a fight if it comes to that."

She frowned despite his attempt at frivolity. "It may very well come to that, Freddie, and you know it."

"Are you worried for me?" He had thought he glimpsed such worry in her eyes but would she admit it?

"Why... *non*," she said defensively. "I just don't want to lose the man leading our mission." She let out an exasperated sigh and her eyes turned the color of storm clouds. "You may play games in Guernsey's taverns, Freddie, but what do you know of war? Or of fighting with that sword you carry for that matter?"

More than you know, he wanted to say. Instead, he met her disquieting gaze and said nothing. Would it help for her to know he was not just d'Auvergne's man but also Evan Nepean's, the British Undersecretary of War? She was intelligent enough to have questioned where he went when he disappeared for weeks at a time. He had always managed to avoid giving her a full answer. Finally, deciding he must say something, he assured her, "I have had the usual lessons and I can use the sword if I must." He would not tell her of his training with the finest sword master in London nor the times he had survived because he was that good with a blade. Another reason Nepean had recruited him.

Nepean's exact words were, "You have skills that the others I could send into France do not, West. Those skills would be wasted on a ship. Why, even I cannot speak French in as many dialects as you. You are also conversant with the codes we use. And then there is the family connection to the Frenchman, Jean Donet. Not a man to be taken lightly, I understand. Now that he is ferrying émigrés to England, you will have transportation when you need it. Of all the choices, you were first on my list. You can serve England better this way than in the Admiralty, as you have proposed."

Freddie had accepted the charge Nepean had given him and Donet had consented to being involved, but neither he nor Freddie had told Zoé he was England's spy.

Lifting the wine to her lovely lips, Zoé took another sip and stared into the pale liquid glistening in the candlelight. "I suppose," she began slowly, "there is much I do not know of your work or why d'Auvergne chose you, an Englishman, for this task." Raising her gaze to meet his, she said, "We have been friends for years and yet, in some ways, you are still a mystery to me, Frederick West."

A knock sounded on the door, relieving Freddie from having to comment. Rising, he said, "There will be time for you to ask me about that in the days ahead, but for now I must go."

Freddie slipped out with Cadoudal, taking the route agreed upon by the Chouans that would bring them to the square in front of the *Palais de Justice*. The moon was a mere crescent against a black sky dotted with stars as they wove their way through the deserted streets. A chill had Freddie turning up his collar and buttoning his coat.

Light from the lanterns hanging from posts set about the square cast faint light on the imposing structure where the *Parlement of Brittany* had met before being closed by the National Assembly. Freddie thought it ironic that a building dedicated to justice now imprisoned those who sought it.

In the ghostly atmosphere, the guillotine took on a sinister appearance as if the monster were lurking in wait, its jaws eager for the blood of its next victim.

Freddie moved with Cadoudal into a darkened corner just as another group of his men took their places on the other side of the square. The six men who had donned the uniforms of the National Guard arrived two by two, coming from different directions to converge on the entrance.

The guards that would have relieved the ones on duty were nowhere in sight. Freddie didn't have to ask what had been their fates. He imagined they were sleeping off a blow to the head in some deserted alley.

With a nudge to his ribs from Cadoudal, Freddie turned to see Chouans disguised as guards climbing the stairs leading to the entrance of the *palais*. They moved like the real ones Freddie had observed earlier that day. Some had added mustaches to their upper lips in the fashion of many of the Blues; others had suddenly grown short-cropped beards making their transformation more dramatic. With straight backs and practiced adjustments of their muskets, they strode to the posts they were to assume, nodding under their bicorne hats to the guards on duty. Cadoudal had told him that in the dim light with their disguises mirroring the actual guards, they hoped their true identity would not be detected.

Few words were exchanged. What Freddie heard sounded more like grunts than speech. Having been relieved, the real guards departed, showing no concern for those taking their places.

Two of Cadoudal's men took up their posts on either side of the entrance, while the others disappeared inside. A short time later, they reappeared with a young girl in tow, scantily clad in a thin blue dress. To anyone in the square, they might have thought her a prisoner being escorted away; however, the Chouans treated her as the precious jewel she was, one on either side of her and two following.

Freddie, Cadoudal and the other Chouans moved from the shadows to follow surreptitiously. As soon as they were off the main street, the ones wearing the republican uniforms disappeared into the night.

The girl's brother, one of the Chouans who had come to the square, wrapped his sister in his coat and embraced her, tears of joy filling his eyes. He stood her away from him, examining her appearance. "You are all right?"

The dark-haired girl nodded as tears ran down her cheeks. A smile formed on her face. "I knew you would come."

"I would never leave you with our enemies, Isabeau. Forgive me for not coming sooner."

Freddie asked one of the Chouans, "How did you convince the guards inside the prison to release her?"

The young man leaned close to whisper. "I told them General Rossignol wanted her for the night. His men know well his twisted inclinations, but even at that, her guard expressed surprise and said, 'The general usually prefers them a bit older', which, *Dieu merci*, told me he had not yet touched her."

Zoé had no intention of remaining behind when Freddie left with the Chouans. Gabe had objected when she told him they would be following but, in the end, he had gone with her mumbling all the while that her uncle would not be pleased she had disobeyed M'sieur West.

Zoé would rather face Gabe's stern disapproval than miss being present to witness the rescue. How could she not be there if things went badly and Freddie needed her help? She didn't accept for one moment his bravado as reflecting the true picture of things. He was brave, yes. That much he had demonstrated in Granville the night he had been shot. And he may have had a few fencing lessons, but that did not prove he could acquit himself in a fight. She had never seen him fire a musket or use his sword.

Checking her pistol, she secured her knife at her hip and set out after them, clinging to the shadows so as not to be seen.

As the rescue unfolded, she watched, fascinated by the precision of the Chouans replacing the guards and the quick extraction of the girl. It had all gone smoothly but still she was glad she had come. When the Chouans led the girl away, Zoé had hurried back to the inn to arrive before Freddie.

"Did I not tell you, mademoiselle," said Gabe, his brooding countenance reminding her he was her uncle's man, "M'sieur West may be *Anglais*, but he knows what he is about."

"Oh, pish," she said, using her aunt's favorite word when presented with something she did not quite believe. "And say nothing of this to Freddie."

Gabe huffed in response and escorted her to the inn's back door where they had departed an hour earlier.

By the time Freddie opened the door to their chamber, she was slicing her apple. "Well, you look to be in one piece," she said, her eyes roving over his body to be sure he had not encountered any soldiers on his return.

"Hale and hearty, as promised," he said with a grin. "Is that apple for me?"

"It is if you want it." She slid the plate toward him. "There is more wine, too. Come let us toast your success. You did recover the girl, *oui*? Your face tells me you did."

He nodded. "Her name is Isabeau and she is downstairs at this very moment eating a bowl of stew and charming the Chouans. A stouthearted little soul."

"How old is she?"

Freddie inclined his head, seeming to ponder. "About twelve, I should think. Not a child exactly but not yet a woman."

Zoé tried to imagine a girl that age being seized by the republicans and confined in their filthy dungeon. "She must have been terribly frightened. Is she well?"

"Apparently her guard developed a fondness for her and made sure she was left alone. When Cadoudal's men allowed him to think Rossignol wanted her, he was most annoyed but there was little he could do."

"I see." And she did see. The general was reputed to prefer young ones. "Perhaps her guard will be relieved when he learns she was plucked from the prison and returned to her family."

"Well, that's just it, Pigeon. Her mother and father were among those killed. She has only her brother, one of Cadoudal's men."

"She can hardly travel with the Chouans. Where will she go?"

"Cadoudal suggested we take her with us to Guernsey. Her brother wants her out of Brittany. She is not safe here."

Zoé considered the idea. "I have smuggled children out of France before but we are not yet on our way home. She would be in danger as long as we remain in Brittany."

Freddie gave her a hopeful look.

Zoé relented. "If it means her life to leave with us, how can we say no?"

A self-satisfied smirk appeared on his handsome face. "I had a feeling you would agree, so I said we would take her. I've asked Gabe to see if he can find her a lad's clothing."

Zoé frowned, annoyed she had proved so predictable, but at least Freddie had thought she would be kindly disposed toward the girl. "Here," she said pouring him a glass of wine, "you can celebrate your victory."

He pulled out a chair and sat, taking a sip of wine before biting into a slice of apple. "We will leave before dawn. Isabeau's brother has volunteered to set us on the path to Fougères. I cannot leave Rennes soon enough. Once Rossignol realizes he's been outwitted by the Chouans, he will be furiously combing the city for us."

"Is Cadoudal worried?"

"Nay, he's taking his men south as we go north."

Zoé finished her wine, feeling fatigued to her bones. "I'm going to get some sleep." She went to the bed and pulled down the cover, tossing one of the pillows to Freddie.

He caught it. "Thanks."

She started to yank off her boots but Freddie intervened. "Allow me to act the valet."

"Thanks." It felt good to let her feet breathe. In her stocking feet, she took off her coat and climbed into the bed.

Freddie moved the small table away from the fireplace to make room for his thin pallet and added a few logs to the low-burning fire, prodding the flames to life with a poker. Snuffing the candle, he settled down on his blanket and drew his coat over his chest.

"Thank you," she said, pulling the cover to her chin.

"For what?"

Fighting a yawn, she looked over the edge of the bed to see

his form silhouetted against the firelight. She lay back down and stared at the firelight flickering on the ceiling. "For returning hale and hearty."

In his exhausted state, Freddie should have been able to sleep, but he could not. His mind whirled with thoughts of the woman who slept a short distance away. He wanted desperately to climb into that bed with her and kiss her. That he might not be able to stop at just one kiss briefly occurred but it mattered not. He could never allow his desire for her to overcome his respect for her innocence. And if they were to become lovers, there might be a babe. One day, he hoped she would give herself to him as his wife. But that day was not today.

On the way back to the inn, Cadoudal had told him what to expect in Fougères. "If he still holds the town, Boisguy will prove a worthy host. He has more than two thousand men under his command. I do not know their needs but they must be substantial as more men join him each day."

Warmed by the fire, Freddie had finally begun to doze when Zoé let out a groan, followed by a shout of *"Non!"*

Concerned Gabe and Erwan might come rushing into their room, believing her shout was directed at Freddie, he leaped up and ran to her bedside.

Tossing and turning her head on the pillow, she fought some invisible foe. *"Non, non, non!"*

He placed his hands on her shoulders and gently shook her awake. "Zoé! Wake up!"

She opened her eyes, dazed from her dream. "Oh, Freddie you are here!" She rose on her knees and swept her hands over him as if to make sure he was really there. Though he knew she was just verifying his existence, the touch of her hands on his shirt might have been on his skin for the effect it had.

Thinking her dream might have been caused by worry for the next day's travel, he asked, "What is wrong? Did you dream of being harmed?"

Staring into his eyes, she whispered. "*Non*, not me. Someone was after *you*. Oh, Freddie, it was so real." Her whole body shook as her hands flew to her face.

"Pigeon, it was merely a dream. We are safe in Rennes." Overwhelmed by the desire to comfort her, he pulled her against his chest and leaned his cheek against her head. Her hair smelled of wood smoke but he didn't mind. It was enough to be with her every day. Was he right in remaining patient, never giving her an indication of what lay in his heart? He thought so, at least for the time being. After all, war was inopportune for love. "As we are leaving in but a few hours, I suggest you try to get some sleep."

He made to lay her back on the pillow but she clung to him. "Don't go, Freddie." She slid over to the far edge of the bed, her hair strewn across the pillow. "There is room here beside me. Not much, but enough. You can sleep on top of the cover with your blanket if you like."

He let out a sigh. It would be torture. But how could he deny her innocent request?

"If it will help you sleep, I'll stay."

Zoé curled into the warmth of Freddie's chest, tucking her head under his chin. Her heart still raced as she tried to recall the dream, certain it was some kind of omen. The vague images quickly faded yet the horror of them persisted. Someone had dragged Freddie away and she had been helpless to save him. Could it have been brought on by her fear when he'd gone to rescue the girl? That might be so but, still, it had been uncommonly real. And frightening.

Freddie's familiar scent and his arm wrapped around her were a balm to her soul, the steady beat of his heart a reminder of his strength. It was like coming home after a long voyage, like smelling the sea breeze on Guernsey after the stale air of Paris, like being tethered to an anchor in rough seas. Freddie, she realized, was her home port.

More than a friend and dearer to her after the night he'd been shot coming to her rescue in Granville, she couldn't imagine her life without her friend.

Bravely, she laid her hand on his chest and had the sudden urge to raise her head and ask him to kiss her.

He would think her a fool. They were cousins, after all, and he'd known her for a decade.

Lulled by the slow beating of his heart, Zoé let go of her wild imaginings and began to drift back to sleep, comforted by the presence of the one man who had never hinted of any interest in her beyond friendship. She knew him to be a man of honor, a man she could trust even if he weren't good with a sword.

She was nearly asleep when he pressed a kiss to the top of her head, telling her he was awake. "Get some sleep, Pigeon."

Nestling into his chest, she pondered the cause of his wake-fulness. Did it speak of his worry for the morrow when he must lead them to Fougères without the Chouans to guide them?

Chapter 8

The next morning as the first rays of dawn slipped in through the wooden shutters, Freddie rose, thinking of the long day ahead. Somehow he would find his way through the unknown forest.

He pulled on his boots while watching Zoé sleep, her mahogany hair flowing out behind her on the pillow and her cheeks rosy with the same blush as her lips.

He wanted to crawl back into that bed with her but not for sleep.

Having held her through what had remained of the night, he'd had little rest. Even with the bedcover and their clothing between them, she had curled against him, her breasts pressing against his side, stirring his body to attention.

Aye, torture, indeed.

He had struggled mightily against the overwhelming desire to initiate her in the ways of love. Having been patient for so long, he could wait a bit longer. Besides, he didn't know if she would want him in the way he wanted her.

A muffled sound from the bed drew his attention. She had turned onto her back. "I trust you are rising sometime this morning, Pigeon."

She let out a dull moan. Her eyes slowly opened and she turned her head to look at him. "You are dressed."

"As I was when I went to bed, silly goose. Best hurry if we are to arrive in Fougères in time to dine with Aimé du Boisguy." Freddie put on his coat. "I will meet you in the common room."

She was just sitting up as he reached the door, her long hair tousled, a temptress rising from her mussed bed like Venus rising from the sea.

With a single glance back, he opened the door and stepped out, closing it behind him. A man could only stand so much.

Several minutes later, surrounded by Chouans in the common room, Freddie introduced Zoé to Isabeau and her brother. From the warm smile Zoé directed at the girl, she seemed pleased to have Giles' sister included in their travel. Because he was a Breton and happy to see one of his own escape France, Erwan had been enthusiastic at the idea of Isabeau joining them. Gabe had merely shrugged when asked his view, but then he was along to guard Zoé. While Freddie worried for Isabeau's safety, he couldn't bear to tell Giles no having seen the fear in his eyes for his young sister.

Cadoudal had advised Freddie that Fougères could be reached in a day, but it would mean a very long day. "At least you'll have many hours of daylight."

Giles knelt in front of his sister, taking her small hands in his. "Mademoiselle Donet will take good care of you, *mon petit chat*. Do as she says."

Tears flowed down Isabeau's cheeks as she nodded, her dark eyes fixed on her brother. The men in the tavern quieted at the touching scene. Isabeau was reed-thin and tall for her age but her modest peasant's clothing, now that of a lad's, made her appear younger than her twelve years.

Freddie studied the girl's face. She was trying to be strong for her brother but the tears flowing down her cheeks made clear she was failing.

In a halting voice, Isabeau said, "I... I have only just got you back."

Giles placed his hands on her shoulders. "I need to know you are safe, Isabeau, somewhere far from Brittany. My friends here will take you to their home on the Isle of Guernsey."

Isabeau regarded Freddie with a look of suspicion. "But he is *Anglais*."

"*Oui*, and one of us," said her brother, rising. "I'm told Guernsey is a wondrous place. You will love it and it is there I will come for you."

Freddie gave the girl a reassuring smile. He hoped it would be as Giles predicted. None of them knew from one day to the next if they would live or die. Too easily, they could join the victims of the republicans' muskets or the guillotines that stood in every major town.

When their goodbyes had been said, Cadoudal handed Freddie a message for Boisguy. "This will vouch for you."

Freddie tucked the folded parchment into his waistcoat and offered his hand to the Chouan chief, thanking him for his help.

Giles opened the door of the inn and led Freddie and his companions out into the misting rain. He was glad for the wide-brimmed hat that kept the drizzle off his face. As an Englishman, he should be used to such weather, but his time on Guernsey had spoiled him. He now preferred sun.

"I will show you the road leading to Fougères," offered Giles. "Then I must leave you. You will know you have arrived when you see the huge stone fortress rising above the town. It is Boisguy's headquarters and where many of his men may be found. Should you want to stop for the night before you reach Fougères, there is a mill house just outside of Combourtillé where you can stay. The miller is a friend of Boisguy and has often been of assistance to the Chouans. He will know the owl's cry." Giles handed Freddie a drawing. "I have made this to help you."

Zoé peered around Freddie and they studied the map together. He resisted the urge to wrap his arm around her shoulder and draw her close. Instead, he concentrated on the simple sketch. The way was clear enough, marked with a few landmarks and small towns.

"This is most helpful," said Freddie.

Giles kissed his sister on the cheek. This time she did not cry but her wrinkled brow betrayed her anxiety.

Turning to Freddie, Giles said, "There are pockets of republican soldiers between here and Fougères. Beware the sham Chouans who are really Rossignol's men. They will be few and will not know the owl's cry. None of them would dare wear a rosary."

Freddie thanked him for his advice. "I won't forget."

At the edge of the city, Giles glanced once at his sister as if to memorize her face and then disappeared into the trees.

"You will see him again," said Zoé, taking Isabeau's hand as they followed Freddie onto the dirt road leading north. She hoped she spoke the truth.

Isabeau returned her a doubtful look.

Zoé understood the girl's plight. She had lost her parents to the revolution and now she believed she was losing her brother. But Zoé could not allow her to focus on her loss. After all, Zoé had once been where Isabeau was. "You are a Breton, are you not, raised in the Church?"

The girl nodded.

"Well then, remember you fight for what is right and you must trust God to keep Giles safe." She squeezed Isabeau's hand. "We will pray for him each night."

With that thin thread of hope, the girl's countenance brightened. She and Isabeau had more in common than the girl knew. "When I was a few years younger than you, with my parents both dead, my uncle became my guardian. He and his English wife, Freddie's sister, became like parents to me. Through my uncle, I have traveled much. You will meet him when we leave Brittany, for we will sail on one of his ships."

"He has ships?" Isabeau asked, her eyes full of awe. "I've never been on a ship."

Freddie turned back to caution them. "Best not to speak more while we are on the road. We cannot predict who we may encounter."

Zoé nodded. How could she argue when he was right? At any moment, republican soldiers could appear out of the woods to question them... or worse.

She had never witnessed Freddie leading others before, but as she observed him, he seemed to grow taller, more confident, truly comfortable in the role. Pride filled her as she realized how easily he had accepted the responsibility for them all.

Hours later, Freddie called a halt and directed them off the road to a small clearing surrounded by oak, yew and beech trees. Above them, the branches teemed with twittering birds. The light rain had stopped and the sun glistened off the wet leaves. Around them, wildflowers appeared wherever the rays of the sun pierced the canopy.

Freddie asked Gabe to stand guard near the road and told the rest of them to find a place to sit.

Zoé handed Gabe some of the dried beef and apples the Chouans had given her and then shared what remained with the others. She found a seat on a large rock as they passed around skins of water.

Casting his gaze first at her and then at each face in their small circle, Freddie said, "If you're feeling up to it, we can press on until we arrive at Fougères. We will not reach the town until day's end but there should be sufficient daylight for us to find Boisguy and secure lodgings."

Zoé preferred not to stop no matter how weary she would be when she finally arrived. She knew by the pace Freddie had set that he, too, was anxious to reach Boisguy. Still, they had to consider Isabeau's ability to keep up.

Freddie must have had the same concern as he studied the girl. "If, at any point, you feel too tired to go on, Isabeau, we can spend the night at the mill house Giles spoke of and resume our journey tomorrow morning."

"*Je ne suis pas fatiguée*," insisted the girl, raising her chin. Considering what she had been through, Zoé thought her a hearty soul to deny her fatigue. Perhaps for her brother's sake she wanted to appear one of the valiant Chouans.

"You have done well to keep up," Zoé told her. "But no one will fault you should you want to stop sooner than Fougères."

A few hours later, they skirted the town of Combourtillé and Freddie asked them if any were of a mind to stop for the night. Zoé inquired of Isabeau, but the girl bravely shook her head. Nonetheless, Freddie suggested that before they pressed on, he should call on the miller to see if he had any messages for Boisguy.

"I'll take Erwan with me since he has the best command of Breton. The rest of you stay here, off the road and hidden among the trees. Gabe will stand guard."

Zoé was about to remind Freddie she could be useful in a fight, but something in his expression told her to hold her tongue.

From the edge of the trees bordering the stream, Freddie observed the two-story stone mill house some thirty feet away. Its chimney rose above a sloping slate roof typical of the countryside. While the house appeared in good repair, the six paned windows were devoid of curtains, a woman's touch clearly lacking here. Smaller buildings of similar ilk but without windows stood nearby. He assumed they were for grain storage, equipment and animals.

An eerie quiet permeated the area. No birds sang in the trees. Even the stream was silent in its sullen passage. 'Twas as if nature was holding its breath.

Freddie's nerves were taut with expectation. "Keep alert,

Erwan."

They were about to step from the cover of the trees when the faded blue door of the mill house burst open and two Chouans strode outside, their jackets bearing the sacred heart patch. Each carried a bayoneted musket. A third man, coming from the side of the house, joined them.

Freddie raised his arm in front of Erwan, holding him back when he would have stepped forward. "Wait."

Sun glinted off the Chouans' clothing revealing what looked like fresh blood splashed across their shirts and waistcoats. Two of the men carried bulging sacks.

"Boisguy's men?" Erwan whispered.

Somehow Freddie didn't think so. "Or men who would have us believe they are."

"The false Chouans?"

"Possibly." When the three men had departed into the woods, Freddie carefully left the cover of the trees, his musket raised. By his side, Erwan drew a pistol. Slowly, they crept toward the mill house.

The front door stood ajar.

No sound emanated from the interior.

Freddie whispered to Erwan, "Inquire in Breton if anyone is home."

Erwan spoke the words loud enough for anyone in the house to hear.

Silence greeted them, and the eerie feeling Freddie had experienced earlier returned. He pushed the door open and stepped inside. Light from the windows and open door filled the large room. The first thing he noticed was the wooden table fallen on its side, the broken dishes it once held lying scattered across the stone floor.

Freddie crossed the room and stooped before the fireplace searching for heat. Warmth emanated from the ashes. "There was a fire here not long ago."

"It seems the Chouans, or whoever they were, meant the mill owner no good," said Erwan.

Freddie scanned the room. The shelves contained a few books, cooking pots and tankards. Over the fireplace was a miniature portrait of a woman.

There was no evidence of blood.

"Take a look at the rest of this floor, Erwan. I'll see about the upstairs."

Freddie took the stairs two at a time, dreading what he would find. Perhaps the man died in his sleep and the men had discovered the body and decided to plunder his home, robbing the dead man of his valuables.

But that would not explain the blood splashed across their clothing.

Inside one of the bedchambers, a gruesome sight confronted Freddie, confirming his worst fears. A man of middle years with lined skin, his brown hair peppered with gray, lay across the bed fully clothed. He had been stabbed in the chest and his throat slit. Blood seeped from his wounds into his clothes and onto the bedcover, the coppery scent of his life's fluid filling the air.

Freddie returned to the top of the stairs. "Erwan, up here."

Erwan gasped as he entered the room and came to stand beside Freddie. The two of them stood over the body, crossing themselves.

Erwan shook his head. "A terrible way to die."

"Aye, a bayonet to the chest and a knife to the throat to make certain the man did not live."

"But why?" asked the Breton.

Freddie could only speculate. "The man's support for Boisguy likely became known. I'd bet this is the work of Rossignol's false Chouans. None that we saw leaving the mill house wore rosaries." Freddie did not wish to linger where their enemies had been. "See if you can find a shovel. We must bury the man. It will take time we can ill afford but Boisguy would expect it. While you find the shovel, I'll check on the other buildings."

In one of the buildings, Freddie found a black mare unharmed. Next to the horse was a dead stable boy lying in the hay, stabbed like his master. Crossing himself, he muttered, "The republicans make no exceptions for the young."

Leaving the lad in the hay, he found Erwan. "We've another body to bury, a young stable boy."

Erwan let out an oath, then held up his hands in which he held shovels. "I found these."

"Good. Oh, and a horse will be joining us. I must tell Zoé and Gabe of our discovery. Once the dead are laid in the ground, we'll continue on." He wanted to get Zoé out of the woods in which the false Chouans might still be prowling. "I am more eager than ever to reach Fougères."

Freddie returned to where Gabe guarded Zoé and Isabeau. Addressing the girl, he asked, "Did you know the man who lived here, Isabeau?"

Beneath her felt hat into which she had tucked her brown hair, Isabeau truly appeared to be a lad. *"Non."*

He was glad for her answer. The girl had suffered enough. "It seems the man has died." He would not speak of murder, not in the presence of one so young. "We will bury him and move on. As he left behind a horse, you can ride."

Drawing Zoé aside, he said, "The man and his stable boy were murdered. Erwan and I will make sure they are in the ground before you and Isabeau join us." To Gabe, he said, "You might see if you can help Erwan."

Gabe nodded and headed in the direction of the mill house.

Zoé looked up at Freddie with trusting eyes. "Do you have any idea—"

He loved her all the more for her unflinching reaction to what had happened. Not many women would nod at the word "murder" and inquire the cause.

"Yes, and we will speak of it later." In a louder voice, he said

121

to her, "Why don't you and Isabeau rest here while we take care of the task?"

"Can I help?" Zoé asked.

"Aye, you can say a prayer over him when we are ready."

With the shovels Erwan had found in a shed, Freddie and the other two men soon buried Boisguy's friend and his stable boy. Zoé said a prayer over the common grave that Erwan, certain they were fallen Chouans, marked with a large stone.

Freddie hoped this was not to be a sign of what was to come.

Chapter 9

Fougères, Brittany

Zoé stood on a hill with Freddie and the others, gazing down at the Château de Fougères. They were exhausted from the day's events and glad to have arrived at their destination. Behind them, the setting sun cast its rays on the sand-colored stone, making the castle appear golden, like some celestial city lowered to earth.

Giles had not been exaggerating when he described the castle as a medieval fortress. The massive edifice, built on a rocky outcrop, stood high above the river that circled its oval base like a moat. Zoé counted thirteen towers built into the stone walls, some very large.

Gabe removed his hat to brush his dark curls off his forehead. "My family is from Le Havre and I have seen many sights sailing with the *capitaine*, but there have been none like this."

"The château is one of the largest in Europe," said Erwan. "It was built to protect Brittany against sieges from her enemies, a warning for them to turn back from our borders. In times of war, the people took shelter behind the castle's ten foot-thick walls."

Zoé's gaze drifted to the stone houses pressed closely together on three sides of the fortress and the small village that lay on both sides of the path leading to the castle's main gate. "Is that why the town grew up around it?"

"*Oui*," said Erwan. "The people wanted to be close if the enemy came in spite of the warning."

"As long as the fortress is held by Boisguy," put in Freddie, "it serves the same purpose today."

Erwan helped Isabeau from the horse and the girl hurried to stand next to Zoé, taking her hand as she looked down at the castle. "I was here once before... with my parents." The sadness in the girl's eyes and her quavering voice spoke of her lingering grief.

Zoé squeezed her small hand unsure of what to say, remembering the day she, too, had been orphaned. The deep wound to her young heart had only been healed by the love of her uncle and aunt, who was then Lady Joanna West. And the friendship of Joanna's younger brother. She had thought Freddie most annoying at first but the passage of years had shown her that he was a true friend.

On her other side, Freddie took off his felt hat and wiped his forehead with a handkerchief. "Let's hope Boisguy will welcome us. A bed and dinner would not go amiss."

"What river is that circling the castle?" asked Zoé.

"'Tis the Nançon," replied Erwan, "and this is the Nançon Valley."

Zoé's eyes took in the narrow valley, a swath of verdant vegetation and forests surrounding the castle. The trees and foliage had flourished in the spring rains. Red, blue and pink wildflowers blossomed from every crevice, reminding her of Guernsey.

"We'd best seek our host," said Freddie, "before we lose the light."

As they began their descent, Zoé looked down at the men milling around the outside wall. "Why has no one approached us?"

"I suspect we are under observation," said Freddie. "As we get closer to the main gate, Boisguy's men will make themselves known."

To reach the gate that would take them past the castle's out-side wall, they had to first walk through the village and then cross a small bridge that spanned the moat. Freddie led the way, Zoé and Isabeau fell into step behind him. Gabe and Erwan followed with the black mare.

The villagers peeked their heads out of doors and windows to regard them with suspicious eyes. The women frowned at Zoé. She assumed it was due to the way she was dressed. Isabeau might pass for a lad but only from a distance did Zoé think her disguise would be convincing. The women of Fougères wore dresses or loose smocks tucked into long skirts, over which they donned short vests or jackets. Most of their hair was hidden beneath white caps, some with lace edges.

One woman pointed to Zoé. *"Un autre Capitaine Victor?"*

If they thought she was another Captain Victor, the woman who led a company of Chouan fighters, it meant she had been here. Zoé grew excited at the prospect of meeting such a woman.

No sooner had they reached the path leading across the bridge to the castle's main entrance than two men bearing grim expressions on their hardened faces blocked their advance. Each carried a musket and wore the sacred heart patch on his coat and a long rosary around his neck.

Freddie gestured to Erwan to join him and the two walked toward the Chouans. Reaching into his coat pocket, he pulled out the message Cadoudal had given him. "For General Boisguy," he said in Breton, bowing slightly.

Erwan spoke a few words to the Chouans, the only one Zoé recognized was "Cadoudal".

Isabeau, who knew French as well as Breton, leaned close to whisper, "Erwan has told them we come from M'sieur Cadoudal and the message is from him."

The man who had accepted the missive motioned for them to wait. Leaving his fellow Chouan to guard them, he crossed the bridge and walked with determined steps through the arched entrance.

When Freddie looked back at Zoé, she asked, "You are not worried?"

"Not yet. When we stopped to rest I asked Erwan to read me the message since it was in Breton. In veiled terms, it describes our mission as seeking information on their weapons and stores, to understand their needs. I assume he wrote it so that we could pretend to be on the side of the revolution should we be searched by republican soldiers. Clever that he should think to do that. As a result, it will take a bit of explaining to assure Boisguy we are here to help."

Only minutes had passed when the Chouan reemerged from the gate and beckoned them to follow. They followed him through the tunnel that cut through the thick outer wall.

Inside, a lad took the horse's reins, leading the mare toward what looked like a stable.

Not wanting to cause Zoé undue angst, Freddie had omitted telling her about the part of the message that urged Boisguy to judge for himself "the sincerity of the government's stated purpose". Left unspecified was which government but, coming from Cadoudal and signed in what appeared to be code, Boisguy would know it was not revolutionary France that Freddie represented.

The guards led them up three flights of damp stone stairs before stopping in front of a wooden door with rust-stained ironwork that led into one of the larger towers.

One of the guards knocked. At the shout of "Entrez!" he opened the door and gestured Freddie, Zoé, Isabeau, Gabe and Erwan inside.

The chamber was circular, like the tower, and smelled of musty leaves and burning wood. In the center of the room was a large desk. Sitting behind it was a young man with intense dark eyes. Freddie noticed immediately his fine blue coat and his elaborate white cravat spilling over his waistcoat. His long black hair fell to his shoulders.

The only sound was the hissing and popping from the fireplace.

The well-dressed young man rose and came around the desk to face them, crossing his arms and leaning back against the desk. Freddie had to remind himself Aimé du Boisguy was "not yet twenty", for the man who stood before him had a noble bearing and an air of authority of a much older man, one who owned the respect of other men.

As he introduced himself, his aristocratic accent and elegant French gave proof of his noble origin. "I am Aimé du Boisguy, general of the Chouans in this area. Who might you be?"

Knowing he had but moments to convince Boisguy of his benevolent purpose, he said, "I am Frederick West, brother of the Earl of Torrington. I come on business of His Majesty the King of England. The government wishes to understand the needs of the Chouans both in Brittany and Maine so that we may provide assistance in your fight against revolutionary France. Our Prime Minister abhorred the murder of your king and means to win the war."

A movement drew Freddie's gaze to the shadows where a rough-looking man leaned against the wall, his disquieting gaze fixed on the new arrivals. He was older than the other Chouans they had encountered, in his mid-thirties, Freddie judged. The man's short hair and long downturned mustache were a dark brown, not unlike that of most Bretons. Freddie might have judged him a farmer for his face, lined and tanned like those who spent their days in the sun. He reminded Freddie of Donet's vineyard workers. However, his wide-brimmed black hat bore the Bourbon white cockade and a white plume, marking him an officer in the Catholic and Royal Army. Around his neck over his white shirt he wore a brilliantly colored scarf splashed with red and a long rosary of black beads. Freddie amended his assessment. This man was no farmer, at least not anymore.

His eyes never leaving Freddie, the strange Chouan left the shadows to take his stance beside the young general. "And these with you?" he challenged Freddie.

Freddie gestured to Zoé. "Mademoiselle Zoé Donet, a friend of the comte de la Rochejaquelein," naming for the first time in her presence the fallen hero she had once idolized.

The young general's dark eyes gleamed as they alighted on Zoé, giving her man's attire an approving smile. "Henri and I were friends from our youth. We fought together as brothers until our enemies took him from us."

Despite the young general's relationship to the fallen de la Rochejaquelein, Zoé had never spoken of the chevalier du Boisguy as someone she knew. Yet, here was another handsome young leader of the royalist cause. Might he be another hero for Zoé to worship? An alarm sounded in Freddie's head. How could he compete in her eyes with such matchless figures?

Zoé offered the general her hand and he bowed over it. "Mademoiselle."

Happy to interrupt Boisguy's interest in Zoé, Freddie gestured to Isabeau. "This child is Isabeau le Gallou, the daughter of two who paid with their lives for their loyalty to the Chouans. Her brother is one of Cadoudal's men."

Isabeau said nothing but moved close to Zoé and stared at the two strange men.

"You are most welcome here," said Boisguy to the young girl.

Freddie then introduced Erwan as a Vendéen soldier and Gabe as a member of the crew of the ship that had brought them to Brittany.

Passing his gaze across the visitors, particularly the men, Boisguy said, "If your words be true, and you are who you claim to be, I welcome you. If they are not, your lives will be forfeit.

Traitors do not live long among us."

"Of course, Mr. West's words are true!" protested Zoé, her furrowed brow and indignant expression making clear she resented Freddie's word being questioned.

Freddie smiled to himself, pleased at the wildcat she became in his defense.

"We come at great risk," she went on, "to provide the English with accurate information of the needs of your growing army to help you fight Robespierre's Terror."

"It is our intention when we are done here," Freddie put in, "to travel to Maine where we hope to meet with Jean Cottereau, the one called Jean Chouan, on this same mission."

Boisguy raised a brow, inclining his head toward the mysterious Chouan standing next to him.

Freddie directed his attention to the young general. "We were hoping you could help us locate him and gain his trust."

A twinkle in Boisguy's eyes matched his amused look. "You will have to gain the trust of Jean Chouan on your own, *mon ami anglais*. But you will not have to travel to Maine to meet him. You are most fortunate to have come when you did. It is Jean Chouan who stands beside me."

Surprised, Freddie shifted his gaze to the man next to Boisguy. "Indeed, this is fortuitous. You have made possible our gaining the needed information in a single meeting. We thank you." He could tell from the skeptical look on Jean Chouan's face that he harbored doubts about the truth of Freddie's stated purpose.

"It is nearly time for dinner," said Boisguy. "You will join us and when the food and wine have been served, we will speak of what England can do for us."

Zoé had been to Versailles with her uncle before the revolution and she had been in fine estates in Saintonge, but she had yet to dine in a medieval castle, particularly one of this size. When she followed Freddie to Brittany to meet with the royalist fighters, she never anticipated being in a place haunted by ghosts of centuries long past. In her mind's eye, she saw the rich tapestries that once hung on the now bare walls. She heard the clang of metal armor and spurs of knights crossing the stone floor.

Light from torches set into the walls and candles on the long tables illuminated the vast stone hall that echoed with men's voices eager for the evening meal. Where once there would have been knights dining with their lord, now were gathered farmers turned into fighting men. They did not fight for riches, lands or glory, as the knights had, but for freedom from tyranny, their faith and their way of life.

She and her companions sat with their host at a table perpendicular to four long tables stretching the length of the hall. As if by magic, peasant women entered the great room from doors on one side. They carried pitchers of wine and platters of venison. The rich meat seasoned with rosemary and thyme sent a mouthwatering aroma into the air. Roasted vegetables, too, appeared in great wooden bowls. After the meager fare they had endured on the road, Zoé was delighted.

"I'm surprised you eat so well."

Boisguy, on her right, leaned in close. "Many of my men are hunters. As long as the forest provides, we dine well."

The men's voices were soon reduced to the sounds of eating.

Freddie spoke from her left. "Best eat while you can, Pigeon. We still have the return trip where food may be scarce."

Zoé needed no encouragement. She eagerly bit into the venison, which was succulent and tender, the herbs making it tasty. The white wine of Brittany, too, was very good.

Setting down his wine, Boisguy said, "We are not often so many at table, but Jean's men have joined mine and there are others who have recently come to us, a few whom you might like to meet." With a poignant look, he added, "Friends of Henri's."

Zoé was impressed that this general of thousands of men was of an age with her. And, even though his ancestral lands were in Brittany, it struck her that his voice and manners were those of a member of the French aristocracy who would have been comfortable in Paris. Likely, he had been educated well and expected to manage his family estate. All that was gone now, of course. The revolution had changed his life forever, as it had hers. Yet he seemed given over to his new purpose without reservation.

"Do you think to win against the Blues?" she asked him.

His eyes lit with an inner fire. "We fight to win. Our cause is just and, thus far, God has blessed that valiant cause. But even should we fail, to a man we would rather die fighting against a godless, bloodthirsty régime than live in a country that would murder its king and priests and refuse its people the freedom to worship as they choose."

She set down her wine and let out a sigh as memories rushed into her mind. She remembered a night in La Rochelle when she and Henri had dined together, a candle between them. Henri's golden face had been lit with the fervor of a righteous man willing to die for a cause he judged more important than his life. "Henri often spoke with the same passion in his voice."

Boisguy's eyes bore into hers. "I can see you understand, Mademoiselle Donet."

Freddie chose that moment to interrupt. "Did you tell the general of what happened at the mill house outside of Combourtillé?"

"*Non.* Perhaps you might, Freddie." She was loath to tell Boisguy his friend had been murdered. Freddie had always been better at delivering bad news than she, his voice remaining steady and calm whereas hers would falter.

Freddie leaned across her to relate the story, including that Isabeau did not know of the gruesome deaths, only that the miller had died, adding at the end, "The villains were just leaving as we arrived. Until I saw the blood on their clothing, I had thought them Chouans."

Boisguy closed his eyes tightly, shaking his head as if to deny the horrible truth. When he opened them, anger had replaced sorrow. "The miller was a man of honor and a great friend to the Chouans. For that, the republican dogs who did this will pay. We must rid Brittany of Rossignol's parasites." Looking about the hall, his gaze came to rest on a tall slender figure standing to one side talking with another man. "Captain Victor!" Boisguy called.

The slender figure, white plumed hat in hand, turned and started toward the general. As the Chouan drew close, Zoé realized this must be the woman Henri had spoken of. Absent her hat, her long dark hair, confined to a plait falling halfway down her back, framed a feminine face with high cheekbones and large dark eyes. But her clothing spoke of her rank in the Catholic and Royal Army: a charcoal-colored coat fitted close to her body, a white neckcloth over a linen shirt, cream-colored breeches and black boots. At her hip was a sword and tucked into her waist was a small pistol.

The female Chouan passed her gaze over Zoé and her companions before turning to Boisguy. "Sir?"

"It seems we have lost Jodoc to the villainy of Rossignol's false Chouans."

For a moment, Captain Victor's face reflected horror, but that gave way to a stony resolve in her dark eyes. "Do you want me to take a patrol and clean out the rats' nest?"

"*Oui*, if you can find them. At first light or tonight, if you prefer." As his captain turned to leave, Boisguy said, "Wait! I want to introduce you to our visitors." Turning to Zoé and the others, he said, "This is Mademoiselle Victorine du Rocher du Quengo, captain of our division in Bécherel to the west."

Freddie and the men rose.

Jean Chouan retained his seat, his mouth curling up in a sarcastic smile. "Only you would have a name longer than the rest of us, Victorine."

The woman he called Victorine smirked. "You can be glad I do not expect you to remember it, Jean."

Boisguy interrupted, "Captain, I believe you will want to meet this first guest. Mademoiselle Zoé Donet was a friend of Monsieur Henri's."

Zoé stood and offered her hand, which Captain Victor accepted while smiling at Zoé's clothing.

"I have long wanted to meet you," said Zoé, her voice full of admiration. "Henri spoke of your achievements with much pride."

"You pay me a great compliment, for Henri was revered among us."

Resuming the introductions, Boisguy said, "Next to Mademoiselle Donet is Mr. Frederick West, who, if he is to be believed, is an emissary from the King of England."

Captain Victor's brows rose as she gave Freddie a studying perusal.

"Mademoiselle," Freddie said in the clipped English of the British upper class.

In a lowered voice, possibly for Isabeau's benefit, Boisguy said to his captain, "You should ask Mr. West for a description of the men who killed Jodoc." Then he pointed to the other side of Jean Chouan. "Over there is young Isabeau le Gallou whose brother serves under Cadoudal and, if I have it right, next to her are Erwan and Gabe."

Captain Victor acknowledged each of them, graciously inclining her head. *"Bienvenue*, welcome."

Boisguy addressed his captain, "They say they have come to learn of our needs so that England might help supply our growing army."

"Ammunition," said Captain Victor without hesitation. "'Tis a critical need."

"Dan ce cas," said Boisguy, "if the time has come for this discussion, let us sit." He called to a serving girl, "More wine!"

The servant returned with a pitcher and, while she was refilling their glasses, Boisguy asked her to take Isabeau to the other side of the great hall to introduce her to those closer to her age eating there.

Captain Victor, Jean Chouan and Boisguy took seats across from Zoé, Freddie and the others.

When their cups were again full and Isabeau had gone off with the servant, Freddie opened the discussion. "Your men are armed with muskets and knives, some with swords. In addition to ammunition, is your need for more of these?"

Boisguy took a long drink of his wine. "Many of the weapons my men have were gained through our victories over the Blues. We could use more, of course, as men join us each day. However, we also have a need for small artillery and horses. We've no cavalry to speak of save for those of us who had horses and were trained to ride from our youth. And the only small mobile cannons we have are ones we seized in a raid."

"We do not fight like the English or even the French," interjected Jean Chouan. "We fight from behind rocks, from between trees, taking care with our shots. Our army is made up of mostly peasant farmers. They are comfortable with muskets and knives. But the general is correct. In an open area we are at a grave disadvantage against the Blues' horses and artillery."

Freddie rested his chin on his upturned palm, his eyes gazing at his wine. Zoé recognized the contemplative look, the one he always got just before deciding whether to share something he'd been hiding from her.

Finally he looked up, meeting Boisguy's steady gaze. In a voice only they could hear, he said, "There is talk of landing a British-backed émigré force off Brittany's coast in which case you would have your artillery and many men to join you."

Boisguy sat back in his chair. "That is, if the British actually make an appearance this time. We have not forgotten Granville, *l'Anglais*."

"A sad chapter, I know," said Freddie looking down at his wine. "Your chiding is well taken."

Jean Chouan huffed. "The supplies and weapons would be welcomed, but even if the British make good on their word this time, I have reservations about émigrés leading a force into Brittany. As I said, we Bretons do not fight like the British or even the French. It is one reason we have been successful."

"Such an operation," put in Boisguy, "would require considerable planning and strategy to be successful. In the meantime, we have needs you can meet."

"Like ammunition," reiterated Captain Victor. "For that, you need no ships or landing forces, only small boats."

Gabe, who'd been silently watching until now, said, "My *capitaine* has delivered supplies for the royalists to the shores of Normandy and Brittany before."

"Who is your *capitaine*?" asked Boisguy.

"My uncle," said Zoé, "Jean Donet, comte de Saintonge, or at least he held the title until the revolutionary government took it away. He has three ships, *la Reine Noire* being his flagship."

"I have sailed with him on all three," said Freddie, "and can vouch for his commitment to the royalist cause."

Boisguy gave his attention to Zoé. "I knew your name sounded familiar. Was your uncle at one time a privateer out of Lorient?"

"He was," said Zoé. "And a smuggler. Now, in addition to his merchant shipping business, he helps Erwan and me smuggle refugees out of France."

Boisguy's dark eyes simmered as he continued to gaze at Zoé. "I sensed you were an unusual woman when I first met you, mademoiselle."

Perhaps he found her snatching men, women and children from the guillotine's jaws a worthy endeavor. It was no more than others had done and less than the sacrifices of many. "Not so unusual in these times, Monsieur le chevalier."

Boisguy rose and offered her his hand. "As you've had a trying day and tomorrow morning will be soon upon us, it might be best if I escort you to your chamber."

Chapter 10

Freddie abruptly stood, placing a protective hand on Zoé's shoulder. "You have been a gracious host, General Boisguy, but there is no need for you to see us to our chambers. If a servant can lead the way, I will be happy to accompany Mademoiselle Donet."

After having seen the desire in the young general's eyes whenever he looked at Zoé, Freddie had no intention of leaving her alone with him. She was too fetching a prize. Then, too, she might be vulnerable to the young royalist hero, who was a dark version of her glorious Henri.

Zoé got to her feet and frowned. "Really, Freddie, I can follow the servant myself. You can both stay."

Gabe stood and addressed Freddie. "I will be attending the mademoiselle, as always. She will not be alone."

By now, everyone at the table was on their feet and the entire situation was becoming ridiculous. Freddie was considering letting Gabe escort Zoé when Captain Victor spoke up.

"Allow me to accompany you," she said to Zoé. "The towers can be confusing and our walk to your chamber would give us a chance to become better acquainted."

"I would like that," said Zoé, smiling at the female Chouan.

Freddie let out a breath. He had hoped for a moment alone with her. "Very good. Sleep well. I will call upon you in the morning."

As the two women walked off, Gabe trailing behind them with a lantern, Freddie took his seat across from Boisguy, whose gaze lingered a bit too long on Zoé.

Drawing the general's attention back to him, Freddie said, "I will make sure my contacts have the information regarding your army's most urgent needs. Men and horses may take time, but small artillery, muskets and ammunition can be transported sooner to Brittany's shores."

Boisguy took a long draw on his wine. "We would be most grateful. I expect the war in Brittany to go on for some time."

"Will you be reducing that list of our needs to writing?" asked Jean Chouan with a suspicious look. The Chouan from Maine clearly did not yet trust them.

"I came prepared to do so," said Freddie. "The writing will be in code, of course, merely a description of the local flora. That way, if I am wounded or worse, my companions can see the list reaches the right hands."

"If they were to take you," said Boisguy, "I can assure you their methods to extract information would be ruthless, leaving little for the guillotine."

Jean Chouan leaned across the table, a wry smile on his lips. "But then the *Anglais* are typically shot."

Freddie shuddered. "Most comforting."

"Perhaps it would better inform you if you were to accompany me on tonight's patrol," said Jean Chouan. "My men and I will be leaving shortly."

Freddie thought the night patrol would be a good opportunity to see the Chouans from Maine in action and he suspected the Chouan leader wanted to observe Freddie more closely as well. He nodded. "I'll be ready."

Zoé followed Captain Victor down a castle walkway to a distant tower where she stopped in front of an arched wooden door. Gabe had trailed behind them and, as they stepped through the doorway, he went to the wood stacked next to the fireplace and offered to light a fire.

Zoé thanked him and took his lantern, placing it on the shelf above the fireplace. The flickering light allowed her to see the chamber's furnishings. They were sparse but adequate, two narrow beds, a small table and two chairs.

"This tower is more remote than the others," said Captain Victor. "You and the girl should have some privacy here. Mr. West and the two other men can stay in the adjacent chamber."

"Thank you," said Zoé. "I expect she is very tired."

Gabe's success with the fire soon produced a steady blaze, warming the small room. "I'll be just outside, mademoiselle," he said, slipping out the door.

Zoé sat on one of the beds and invited Captain Victor to sit on the other. "Captain Victor, might you tell me how you came to join Boisguy's forces?"

"Call me Victorine, if you like. The story of how I came to serve under General Boisguy is not a terribly exciting one, but I will tell you." She flicked her long plait behind her.

Zoé leaned forward, anxious to learn more about this intriguing woman.

"My family is a very old one, loyal to the king and the Church for many generations. When Brittany rebelled against the conscription that would have had its sons fighting for the revolution, many men joined the loyalist cause. I watched them go and wondered what I could do. But when the Committee of Public Safety ordered the deaths of priests and murdered the king and queen, I could no longer stand idly by. Like Boisguy and Henri and the other nobles who were persuaded by the peasants to lead them, I could shoot and ride. I had to decide whether to leave with the other émigrés or stay and fight. I chose the latter."

"Your parents must have been horrified."

"By then, my mother had died. My father just shook his head. I think he knew eventually I would go. Saying goodbye was hard, knowing I may never see him again, but I shall always remember the pride in his voice and the sadness in his eyes when he bid me 'Godspeed'. Like you, I chose to wear a man's clothing. 'Tis more practical and easier for the men to take orders from a woman who is not wearing skirts."

Zoé gazed into the fire seeing again Henri's face lit with the passion of the royalist cause. "For this trip deep into Brittany, a man's clothing seemed in order. But I most often dress as a peasant woman to blend with those in the villages." Shifting her gaze to Victorine, she said, "You see, 'tis my way of avenging Henri. I had only my uncle and aunt to convince that I should be allowed to rescue those destined for the guillotine. My uncle well understood my desire to join the cause, being something of a rebel himself. My aunt, who is Mr. West's sister, grudgingly accepted my nighttime excursions."

"Ah, M'sieur West, *l'Anglais*. He speaks French like one of us but he has the unmistakable air of an aristocrat. Handsome, too. Is he your man?"

"*Non*," Zoé replied quickly. "We are just friends." At the back of her mind stirred a restive thought that they might be more. The attractive Chouan leader's interest in Freddie did not sit well. "He truly wants to help the royalists."

"He takes his life in his hands to do so."

Zoé met Victorine's dark gaze. "We all know the risks, don't we? And the dangers. Yet, how could we not join the cause when so much is at stake?"

"I asked myself the same question and here I am."

"Are there many women in the Chouan army?"

"A few but no others who serve as an officer under Boisguy. Women can help in ways other than fighting. We need them as spies in the villages and towns where the republicans congregate, to hide priests and the wounded and to care for the Chouan army." She laughed. "As you saw tonight, we've a lot of men to feed who are not tending their farms." She let out a sigh and got to her feet. "I'll let you get some rest. Dawn comes early. You can bolt the door if you like but you will be safe. No one would harm one of the general's guests. I'll see if the one who guards you can be persuaded to bring Isabeau to you. By the way, how is it she came to join you?"

"It was her brother's request when we left him in Rennes. He wants her out of Brittany. So, we agreed to take her with us to Guernsey where my uncle and aunt live."

"Ah, Guernsey," said Victorine, reaching for the door. "I was there once. Quite a lovely place. I'd like to think I might see it again but something tells me I shall die in Brittany."

And with that, the woman slipped through the door like a shadow and was gone.

By the time Jean Chouan and his men took to the woods of Fougères, the half-moon had risen, casting its pale light on the path, that is, when it did not disappear beneath dense leaf-covered branches. Except for the occasional hoot of an owl, or the stirring of the leaves in the night wind, the woods were silent.

Not more than a half-hour had passed when the Chouan leader drew to a halt and held up one hand. Behind him, Freddie came to a standstill, tuning his ears to the subtle night sounds. At first he heard nothing, but then in the distance there came a rhythmic thumping of boots treading through the forest.

Jean Chouan pointed his finger toward the sky, circling over his head.

In response, his men spread out, moving from the path into the woods where they vanished. Not wanting to be left a standing target, Freddie slipped in among the trees. He had no sooner crouched beside Jean Chouan than a company of Blues, their white waistcoats and breeches glowing in the moonlight, briskly strode past, heading in the direction the Chouans had come.

The Chouan leader stood, watching the last of the soldiers disappear down the path. His men gathered around him awaiting orders. "They are heading toward Fougères and we cannot have that. Pick them off and gather the weapons."

His men hissed, *"Vive l'roi!"* and took off after the soldiers. Louis XVI might be dead but the battle cry still stood. *Long live the king!* It spoke of the Chouans' commitment to one day see a Bourbon restored to the throne of France.

Jean Chouan dashed after his men and, a minute later, the sound of gunfire echoed through the woods.

Eager to see how the Chouans fought, Freddie ran after them. Taking cover behind a tree, he watched them carefully picking their targets. Jean Chouan had been right; they did fight differently. Outnumbered as they were, every shot had to count. They were aided in their accuracy by the flashy white of the enemy's uniforms, which made them easier to spot at night. As far as he could tell, the Chouans did not miss once.

Freddie took a step forward only to be seen by a fleeing soldier, who turned his musket on Freddie. He whipped his pistol from his sash and shot the Blue in the forehead. The soldier sank to the ground, his eyes frozen in shock.

Leaning against a tree, Freddie's chest heaved. The soldier had been no older than he. Freddie reminded himself this was war and he had chosen his side long ago. Too, the republicans had committed many atrocities in the name of their revolution and these were headed to Fougères where Zoé slept in the château.

Jean Chouan gave orders to pull the bodies into the woods away from the path and to harvest any uniforms that were not stained with blood.

"Does this typically happen on a night patrol?" Freddie asked the Chouan leader.

"More often here in Brittany than in Maine," he said, fingering his dark mustache. "Rossignol is eager to retake the château, but he lacks the men and the cunning to do so."

Zoé tossed on her small bed, worried about Freddie. When Gabe returned with Isabeau, he had told her that Freddie had gone on patrol with Jean Chouan, leaving both Erwan and Gabe behind. Victorine, too, was out there somewhere with her men, searching for the false Chouans. Did no one sleep here?

Sitting up, she flung her feet to the floor. Across from her, Isabeau enjoyed the dreamless sleep of youth.

"I might as well be up," Zoé muttered. Perhaps the patrols had returned. Since she had slept in her clothes, she had only to pull on her boots and light a lantern to be ready. Opening her door, she encountered Gabe lying across the threshold beneath a blanket. He would be displeased with her should she not wake him.

"Gabe," she whispered, nudging his shoulder, "I'm going down to the hall to see if the patrols have returned. You can stay and keep an eye on Isabeau. Where's Erwan?"

He answered in a groggy voice. "Sleeping in the hall with Boisguy's men. He has friends among them." Groaning, Gabe got to his feet. "If you are going, so am I." Raking his fingers through his dark curls, he said in a sleepy voice, "I'll send a servant back to sit with Isabeau."

To have Gabe by her side was a little like having the shadow of her uncle watching over her. "*Très bien*," she said, handing the lantern to Gabe. "Let's see if we can find our way to the hall."

The stone walkways connecting the thirteen towers were winding and convoluted so that one could easily get lost, but she kept the central hall far below in her sights, glad for what light the moon afforded.

They arrived in the immense chamber, which, even at this

late hour of the night, was crowded. At one end of the hall, men slept on pallets. The other end was a hive of activity with men standing around engaged in low-voiced conversations and stacking weapons on a table. She could not see Freddie among them, but she recognized Victorine who was speaking with Boisguy.

"I'm going to talk to General Boisguy," she said to Gabe as she walked away.

Boisguy smiled as she approached. "What has you up in the middle of the night, mademoiselle?" He seemed remarkably awake for the late hour and pleased to see her.

Glancing at Victorine, she said, "I was hoping for news of the night patrols." She said nothing of her concern for Freddie.

"Jean Chouan has yet to return," said Boisguy, "but, as you see, Captain Victor is here with her men."

Victorine looked as if she had been in a fight, her cheeks and jacket besmirched with dirt and her hair, so neatly plaited at dinner, now had loose strands dangling to her shoulders. "How did the search for the false Chouans go?" Zoé asked.

Victorine returned her a smile of success. "I was just telling the general. We found them and, after a brief skirmish, made sure they will never again harm one of ours."

"Any of your men wounded?" inquired Boisguy.

"One man took a bayonet in his arm. He will recover."

The sound of men's voices caused Zoé to turn toward the hall's entrance. In strolled Jean Chouan followed by his men. Several carried extra muskets. Her eyes raked over the Chouans who, like Victorine, bore the evidence of their excursion.

"All's quiet?" asked Boisguy of the Chouan commander.

"It is now. We took out a company of Blues heading toward Fougères."

At the end of the line of Chouans filing into the hall was Freddie. Zoé's heart leaped to see him unscathed.

She rushed to meet him, touching his shoulder. "You are

well?"

"I'm fine, Pigeon. The Chouans are good at their jobs. They are stealthy fighters and crack shots. I did manage to dispatch one of the Blues who had his musket trained on me."

She looked into his eyes but saw no trepidation, no regret. He spoke of killing a man, albeit a despised enemy, with a coolness that surprised her. How could he be so nonchalant? "Oh, Freddie, you might have been killed!"

"Do not dwell on what might have been, Pigeon, only what is." With a broad smile, he said, "I have returned hale and hearty."

She slapped his shoulder. "And as arrogant as ever."

Freddie fell asleep with a smile on his face as he remembered the look of concern in Zoé's beautiful eyes.

He rose a few hours later. Since the war began, his sleep was fitful and often disturbed by vivid dreams. He could not always remember them but the sense of foreboding he had upon rising told him the cause had been a dream.

He intended to spend the day talking to Boisguy's men about their particular needs and to get an idea from Boisguy as to the routes he preferred for delivery of the supplies Freddie arranged when he returned to Guernsey. He had yet to reduce to code what he had learned thus far, but he would this night. Captain Victor had been right about their ammunition running low. The lack of artillery and cavalry might make them less effective in the open, but without ammunition, they could not fight at all.

It was his plan to leave for Lorient tomorrow. If all went well, they would arrive earlier than expected since they weren't traveling on to Maine. The trip to the coast would take them a week, maybe longer depending on what they might encounter. Donet had told them he'd bring his ship close to shore each night for the week before they were expected—and the week after, should they be delayed. Hopefully, the timing would be right for *la Reine Noire* to take advantage of the dark of the moon.

Stuffing his notes into his satchel, Freddie left his chamber for the hall. On the way, he knocked on Zoé's door, but there was no answer. Seeing no sign of Gabe, he assumed she had already risen. He suspected Zoé slept little at night. After all, she and Erwan were combing the streets of Granville and other port towns at that time to meet fleeing émigrés. Several times he'd observed her napping in the afternoon on the aft deck when they were at sea, doubtless making up her lost sleep.

The hall was bustling with men when he arrived, some breaking their fast while others were dividing into squads, receiving orders. A small group of priests stood in one corner, conversing in hushed tones. They would be the priests who had refused to take the oath of allegiance demanded by the National Assembly, thereby subjecting themselves to Robespierre's terrible vengeance. At least these were protected by Boisguy. Freddie had not asked but it seemed likely the priests said mass for the Chouans each morning.

As he gazed about the hall, he spotted Zoé sitting with Boisguy. The young general leaned across the table to whisper something to her that made her blush. Freddie narrowed his eyes on the handsome aristocrat, immaculately attired in his coat, waistcoat and white cravat. Freddie was suddenly aware of his own creased, slept-in common garb, annoyed that he appeared shabby by comparison.

He decided it was past time for him to speak to Donet about courting Zoé. Donet could hardly protest the suit of an English Anglican since he had married one, but Freddie was no peer, only a younger son with little to show for his years serving the Crown. No naval officer's uniform, no estate of his own, and his prospects were more limited with the war. He had been Donet's partner in trade before the revolution. Perhaps that might continue.

If they could just get home to Guernsey, he would pursue a

deeper friendship with Zoé, one he hoped would lead to love on her part. The war might last for years but he didn't want to wait years to claim the woman he had loved for so long.

She raised her head at his approach, bringing a smile to his face. Her bright eyes gave no hint of fatigue, though her clothing bore the signs of all she'd been through. Matching Freddie's appearance, she looked like a crumpled Chouan, her waistcoat stained from their travels, her shirt wrinkled and besmirched and her boots scuffed and splattered with mud. It mattered not. He would take her dressed in lace and satin or in a dirty coat and muddied breeches.

"Freddie," she scolded, "are you finally awake?"

He laughed and slid onto the chair beside her. "It seems no one here needs sleep. Morning, General."

"Good morning to you, West."

"Where is Isabeau?" he inquired, looking about the hall.

"She has made friends," said Zoé, pointing to a far table where the girl sat laughing with some younger Chouans.

"A pity you can't leave her with us," put in Boisguy. "We can protect her, you know."

"We promised her brother we would take her to Guernsey," Zoé reminded him.

"Very well," said Boisguy. "I will not press. How long do I have the pleasure of your company, mademoiselle?"

Zoé turned to Freddie, brows lifted.

He answered for her. "I am hoping to garner what more I need today, put my notes into code tonight and be off with the dawn."

A look of regret crossed Boisguy's face as his gaze met Zoé's. "Alas, war separates what life would join. When this wretched revolution is over, if I still live, I will seek you out, mademoiselle."

This time Freddie was certain Zoé blushed, but pleasure infused his soul when the regret he glimpsed in Boisguy's eyes was not mirrored in hers.

"While you are gathering your facts," she told Freddie, "I plan to join Captain Victor today. I might learn something about the challenges she faces as a woman fighting with the Chouans."

Freddie frowned. "Do you mean on patrol?" He didn't like the idea of her being exposed to more danger just as they were preparing to leave.

"Well, yes, if she is to lead one."

"Mademoiselle Donet will be fine," Boisguy assured Freddie. "Captain Victor takes no unnecessary risks."

It was the necessary ones Freddie worried about, but seeing Zoé's enthusiasm for her last day with the female Chouan, he made no objection.

Zoé placed her hand on his sleeve. "Don't worry, Freddie. I'll be careful and you know Gabe will insist on coming."

"All right." He rarely said no to her. Found it near impossible, as a matter of fact, especially when she turned those dove gray eyes on him. It was one of his many weaknesses where she was concerned.

Zoé watched Freddie stride across the hall toward a group of Chouans, his broad shoulders and height standing out amidst the smaller Bretons. She couldn't remember just when he'd grown so tall. Perhaps it was—

"I have told the men to give your English friend their candid assessment as to what they would ask the English to do for us," said Boisguy, interrupting her thoughts. "I think I heard one mention uniforms. Unnecessary to my thinking but important to some."

Zoé gave the general her full attention, her mouth hitching up in a grin. "But you wear a uniform of sorts, do you not?"

Boisguy shrugged. "My men think so. Like me, many of the officers come from the nobility, asked to lead the fight by their tenants and villagers. We merely retain the dress we started with. That and the white cockade set us apart for our men."

Zoé allowed her mind to wander back to the last time she had seen the dashing comte de la Rochejaquelein sitting atop his chestnut stallion as he rode off to join the Royal Guard of King Louis XVI. "Henri dressed like you, monsieur, impeccably attired even when he was riding off to battle. Beneath his crowned hat, his golden curls were never out of place."

"Ah, *oui*, de la Rochejaquelein was the perfect soldier, the perfect officer, a brother to his men, eating their food, sleeping on the ground under the trees. And happiest with a pistol in one hand and a sword in the other. Of course, all the women threw their handkerchiefs at his feet, sent him love notes and tokens of their affection. So foolish. Henri and I used to laugh about them over our wine."

A knot formed in Zoé's throat. Had they laughed about her? She had sent Henri notes and given him small tokens to carry with him, a ribbon from her hair, a ring he wore on his smallest finger. "But surely, Henri had someone who was close to his heart, someone whose token he treasured?"

"*Non*, mademoiselle. I assure you, he did not. The sacred heart patch was his Madonna. He had no room in his heart for a mere female. Women like Captain Victor were useful to him and therefore he admired her skill with a sword, but he never loved a woman. Most he considered a nuisance."

The scales fell from Zoé's eyes, as she realized why Henri had never given voice to the words of love she had longed to hear. Not wanting Boisguy to see how his barbs affected her, she hid her despair beneath a cough. Her gut twisted to think she was among the women they had laughed about. Boisguy might not know her name as one of Henri's devotees but she felt the shame as if he did. She could not chide Henri for his indifference for he was gone. But here was another. Was Boisguy just like him?

"Are you of the same opinion as Henri, monsieur?"

Her hand was on the table. Boisguy covered it with his own, his warm skin pressed against hers in too intimate a gesture for their brief acquaintance. *"Non*, mademoiselle. I am not like Henri. I make room in my heart—and my bed—for women I like." His eyes took on a dark, predatory gleam. "Particularly one as lovely as you."

Zoé pulled back her hand and slipped it under the table.

"Have I made you uncomfortable?" he asked with feigned innocence. "You see time is so short for us. We've only this night to know each other better. There may be no time for love but there is always time for pleasure."

Disgusted, Zoé got to her feet, looking down at him. "You have, indeed, offended me, monsieur, but then you do not know me well. I am not one to fall at the feet—or into the bed—of the heroes you speak of. For that, you will have to seek out another."

She turned and, with her chin in the air, took her leave.

As she walked away, she heard him chuckle before saying, *"Quelle femme!"*

She wanted nothing to do with so-called heroes like Henri and his friend Boisguy. They lived for today and for a cause or, in Boisguy's case, their own needs, using whomever they would without regard to the hearts they broke along the way. Zoé might admire their courage and their leadership among men, but she would never want to be the woman of such a man. She wanted to be the world for the man she loved, be it in the middle of war or in peace. Her uncle had taught her such was possible and she did not want less for herself.

Chapter 11

Freddie did not question Zoé when she asked if she and Isabeau could take dinner in their chamber, saying she wanted to retire early. Perhaps she was tired from her excursion into the woods with Captain Victor and little sleep the night before. He was just glad she had returned unscathed, the patrol without incident. The journey tomorrow would be long and she would need her rest. Besides, the evening allowed him time to transcribe his notes into code.

The next morning brought a steady rain as they readied for their departure. Despite the weather, Freddie was anxious to leave. Now that he had the information he had come to collect, there was no reason to linger. Boisguy's repeated urgings for Zoé to stay had, to Freddie's great pleasure, fallen on deaf ears.

At the castle's entrance, Jean Chouan and Boisguy waited to see them off. The Chouans had made sure the departing visitors carried food for the journey, the kind of portable rations Boisguy's men took with them on long excursions: dried meat, berries, hazelnuts and the white wine of Brittany. They were also provided with a map, Jean Chouan suggesting they return to Lorient by another route, skirting Rennes to the west.

"You're in charge of the map," Freddie said to Erwan, handing him the drawing. "Keep us on the right path."

Erwan nodded, his finger tracing the route Boisguy had

marked out before stuffing the map into a watertight pouch.

As before, Isabeau would be the only one of them to ride. Freddie helped her to mount. She sat atop the black mare she had named Sabre on a thick saddle blanket, crouched beneath her wide felt hat and huddled under her coat.

Handing the reins to Gabe, Freddie said, "I'll leave you to watch over Zoé and Isabeau and lead the mare."

"Very well, sir."

"Ready everyone?" Freddie inquired. Their nods caused rain to cascade down from the brims of their hats.

Turning to the two Chouan leaders, he thanked them for their hospitality, vowing to see the needs of the Chouan army would be met. To complete the mission, he had only to get Zoé and the others safely to the shores of Brittany's western coast.

Their first day on the road was long and monotonous, which encouraged Freddie to think they need only suffer four more days of the same to reach the coast and Donet's ship. The rain ceased at noon and the sun showed itself, drying their soaked clothing.

They had stopped twice for brief periods to eat and rest but, otherwise, kept up a good pace.

Freddie planned to avoid Rennes by following Boisguy's advice to go around the city to the west. Even so, about dinner-time, with the city just to the east of them, he felt the hair on the back of his neck stand up. Casting his gaze about the forest, he felt as if a thousand eyes were focused on them.

He gave the signal to stop and waited for a long moment. Nothing moved amid the wall of green trees and he heard nothing save the birds in the canopy above them.

However, the foreboding did not leave him.

Twice he'd ordered his charges into the trees to avoid Blues on patrol. When the last company marched by them, he whispered to Zoé, "I don't like it. The woods are crawling with Rossignol's men." Turning to Erwan, he said, "Scout ahead and see if the path is clear for us. We've hours of daylight remaining but I'd prefer to stop sooner for the night if we can find a safe place. Until you return, we'll continue but more slowly."

Erwan nodded. "I'll find you." He disappeared into the trees, his Breton clothing and long brown hair blending with the underbrush that closed around him.

Freddie looked at those who remained, assessing their strength to go on. Zoé leaned against a tree, obviously tired but uncomplaining. He suspected she wanted to remove her boots and give her feet some air, yet she had not done so. Perhaps she, too, felt uneasy at being so near Rennes. Gabe gave no sign of exhaustion but he watched his mistress closely. Atop the black mare, Isabeau gripped the reins yet her eyes bespoke her weariness. They all needed rest but Freddie could not risk stopping here. "Come, we will go on until Erwan rejoins us."

They had not gone far when a shouted order in a gruff voice echoed through the woods. Though it came from some distance away, he thought he heard the command, *"Fouillez partout!* Search everywhere!"

Gesturing his companions off the path with a sweep of his hand, Freddie drew his pistol and crept toward the direction of the voice. Not far on, he spotted a large number of republican soldiers fanning out to search the bushes, parting the undergrowth with the butts of their muskets. Looking for some poor Chouan, no doubt.

Freddie's heart pounded as he realized the tide of Blues was sweeping toward them. There were too many to engage in battle and fleeing in haste would only draw their attention. Soon the company of soldiers would be upon them.

Retreating as fast as he silently could, he joined Gabe guarding Zoé and Isabeau, already knowing what he must do. "There's a company of Blues coming toward us. Take Zoé and Isabeau ahead," he ordered Gabe. "I will try to divert the soldiers away from you."

"Non!" Zoé protested. "They will shoot you the minute you

153

are seen."

He took her by the shoulders. "There is no time, Pigeon. I cannot let you and Isabeau fall into Rossignol's hands." Hoping to convey with his eyes what he could only hint at with words, he said, "You know what it would mean for you and the girl. I cannot let that happen."

Her eyes welled with tears as she grabbed onto his coat. "But, Freddie—"

Taking the coded information from his satchel, he stuffed the papers into her hands. "There is no time to argue. You must get this to d'Auvergne on Jersey."

She took the papers, tears streaming down her cheeks as she frowned her dismay. "They will kill you; I cannot bear it."

His eyes bored into hers. "And I cannot live in a world where you are not." This was the last time he would see her, his only moment to show her how he cared. He pulled her to his chest and kissed her full on the mouth, putting all his love into the only kiss he would ever give her.

She made a slight gasp as he forced himself to end the kiss. Bringing her fingers to her lips, she stared at him wide-eyed, on her face a look of wonder.

"I will try and convince them that I am too valuable to Rossignol to die here without ceremony. Perhaps I will live for a time." And with that, he said to Gabe, "Take them away; don't let her follow."

Gabe nodded, in his eyes a solemn promise to do as Freddie bid him.

"Freddie, don't do this," pleaded Zoé. "Don't go."

With a last look at the woman he loved, Freddie turned and strode toward the oncoming company of Blues.

Gabe tugged at her coat sleeve but Zoé resisted. She had to know

Freddie's fate.

Stupid heroic Englishman.

Her lips still stung from his kiss. It had not been the gesture of a parting friend, one who was saying goodbye as he sacrificed his life for hers. *Non*, in his eyes she had glimpsed a depth of affection she had not seen before. Feelings for her he'd kept hidden until now. She remembered the first time he'd kissed her, the night of the *Fête de la Fédération* when fireworks exploded in the sky above them. That had been the innocent kiss of a friend, but this...

"I must know what happens," she whispered to Gabe.

"One moment only, mademoiselle."

Zoé strained her ears to hear what was taking place some thirty feet away.

"*Halte-là!*" came a shout. "Identify yourself!"

Speaking the terrible French of an Englishman acting in a comedy on stage, Freddie said, "Why, I am Frederick West, lately of England. Perhaps you might be of assistance. You see I seem to have become lost in these damn fine woods you Frenchies have."

"Insolent cur!"

She heard the smack of a blow and flinched, touching her hand to her cheek where she could almost feel the pain of the impact.

"No need to be rough, good sir," Freddie intoned. "I am but a humble public servant like yourself, a professor of botany to be precise."

"Kill the English pig!" shouted a coarse voice.

"Now, do not be hasty," advised Freddie. His voice sounded calm but, for all his brave front, Zoé believed his bluster masked fear.

Oh, Freddie.

"And why not kill you?" came a drawl.

"Well, for one thing," Freddie replied, "I would very much like to meet your General Rossignol about whom I have heard so much. What's a trip to Brittany without a visit to Rennes, *n'est-ce pas*? After days wandering about with only plants for company, to see the city I've heard so much about would be a treat."

"He's a spy!" exclaimed one of the men.

"Whether he is a spy or not," said another, "he is most certainly English. Perhaps we should deliver him to the general and let him decide what to do with this lying English dog. Take his weapons."

With that, she heard some muffled sounds and then boots moving off through the trees.

The woods fell silent. Even the birds held their songs.

Freddie was gone.

Zoé turned to face her friends, closing her eyes and shaking her head. Freddie had wanted her to go on and she would. But she would not give up. Surely there was a way to free him. Leading Isabeau's horse, she followed Gabe down the path, wiping tears from her eyes.

"Will Monsieur West be all right?" Isabeau inquired in a shaky voice.

"We must pray that he will live, Isabeau. Pray very hard."

Zoé knew royalists, particularly English ones, did not live long in Rossignol's headquarters or Robespierre's Paris for that matter, but she had to hold on to the hope that Freddie might survive. He was clever and smart. Her brave Englishman would live.

She touched her fingers to her lips still tingling from his kiss. Freddie loved her. She had seen it in his eyes and felt it in his kiss. And though the knowledge had only just come to her, she loved him, too. Perhaps she always had.

She could not lose him now.

Some distance down the path, Erwan joined them. "The path ahead is clear of any soldiers," he informed them. "Where is M'sieur West?"

"The Blues have taken him," said Gabe.

A look of shock crossed Erwan's face. "Taken?"

"He gave himself up to save us from discovery," said Zoé. "Erwan, take some food and go to Rennes. See if you can find out what they intend to do with him. If Cadoudal is still in the area, he might be able to help you. We must go on, but will wait for you at Lorient. Bring us word he lives, I pray you."

Erwan shared a look with Gabe before nodding. "I will do as you wish."

Rennes, Brittany

Freddie wiped the blood from his chin. The cut lip and bruises were mere trifles given what he might yet suffer at Rossignol's hands.

The Blues had summarily dumped him in a cell in the bowels of the *Palais de Justice* with only a rickety bench for a bed. A lantern, hanging from a rafter a short distance away, cast flickering shadows onto the stone floor around him.

Surprisingly, though musty, the cell did not reek of human waste nor was it as soot-ridden as he expected. Perhaps the swept clean appearance was due to the short time General Rossignol's prisoners were typically held. The guard had taken special pleasure in telling Freddie his stay would be brief, that he would either meet the guillotine awaiting him just outside or join his fellow spies in a worse place.

Freddie would have to tell Zoé he'd encountered no rats. That is, if he ever saw her again. He did not regret sending her away and using Isabeau's presence to ensure she went. As long as Zoé was safe, he could face death without regret. The kiss had been an afterthought, one he could not deny himself—or her.

He wanted her to know what was in his heart.

"Bring up the Englishman!" yelled a guard. "The general wants to see him."

His hands locked behind him in irons, Freddie was hauled

from his cell, forced up two flights of stairs and shoved into an opulent room with a red flowered carpet and a carved mahogany desk. The walls were graced with paintings and a gilded mirror over the fireplace. Apparently the revolutionaries kept some luxuries from the prior régime for themselves.

Rossignol stood with his back to Freddie looking out a window to the square below, but Freddie was certain the general knew his prisoner had arrived. What better way to snub the brother of an English earl than to ignore him?

Keeping up his guise as a witless Englishman who had lost his way in the woods, Freddie said, "Good day to you, General Rossignol. I was hoping to make your acquaintance. Wandering in the forest for days can be dreadfully dull. Might you be able to assist me in finding my way home?"

Rossignol whipped around, his dark eyes narrowed on Freddie, his lips curled into a sneer. Trained to notice the smallest detail, Freddie's gaze took in the lapels of the general's dark blue uniform, embellished with gold embroidery, and the artful arrangement of his brown hair with curls around his face.

So, the general favored by Robespierre is as vain as he is debauched.

"Are all Englishmen so stupid as to wander into revolutionary France, Mr. West? Or, are you the spy my men believe you to be?" Not giving Freddie an opportunity to reply, he said, *"Oui, I think you are un espion anglais,* an English spy."

"Oh, *non, bon général,"* Freddie protested, "unless you consider Arthur Young's venture into France to observe agriculture a few years ago to be spying. He did keep a journal in which he wrote of his travels, which you might like to read. I found his musings quite fascinating. My own interest is botany and the plants that grow without human assistance." Freddie had become familiar with botany for his code work and could have expounded for hours on Brittany's vegetation.

"Ça suffit!" Rossignol glared at him with suspicious eyes. "Lies and subterfuge!"

Freddie tried to summon an indignant look. *"Non, non, je vous assure."* Retaining a placid expression and mimicking the bloody bands of sans culottes he had observed arguing in favor of the revolution, he placed his palm over his heart, *"Liberté, Égalité, Fraternité* is my motto. I expect one day soon, England will come to see the revolution for what it truly stands for." To Freddie's mind that would be a thirst for blood and a disdain for everything true Frenchmen valued.

"Your ruse is entertaining, I give you that, *l'Anglais*. But already I grow tired of you. Normally, that would mean the guillotine here in Rennes, but it so happens I owe Robespierre a favor of some import. An English spy served up on a silver platter might be just the offering I need to demonstrate my gratitude. *Oui*, I think you shall go to Paris to answer to him. Should Robespierre decide it best, you can meet Madame Guillotine there before the English-hating *citoyens* who enjoy a good show."

On board la Reine Noire off the coast of Lorient, Brittany

"Well?" Zoé anxiously inquired. "What have you learned?"

Erwan had just climbed up the manrope from the ship's skiff, looking bedraggled from his days of hurried travel. "The morning I arrived," he began, pausing to take a breath, "a contingent of republican soldiers was leaving the *Palais de Justice* with M'sieur West. I asked one of the crowd gathered to watch where they were going and was told 'Paris'." Erwan dropped his gaze, avoiding Zoé's eyes. "I overheard one of the soldiers taunting Mr. West with the name *la Conciergerie*."

Zoé closed her eyes, her heart sinking along with her hope. The Conciergerie, a medieval royal palace, now a prison, was one step from death. Its rat-infested dungeons were the oldest in France. The tales told of dirt, disorder and disease had given Zoé nightmares.

159

The turnkeys, often drunk, ruled over the prisoners with a pack of savage dogs, granting favors for food and a bed if the prisoners could pay the going rate. She had read one account of a survivor who dubbed the prison "the vast antechamber of the guillotine."

Her mind still reeling, Zoé heard her uncle give the orders to set sail and the deck moved beneath her feet. "Come," she said to Erwan, "we must ask *mon oncle* what can be done." She would not give up what hope remained while Freddie yet lived.

In the *capitaine*'s cabin, her uncle, Erwan and Émile Bequel gathered to discuss Freddie's situation.

"It is possible to bribe one's way in," said her uncle, "but not so easy to bribe one's way out, particularly if one has a prisoner in tow. And you say, West is being held for Robespierre?"

"From what I was able to learn in Rennes," offered Erwan, "Rossignol was sending M'sieur West to Robespierre as a kind of gift."

"More like a sacrificial lamb to be slaughtered," put in M'sieur Bequel.

Zoé cringed and he patted her hand. "Do not despair, little one. There is some good in what Rossignol has done. At least he has provided us time to intervene."

"Time, yes," her uncle said, "but not much. We must get to West before he is called before the Revolutionary Tribunal. The sentence would almost certainly be death to be swiftly carried out."

"Are we sailing to Le Havre, *Capitaine*?" asked M'sieur Bequel.

"*Oui*, I have set a course for that port. It will take Rossignol's men a week to get to Paris. We can make it there nearly in the same time if the wind is with us and we have a fast carriage from Le Havre."

For the first time since Freddie had been taken, Zoé began to believe a rescue might be possible.

Her uncle pursed his lips, deep in thought, muttering to himself, *"Oui,* he might be of use..."

"Who, *mon oncle?"*

He looked up, his countenance brightening. "François de Dordogne, a lawyer in Paris who owes me his life. That is to say, I refrained from killing him when his betrayal gave me good cause."

M'sieur Bequel nodded. *"Oui, c'est parfait.* He owes ye much, *Capitaine."*

"Indeed. I still protect his secret. Most convenient for our purposes," her uncle added, "I believe he is now working for the Committee of Public Safety."

Chapter 12

La Conciergerie, on the Île de la Cité, Paris, early May, 1794

Despair settled in the dungeons of the Conciergerie like a thick fog, permeating even the cold stone walls. At one time, the palace above had been the home of kings and perfumed air. Not so the prison below where Freddie was confined. Here, the stench of rats, disease and urine made it nearly impossible to draw breath.

Moans of misery surrounded him yet even here there was hope, not so much for life as for what human kindness the prisoners could show each other in the face of death. Oddly, the equality the revolutionaries preached on the streets of Paris but never achieved was demonstrated in the Conciergerie every day. Here, nobles, clergy, merchants and peasants, even sans-culottes out of favor, had become one family and looked out for each other.

Beside Freddie languished the orphan boy he had managed to rescue from a drunken turnkey's humorless joke the day he'd arrived.

"Hungry, are ye?" The turnkey's slurred words and sardonic smile aimed at the starving lad had warned Freddie to rise. The rags the boy wore for clothing revealed his frail skeleton, tearing at Freddie's heart.

The lad's soot-covered face looked up at the too well-fed

guard with eager anticipation. *"Oui,* sir. *J'ai faim.* Is there food?"

The turnkey withdrew a fish he'd been hiding behind his back, and tossed it at the boy. From where Freddie stood a few feet away he could see maggots devouring the long-dead fish where it lay at the boy's feet. Amidst the other foul smells, the reek of the decaying fish rose to Freddie's nostrils causing him to wince.

Summoning courage that must have been long buried, the boy picked up the fish by the tail and grimaced. Hurling it at the guard's face, he spat back, "'Tis not fit for us; you eat it!"

The turnkey bellowed his rage and grabbed the boy by his shirt, ripping away what little cloth remained. Rearing back, he was about to ram his heavy fist into the small lad's face when Freddie stepped in, shielding the boy with his body. Keeping up the ruse of a naïve Englishman engaged in comedy theater, he said, *"Mon bon ami,* surely this is not necessary. He is only a boy and cannot be faulted for failing to observe your kindness in providing him food." Taking a coin from his pocket, Freddie offered it to the fat guard. "Have an ale on me. 'Twill soothe your understandable anger."

Muttering an oath, the turnkey cursed to Hell rude boys and idiot Englishmen. "He'll meet the guillotine for this, see if he don't." But, as Freddie had hoped, the turnkey took the coin and stumbled away.

The fish lay on the stone floor, untouched by the watching prisoners. The jailor's dogs sniffed at the carcass and turned away.

The boy looked up at Freddie. *"Merci."*

"I am happy to help a fellow prisoner." He offered his hand and a smile. "I'm Freddie. What's your name?"

The boy placed his small hand in Freddie's. "Pascal, but most call me Pax."

He was near the same age as Jack but thinner and his eyes were old and haunted. As Freddie was to learn, the boy had been living on the streets when he was sent to the Conciergerie for insulting a republican soldier. Now, he would be sentenced to death. But then, wouldn't they all?

With the money he had kept in his boots, Freddie could afford the bribes paid to the abusive jailors for food and a comfortable bed, but he preferred to share the large cell with the others and use what money he had to buy food for those who could ill afford to pay.

He and his fellow prisoners endured all the horrors, physical and mental, of Robespierre's heartless régime. Cast aside and left to shiver in dark and naked cells, they were sick, hungry and cold, many suffering untreated wounds. They arrived with cuts and gashes from the republicans' bayonets that only festered in the wretched conditions of the Conciergerie. Even if they arrived unscathed, they would soon have wounds inflicted by the ever-present rats that gnawed on their exposed flesh while they slept.

Worse than the physical wounds were the wounds to their souls. They had no hope of a fair hearing by an upright judge for the guillotine's blade hung suspended over all and the prosecutor, the sinister Fouquier-Tinville, did not even pretend to be impartial. Instead, he taunted the condemned, then happily sent them off to be executed.

But the prisoners had each other for company and stories to inspire them while they waited for the end. They still talked of the silent courage of Charlotte Corday as she went to the guillotine.

For Freddie, the golden moment he clung to was the kiss he had given the woman he loved, a sweet memory of Zoé he would take to his grave. He did not allow his mind to linger on her tear-filled eyes or her protests when he had sent her away. He could not have done otherwise. In time, she would find another to love. There would be many men eager to take Freddie's place in her heart. A frown creased his brow when he realized that Boisguy, if he survived the war, would be one of them.

To occupy their time, some of the more learned prisoners had brought books with them, which they read aloud to an enraptured audience. And, in what Freddie thought a macabre effort to prepare them for what was to come, a mock court dubbed "Tinville's Tribunal" was arranged. Eloquent arguments were made on both sides, a decision rendered and a guillotine of chairs and laths set up with a wooden blade.

The game went on most of the day.

Freddie nervously watched the entrance to the dungeons expecting to be summoned. He had yet to come before Robespierre or his inquisitors. Perhaps the man was too busy to deal with a mere Englishman, even a spy. According to one prisoner, who had learned it from a guard, having ended religion in France, Robespierre had decided faith might be important. Now he was busy introducing a new Cult of the Supreme Being, henceforth to be the civic religion of France.

In the Conciergerie, the prisoners fared better; they had the devoted priest abbé Émery to see to their souls.

How ironic it was that the celebration of Robespierre's new religion was to take place on the Champ de Mars, the same place the *Fête de la Fédération* had been held four years earlier where hundreds of priests had said Mass.

The Donet Townhouse, Paris

As the simple black carriage drove through the arched *porte-cochère* of her uncle's townhouse, Zoé noted how unchanged it was from four years before. The fawn-colored stone, tall paned glass windows and scrolling wrought iron balconies bespoke a France untouched by revolution and chaos. Built in a rectangle with an inner stone courtyard decorated with potted topiary, the Paris townhouse was the most fashionable of her uncle's three homes. Her spirit brooded when she recalled how Freddie had loved it when they came for the *Fête de la Fédération*.

Trying not to show her grief, she asked her uncle, "How have you managed to keep the Paris house?" He was sitting across from her with M'sieur Bequel. "I should have thought it gone with your title."

"It might have been were it not for the fact I deeded the townhouse to Gaspar, my former carpenter on *la Reine Noire*, at least for the time being. And Flèche, who you'll remember as my butler and former gunner, still reigns supreme over the household. I sent word for them to expect us."

In his clothing at least, her uncle looked more like a merchant than the nobleman he was. A white cravat was the only adornment to his black coat, waistcoat and breeches. Zoé, too, had changed her clothing and now wore a gray dress of simple design.

Once the carriage passed through the arched entrance to the courtyard, it stopped in front of glass doors leading to the salon. Her uncle climbed down and greeted Flèche, who beamed his delight at the sight of the man he still called *"Capitaine"*.

Taking her uncle's hat and sword, the butler passed them to a waiting footman. Where once Flèche had proudly worn a wig and elaborately embroidered waistcoat, now he dressed in a simpler style, as did the household servants, so as not to raise suspicions of wealth when they traveled about the streets.

Her uncle handed her down from the carriage and Zoé set her hat aright with its mandatory tricolor cockade. Surveying the inner courtyard, she wondered at the peaceful setting in a city where so much turmoil prevailed.

"Lest you worry," said her uncle, "it might interest you to know that Robespierre moved in the last few years to a rather elegant apartment on rue Saint-Honoré. Not every revolutionary lives in squalor."

Émile climbed down and muttered to Flèche, "'Tis good to be back," before handing his tricorne and sword to the waiting footman.

As they entered the salon, Zoé took off her hat, marking the few changes in the room she noticed. The walls were still paneled in bird's-eye maple inlaid with slabs of cream-colored marble. The red velvet chairs and comfortable salmon-colored sofa remained around the fireplace, but the silver candlesticks and her uncle's gilded desk had been removed to Guernsey.

"Gaspar will be along shortly," Flèche informed them before directing the footman to serve coffee and tea.

Her eyes darting from M'sieur Bequel to her uncle, Zoé accepted a cup of tea but did not take a seat. She was anxious to be about Freddie's rescue.

In a grave tone, her uncle said, "We come on a matter of dire importance, Flèche, to rescue one of our own from the Conciergerie."

The butler's eyes grew wide and his mouth dropped open. "Why, that prison is one step from the—"

"To be specific," her uncle interrupted, "the man we hope to rescue is my wife's brother, Frederick West."

In other words, thought Zoé, they were committed no matter the danger. For that, she was grateful.

"*Mon Dieu!*" exclaimed Flèche. "An Englishman in the Conciergerie. We must make haste."

"Pray we are in time," said her uncle. "Meanwhile, I intend to call in a favor owed me by François de Dordogne to see what can be done."

Flèche scratched his head of dark curls as if puzzled.

"If the name is familiar," put in M'sieur Bequel, "'tis the scoundrel who was to marry the *capitaine*'s daughter, Claire, but was discovered to be a sodomite wanting to disguise his forbidden life with a respectable marriage."

Dawning recognition appeared in Flèche's eyes. "Ah, *oui*, I do remember him. He still lives after that?"

"Fortuitously, I allowed him his life," said Zoé's uncle, his dark eyes flashing with remembered anger. "As it happens, he now works for the Committee of Public Safety. Send him a message to call upon me immediately."

The butler bowed. "Consider it done, *Capitaine.*"

Gaspar arrived a few minutes later to warm greetings from the men with whom he had once served on *la Reine Noire.* Zoé had not met him but was soon introduced.

M'sieur Bequel patted the former ship's carpenter on the back. "Ye appear prosperous even in this time of revolution, old friend."

"Well," said Gaspar, his face brown from his time in the sun, "for some years, my work involved cabinets for the aristocracy and desks for the lawyers, a lucrative business. Now, of course, I make carts to transport the revolution's victims to the guillotines and coffins for those who can afford them. A sad business but one has to feed one's family. I now have five children."

"You are blessed with a full quiver," said Zoé's uncle, "but the tales of your family will have to wait. We come on a matter of great urgency. Let us move to my study."

Her uncle greeted visitors in the salon, but it was in his study the real business took place, be it privateering or plotting revenge. The shutters in the book-lined room were open to allow light to fall on his large desk where he unrolled a map of Paris.

Pointing to the ancient palace on the Seine River, he asked Gaspar, "What do you know of the dungeons of the Conciergerie?"

"Nothing good, *Capitaine.* There are many prisons in Paris, all overcrowded thanks to Robespierre and his friends, but that one is the worst. To be transferred there means a prisoner will soon meet the tribunal and then the guillotine, sometimes in the same day."

"I meant," said her uncle, "what can you tell me of its rooms and corridors, its procedures. We have a prisoner to rescue, my brother-in-law to be exact."

Gaspar's eyes grew wide. "*Sacrebleu!*" Gulping down a swig of his coffee, he said, "I have delivered benches and a few beds to the Conciergerie. I can tell you what I know." All eyes focused on

Gaspar as he continued. "There is a principal jailor who sits by the entrance to the immense room above the dungeons. He determines what visitors will be allowed inside. It depends, of course, upon his mood, the assignats offered him and," with a glance directed at Zoé, "whether the visitor be man or woman."

"And the cells?" asked her uncle. "Are they kept locked?"

"At night, *oui*, but during the day, unless a turnkey locks a prisoner in on a whim, they are allowed to walk about the gallery. At sunset, visitors, even tradesmen like myself, must leave. That is when they call roll. Since many of the turnkeys cannot read and are often sated with drink, the prisoners have to help them. 'Twould be easy to add or delete a name."

Zoé watched the men carefully, looking for a sign they saw the mission as promising success. She would not leave Freddie's fate to others. If there were any possibility he still lived, she would go after him, compelled to save the man she loved. "I will go, *mon oncle*. The jailor at the door may find me pleasing." With tears welling in her eyes, betraying her heart, she added, "I must find Freddie if he yet lives."

Her uncle gave her a knowing look. Did he see her desperate need to rescue her friend, now her love? Heaving a resigned sigh, he said, "I expected you would not be kept back."

"I can go with her," insisted M'sieur Bequel. "Killing the swine who imprison good men and women would bring me great satisfaction. 'Twould be like the old days."

Her uncle smiled. "I may need you to remain outside to assist our escape, Émile."

The quartermaster nodded. "As ye wish, *Capitaine*."

"'Tis better if I go with the mademoiselle," said Gaspar. "I know the prison."

Her uncle nodded. "*Oui*, your knowledge will be most welcome, Gaspar. That is, if you are willing to take the risk. But I must be the one to lead the effort. I do not know the prison, but I can convince them the English dog they hold has dishonored my daughter and must pay for the child she is expecting."

Gaspar chuckled. "Clever, sir. It might work. You would have the jailor's sympathy, particularly if you and your daughter... er, niece appear supporters of the revolution."

Zoé bit her lip in contemplation. "I'll have to explain just how it was a patriot of the revolution succumbed to a charming English dog."

Her uncle smiled. "You could always say you thought he was French."

La Conciergerie

Each morning, the prisoners were assembled in the main gallery and an officer of the court appeared to read the list of those whose cases were to be heard by the tribunal the next day. Freddie had thought he had witnessed despair before, yet these sessions were worse.

The reaction of the prisoners whose names were called differed. Some wailed and turned to give their last farewells. Husbands and wives sat on benches placed against the stone walls, embracing for the last time. Others seem to welcome the anticipated end to a miserable existence, saying goodbye to the friends they had made as if leaving on a holiday. Those who had possessions gave them away. A favorite book might be entrusted to one who promised to read to the others. A few turned aside to write a last letter, which the intended recipient would, no doubt, never receive.

When his name and that of the boy he had befriended were called, Freddie slid his arm around Pax's shoulder. The lad had become his constant companion. "Well, Pax, we knew this day would come. We must face it with courage, trusting God to deliver our souls to Heaven, *n'est-ce pas?*"

"*Oui*, M'sieur." The boy's voice quavered as he looked up at

Freddie. "Will you be with me?"

"*Bien sûr*. I will be with you as we face the tribunal and I will not leave your side as we travel in the cart to the *Place de la Révolution*, whether it be tomorrow or the day after." Freddie vowed to shield the boy from the mud the indignant onlookers were known to fling at the revolution's victims in the hour-long ride to the guillotine.

The call for Freddie to appear before Robespierre had come the night before. Dressed in a fine suit of clothes and an ornately tied cravat, the master of the Terror sat behind a gilded desk in a room lit by chandeliers one might expect to see in Versailles. The sausage curls of his white wig curled up over his ears. Yet for all his finery, he seemed harried and more concerned with the stacks of papers piled in front of him than with Rossignol's "gift" of an Englishman. His pockmarked face was unlined but Freddie thought he looked older than a man of thirty-six years.

"What have you to say for yourself?" Robespierre demanded impatiently. He did not invite Freddie to sit, nor did he rise to greet him. A guard stood at the door should Freddie have any thoughts to attack the man who effectively now ruled France. Not that he could do so with his hands in irons.

"I came to see the vegetation of Brittany and now wish to return home to England. General Rossignol was not accommodating, which was most disappointing. 'Tis rare that one who comes to learn about the plant life of another country is treated so rudely. But I am willing to forgive this injustice if I may now depart."

"*Ça suffit!*" Robespierre shouted, holding up his hand. "I have no time for such prattle. What can you tell me of the *Chouannerie*? If you are forthcoming, I might be persuaded to let you live."

Freddie harbored no illusion that he would be allowed to leave France and he had no intention of betraying those he had come to serve. When he had kissed Zoé in the woods outside of Rennes he had understood it was goodbye. "Alas, I know nothing of whatever that is. As I told the good general, I became lost in the woods and approached his soldiers for help."

Robespierre gave him a studying perusal as if trying to decide if, under torture, Freddie might be persuaded to give different information "That was very foolish, Mr. West. Very foolish. I shall think on your case. If my inquisitors are available, I may send you to them to see if they can loosen your tongue."

"Are you certain you want to do that, sir?" In Freddie's light-hearted tone there was an edge of steel. He was not aware of any English aristocrat who had been tortured in France after the revolution had begun. "After all, I am the brother of an English peer and Prime Minister Pitt might not take lightly the torture of an English aristocrat." *Kill them, yes, but torture them, perhaps not.*

Robespierre blinked rapidly, then looked down at the papers before him. "I care not what the English think. In any event, you will face trial and, I daresay, the guillotine. The good *citoyens* of Paris would relish throwing mud at one such as you."

Freddie expected to die but he dreaded the thought of torture. Better men than he had cracked under the horrors inflicted by France's inquisitors. So, when his name had been called for trial, he'd felt an odd sense of relief.

To lose his head was one thing; to lose his integrity was quite another.

Chapter 13

"And just where do ye think ye are going, little one?" M'sieur Bequel's gruff voice startled her, staying Zoé's hand on the door leading from the townhouse to the courtyard where the carriage awaited.

"Out," she replied, slowly turning around.

The quartermaster stood with his fists on his hips and a scowl on his leathery face making his dark eyes ominous beneath his heavy brows. If she hadn't known him since she was ten, she might have been frightened. Émile Bequel had a savage look about him. He must have just left the study where he had been confined with her uncle. He wore no coat and his waistcoat of brown leather was only partially buttoned over his linen shirt.

"Just for an hour," she pleaded. "I have a thought as to how I might learn something more about the Conciergerie."

His scowl deepened. "The *capitaine* is meeting with that macaroni, Dordogne, and would not be happy if he discovered ye gone when he's finished. Ye'd best stay close as he plans to gain entrance to the prison today. 'Sides, the streets of Paris are not safe for one such as ye, even in the daytime."

"But I must go. Those I intend to call upon might know something others don't."

He huffed. "If ye insist on going out, I will go with ye."

"All right, but be prepared to meet women of pleasure."

Émile's mouth dropped open. "And what would ye know of such women, little one?"

"Enough to suspect they service both guards and prisoners and see more than most. When *Oncle* Jean had the carriage drive by the Conciergerie this morning, I saw women lingering near the front door, smiling at the men going by. I know who they are."

"We'll go, but ye'll not be lingering, or the *capitaine* will be ordering lashes for me."

The carriage M'sieur Bequel hailed pulled up several feet from the entrance to the prison. Two women of indeterminate age leaned against the stone wall of the Conciergerie, looking bored. Their faces were painted, their hair long and unkempt and their chemises barely covered their nipples. Zoé had dressed plainly so as not to draw attention. She might have been a nun next to these women.

Bidding Émile to wait by the carriage, which he only reluctantly agreed to do and then with one hand on the pistol shoved into his belt, Zoé approached the two women. "Mesdames," she said, "might I beg your assistance?"

Their eyes rudely raked her up and down before glancing over her shoulder to where M'sieur Bequel stood wearing a dour expression. "If ye're lookin' to ply yer trade here, *ma belle*, ye might think again. Ye're pretty enough but these are crowded waters and none too calm."

"Ye're too fresh for these men," said her companion. "Tell yer man watching ye to look elsewhere."

"*Non, vous ne comprenez pas.* I do not wish to join you. *Mon frère*, my brother, is one of the prisoners and I need to see him. Can you tell me when 'tis best to visit so as to gain entrance?"

"Well, now, we can help ye with that," said the first. "*L'après-midi*, the afternoon, is best."

"And why is that, may I ask?"

"The jailor who guards the entrance is a bad sort, but by then, he will be drunken as will the turnkeys below. *Les prisonniers* will be in the gallery. They won't hurt ye; it's the guards ye must be wary of."

"Them and their dogs," added the second woman. "One gave me a nasty bite."

"We'll be going in ourselves then," said her friend, "to see our regulars."

Zoé thanked them and hurried back to M'sieur Bequel and his scowl.

The trial before Fouquier-Tinville went forward amidst crowds of spectators that included the abusive turnkeys. Prostitutes mingled outside the courtroom making Freddie think of a backstreet in London's St Giles.

The verdict was a foregone conclusion. All were found guilty of being traitors to the revolution and condemned to die, including him and Pax.

In his mind, Freddie heard a door slam.

He had known this was coming but for the boy, it was worse. Freddie had lived some and known a wonderful woman who had given him memories to cherish, but the boy had yet to live. A revolution that devoured its children would not end well.

After the trial, they were shuffled back to the prison and told they would face the guillotine on the morrow.

"What shall we do now?" Pax asked, despondent, his large brown eyes looking up at Freddie as if he alone controlled their choices.

Freddie had been thinking of how to spend their last night and so he was prepared for the question. "How would you like to hear a story of a boy your age who felled a fierce giant?"

Pax nodded vigorously. "I would like that very much."

"Good. We shall spend my remaining assignats to buy us a fine dinner, well, as fine as this establishment is capable of

177

producing, and then I will tell you the story before you go to sleep."

The boy's eyes lit with expectation. Neither of them spoke of what would happen the next day. Freddie planned to tell the boy the story of David and Goliath and the shepherd boy who became a great king. It seemed appropriate since they would soon be meeting David's God.

"François de Dordogne has agreed to meet us at the Conciergerie," said Zoé's uncle. "He tells me West still lives, at least as of today."

Early that afternoon, her uncle, M'sieur Bequel, Gaspar and Flèche had gathered in the study to go over the details of the rescue. Set before them on the desk were the plans of the prison.

"What will this lawyer do for us, *mon oncle*?"

"He is to gain us admission without the need for a story about you being dishonored, and he has promised to bring papers allowing us to remove a prisoner."

"Is he trustworthy?" asked Gaspar.

Her uncle exchanged a look with M'sieur Bequel. "He has not been in the past, but this one time I believe he will be—for his own sake. He is well aware of my reputation. And, with this favor, he will be released from his debt to me." Turning from the drawing of the prison, he said, "There is another reason I wanted to use him. I intend for us to carry weapons and I don't want to be searched. We can be glad 'tis a chilly day as we'll all need to wear cloaks. With Dordogne waiting at the door, Émile can enter with us."

Shooting their way out of the Conciergerie with armed guards and vicious dogs in pursuit had little appeal for Zoé but she could throw a lethal knife and would if it came to that. Freddie would have no weapons, of course. He would have her uncle,

M'sieur Bequel and Gaspar to defend him. The three of them were good with a sword and crack shots with the French pistols they carried. She, too, would carry a pistol, a small one her uncle had given her.

When the carriage finally departed the townhouse, it was with eager anticipation more than fear that Zoé looked out the window to a fair day and busy streets.

She had not seen Dordogne arrive for the meeting with her uncle. But the man who paced in front of the prison dressed in a black suit with a great mound of lace at his neck and cuffs had to be the lawyer who once crossed her uncle. He was slender, almost feminine in appearance, and not much taller than she. His dark hair, longer than that of most Frenchmen, was tied back at his nape.

They stepped out of the carriage and François de Dordogne greeted her uncle with anxious eyes. It was clear he was not pleased to be about the task set before him. "I have come as you asked, Donet." Working as he did for the revolution's leaders, Dordogne could not utter the forbidden "Monsieur" of the *Ancien Régime* nor would he dare label her uncle a *citoyen*. In turn, her uncle did not introduce Zoé, Gaspar or M'sieur Bequel. "This way," Dordogne said, gesturing them into the entrance hall. As he did, he paused, giving her a puzzled look.

To the thin jailor wearing a red cap who sat at the door, Dordogne gave his name, "François de Dordogne from the Committee of Public Safety" and handed the doorkeeper some folded papers.

Whether the jailor could read or not, he gave the papers a quick perusal and handed them back. "All seems in order, *citoyen* Dordogne. You may enter."

The lawyer gave her uncle another paper and waved them ahead. "This may help. I will wait for you here. Be quick."

Gaspar led the way down to the dungeons below. The stench of urine and rats nearly overwhelmed Zoé but the thought of seeing Freddie brought tears to her eyes and kept her moving forward. *Soon, my love.*

As they reached the lower level, a guard approached Gaspar, who offered the paper her uncle had passed to him. "We come for an Englishman wanted for further questioning by the Committee of Public Safety."

"And the woman?" asked the guard, who reeked of strong liquor.

"To identify him," said her uncle.

The jailor's dogs sniffed at them, growling low in their throats, the beasts' eyes predatory and fierce. Zoé felt like she was looking into the face of evil itself.

They paid most attention to Gaspar. Why soon became evident.

He reached into his coat pocket and pulled out some raw meat, tossing it to the dogs. They fell upon it voraciously, snarling at each other.

"Aye, they do love fresh meat," mumbled the guard, the smell of liquor strong on his breath.

From his waistcoat, her uncle lifted out a wad of assignats. "Here, for your trouble."

Apparently satisfied, the guard nodded and pointed the way to a large area where many prisoners had congregated.

Searching the faces of the men, Zoé did not recognize Freddie until he stood and shouted, "Zoé!" A small boy held on to his coat or what was left of it. She could hardly believe the soot-covered man who stood before her, tears streaming down his face, was her childhood friend, her Freddie. Her love.

At his approach, she saw his clothing hung in tatters, filthy and stinking, his torn shirt stained with blood. He was thinner than when she'd left him outside of Rennes.

She reached out to hug him and he stepped back. "I am not fit to embrace you."

Her uncle held out his hand to Freddie. "You have survived,

West. That is all anyone can ask."

Reluctantly, Freddie shook her uncle's hand.

"Meet Gaspar," said her uncle.

The former carpenter nodded his head.

Unable to hold back one minute more, Zoé flung herself into Freddie's arms. "Oh, Freddie. I don't care what you look like, what you smell like. God has answered my prayers. You are alive!"

"I am, aren't I?" he said. "Though not quite hale and hearty this time."

"Come," urged her uncle, "We must go. Our presence here was gained on a pretext and I cannot be sure how long it will hold."

They turned toward the stairs but Freddie stopped. "I'll not go without Pax."

All eyes turned to the boy still clinging to Freddie's coat.

Her uncle considered the small lad. "Pax, is it?"

The boy nodded, his eyes full of fear. He must have believed he would be left behind.

"Very well," said her uncle with a smile for the boy, "you shall come, too. Somehow we will explain you are necessary."

"We were both to be executed tomorrow," said Freddie as they headed to the stairs, one hand holding the boy's and one hand holding hers. He looked back at the other prisoners. "I wish we could take them all. Some have become my friends."

"Alas, we cannot," said M'sieur Bequel, heaving a sigh. "Ye are enough trouble, Mr. West. Come now. Ye, too, Pax."

In the entrance hall, M'sieur Bequel paused, muttering an oath.

Zoé realized something was terribly wrong. François de Dordogne no longer waited at the door and the jailor suddenly rose from his stool to hold out his palm. "Not so fast, *citoyen*. The man who brought ye left with another. When I asked, he failed to vouch for yer departure. 'Sides," he added with a disapproving glance at Pax, "there was no mention of a boy."

Zoé's uncle flicked his cloak over one shoulder and placed his hand on the hilt of his sword. "That is most unfortunate, *citoyen*, for it means we shall have to persuade you." Her uncle withdrew another sword from his cloak and tossed it to Freddie. "I trust you remember how to use it, West."

"Indeed I do," he said, giving Pax's hand to Zoé. "Guard the boy, Pigeon."

Suddenly a half-dozen soldiers emerged from the wings of the cavernous entrance hall, with drawn swords and shouts of *Arrêtez!*

M'sieur Bequel whipped his cloak behind him and yanked his sword from its sheath, bracing his legs. "Our four to their seven, *Capitaine*, assuming the drunken jailor can even fight. Hardly seems a worthy challenge."

"Then take two!" shouted her uncle with a grin. "That's my intention."

M'sieur Bequel chuckled. "Like old times, *Capitaine*."

The entrance chamber with its arched ceiling echoed with the sound of crashing steel and men engaging each other's swords. She pulled Pax away from the fight exploding around them just as Gaspar stepped sideways to deflect the blade of the soldier he was matched with.

Frustrated, the arrogant soldier threw taunts at Gaspar, disparaging his origins.

The former ship's carpenter merely smiled. "We shall see, *mon ami*. It is not where you begin that is important, but where you end."

She had seen her uncle and M'sieur Bequel fight before as merchants defending their cargo and she knew they had once been pirates, so she was not surprised by their prowess with a blade. From the smiles on their faces as they confronted the stiff republican soldiers, they appeared to be enjoying themselves.

Dressed all in black, her uncle untied his cloak and let it fall to the ground. Like a menacing storm, he advanced on his prey, teasing them with his shimmering blade. Outnumbered, her uncle and M'sieur Bequel fought side by side, slicing their blades across their opponents' swords, causing them to retreat.

Zoé placed herself in front of Pax, guarding the boy with her knife, but the men were too consumed with their fighting to notice her or the lad.

To her amazement, Freddie handled his sword adeptly, confident in his moves as if he'd fought many times before. He swiftly parried the soldier's thrusts. Much like her uncle, his movements were precise, his style fluid, almost graceful. Twice he turned so rapidly his blade made a rushing sound as it whipped through the air, astounding his opponent.

Where did he learn to fight like that?

A soldier managed to cut the cuff of her uncle's sleeve. He paused to glance down at the frayed cloth. "Alas, 'twas one of my favorites." Turning back to the two soldiers who had stopped to gloat, her uncle said, "Enough of this banter! We have no time to teach you braggarts how to fight." He pulled a pistol from his waist and shot one soldier dead, then quickly dispatched the other with a thrust of his blade.

"Well, if it's to be like that," said Émile Bequel, obviously disappointed.

One of his two opponents lunged toward him. M'sieur Bequel snatched his pistol from his waist and fired into the man's head at close range. The other soldier stared at his fallen companion while Émile slid a knife from his sleeve and threw it at the soldier's neck. He sank to the stone floor, a gurgling sound emanating from his throat.

Zoé's mouth dropped open, amazed at how the fifty-year-old quartermaster had fought like a much younger man. She turned to see Freddie sinking his sword into the flesh of the soldier he fought. The man dropped to his knees.

"Well, that's done," he said smiling at her.

The last soldier standing was no match for Gaspar. Surveying the field of dead Blues and realizing he was the only one of Donet's men still fighting, the former ship's carpenter forced his opponent to the wall, knocked his sword from his hand and sliced the man's throat. "I wouldn't want to keep you waiting," Gaspar said to her uncle as he quickly wiped clean his sword and sheathed it.

Turning his attention to the jailor huddled against the wall, worrying his red cap in his hands, her uncle said, "Care to engage one of us?" Sweeping his arm in front of his companions, he said, "You can take your pick. We are very accommodating. We will even lend you one of our swords."

The jailor vigorously shook his head, his eyes huge with fright.

"Then be gone with ye," said M'sieur Bequel.

The thin man disappeared out the front door.

Freddie offered his hand to Zoé and she took it.

"You did well," said Pax, gazing up at the Englishman he obviously adored.

Zoé squeezed Freddie's hand, glad to be assured he lived. No matter he smelled like filth and rats. He was here with her. Not for the first time, she thanked God for this man who had offered his life for hers. "I thought you were wonderful."

At her uncle's shout, they raced out the door and piled into the waiting carriage, the men's chests still heaving with the exertion of their fight.

Her uncle took out a handkerchief and wiped the sweat from his brow. "I would have preferred a quiet exit, but perhaps the prisoners will take this opportunity to escape."

"They were already creeping into the entrance hall before we left," said Zoé.

As the carriage traveled down the street, the horses' hooves clattered over the cobblestones. Freddie leaned across her to peer out the window, looking back toward the Conciergerie. "A great flood of them is flowing out the door." He leaned back against the

184

seat and let out a breath. "I am more than pleased at least some of the prisoners made it to freedom. Perhaps they can slip into the crowds, unnoticed."

Zoé smiled at him and then looked across him to Pax, who clung to Freddie's side like a limpet securely attached to its favorite rock. With Isabeau, who had remained safely behind on *la Reine Noire*, there would be two children returning with them to Guernsey. Playmates for Jack, she supposed. Pax was about Jack's age but Isabeau was older. She smiled thinking that would not deter Jack from ordering Isabeau about.

"I wonder who came for Dordogne," said M'sieur Bequel, his dark brows furrowed in contemplation.

"Assuredly, one of his own," replied Gaspar. "Fearing the *capitaine* as he does, he would not have left except at the command of one to whom he was accountable."

Remembering the odd look Dordogne had given her, Zoé said, "*Oncle* Jean, that man, François de Dordogne, gave me the strangest look when he first glimpsed me. Why?"

Her uncle gazed out the window, scanning the street, as if still worried about pursuers. "I suspect 'tis because you look very much like my daughter, Claire. She was your age at the time Dordogne was contracted to wed her. Though her eyes are blue and yours are gray, you both have the Donet hair and it's been years. At the time, I was unaware that Dordogne had deceived me, that he hid a secret that would forever keep him from being a proper husband."

"Aye," said M'sieur Bequel, his mouth twitching up in an uncharacteristic grin. "Must have brought back some bad memories for him. He might even have thought the *capitaine* brought ye along to remind him of his perfidy."

Freddie raised Zoé's hand to his lips and kissed her knuckles.

His warm lips on her skin reminded Zoé of his kiss in the forest that had caught her by surprise and forever changed the way she looked at him. Returning him a contented smile, she breathed a sigh of relief. Finally, Freddie was safely returned to her and soon they would be sailing to Guernsey. The future opened wide before them. Not that the war was over, but they could face it together, no longer merely friends but more. Did her uncle and the others notice the more intimate nature of their friendship?

Still holding her hand, Freddie leaned toward her uncle sitting across from them with Gaspar on one side and M'sieur Bequel on the other. "I know this may seem sudden, sir, and I am not dressed for the occasion, but I have waited years to approach you on a certain subject. I can wait no longer."

All eyes on Freddie, his gaze paused on each man before continuing. "Now that it appears I'm to live, if you give your permission and Zoé will have me, I would like to ask her to become my wife."

Zoé beamed her happiness at hearing Freddie's intention and squeezed his hand. She could think of no other man she would rather have. Her best friend had become the man of her dreams, the one man she wanted by her side forever.

Her uncle glanced at her with raised brows. "Zoé?" Beside him, M'sieur Bequel nodded his approval.

"Oh, *oui, Oncle* Jean. I love him!"

Freddie flashed his white teeth in a broad smile aimed at her. "And I you."

"I daresay your aunt will be pleased," said her uncle. "She hinted of this to me not long ago. You did not mention a dowry, West. I assume it is of no matter to you?"

"None at all, sir."

"Well it matters to me!" Zoé spoke up.

Her uncle chuckled. "I thought it might. 'Tis a considerable one, West, large enough to buy you and my niece a nicely appointed house on Guernsey, should you choose to live there. Or, if you prefer, a ship of your own."

His words pleased Zoé. She would not go to Freddie a pauper. "Thank you, *Oncle* Jean."

Freddie smiled. "Very generous of you, sir."

"So be it," her uncle said, "you have my permission, West. But I must insist on a Guernsey wedding, else your sister will have my head."

Laughter filled the carriage at her uncle's macabre humor. It was clear they were all relieved to be quitting Paris.

Pax looked up at Freddie, his dark eyes speaking confusion. "Are we going home now?" he asked in a small but hopeful voice.

"Indeed we are," said Freddie, pulling the boy to him. "To paradise, I'm thinking."

Chapter 14

Onboard la Reine Noire off the northwest coast of Brittany, France, 30 May

Freddie peered through the spyglass, seeing only dense fog but sensing ships lay hidden within the heavy mist. "They're out there, I can feel it."

He handed the glass to Donet, standing at his side.

Donet frowned, his black eyes speaking his displeasure at the delay caused by the fog. "Admiral Howe would not have sent the message requesting my presence on the *Queen Charlotte* were he not intending to be here. 'Tis a far distance from Brest but I am certain the French fleet is close by as well."

Freddie had read the message waiting for Donet when they'd arrived on Guernsey in which Howe said Prime Minister Pitt thought Donet could provide useful intelligence on the French Navy. Dispatched from the port of Brest under the command of Admiral Villaret, with whom *la Reine Noire* had tangled on the Channel months before, the French fleet was to protect an American convoy carrying corn to famine-threatened France. Howe's orders were to block the grain shipment from reaching its destination.

Freddie looked toward the aft hatch. The woman who would soon be his bride slept belowdecks. He had wanted Zoé to stay on

189

Guernsey but all his persuading was to no avail. "Pigeon, my sister is eager to help plan the wedding. Why not stay and oblige her?"

"How can you ask me to stay behind when I have only just got you back? *Non*," she said, pouting her perfect lips. "There will be no sailing away without me. I am going with you."

When he told Donet that Zoé intended to sail with them, her uncle shrugged. "As French merchantmen flying the flag of the Republic, we will not be subject to an attack by Villaret and we are expected by Howe. Our business can soon be concluded and we will return to Guernsey."

Freddie's time on the island with Zoé, though brief, had been sweet. Whenever they could, they escaped into the gardens to be alone. She had welcomed his kisses, whetting his appetite for the honeymoon he had long dreamed of. Now that he was assured of her love, he wanted her safe, away from the war.

But the French temptress could be stubborn when it came to dismissing risk.

Once on board *la Reine Noire*, she had advised him if fighting began she would not again be sent to the orlop deck. *"Absolument pas!"* The fury in her gray eyes only made her more beautiful rendering his objection a faint protest he soon abandoned.

He could hardly refuse Donet's request to join him after the daring rescue he had undertaken on Freddie's behalf, snatching him from the jaws of Paris' guillotine. At least Freddie had managed to leave Pax and Isabeau in his sister's care on Guernsey, which delighted Jack, who assumed the new arrivals were for him to supervise.

And so, here he was, sailing into what might be the largest naval battle of the war, worrying about Zoé every minute.

When Donet heeded Admiral Howe's call, Freddie had asked about the ships in the British Channel Fleet and learned that the HMS *Orion*, on which Zack Barlow's son, Danny, served was among them. Freddie remembered telling Zack he would bring him a report on his son but he never expected to be an eyewitness to a battle in which Danny might play a role.

"Do you think those French ships that passed us yesterday were a part of the grain convoy?" he asked Donet. Since *la Reine Noire* flew the Republic's flag, the French ships of the line had sailed right past them, heading for Brest, their home port.

"*Non.* The grain convoy, I suspect, has yet to arrive. More likely, Villaret was sending the ships we saw to Brest for repairs. At least one had received serious damage from what I could see."

Freddie stared into the fog trying to imagine a ship lurking in the gray mist. "Then the battle has already begun."

"Most assuredly. At least a skirmish or two."

The next day, to Freddie's relief, the fog lifted and the day after, the first of June, early in the morning they found the Channel Fleet and Admiral Howe's flagship, the *Queen Charlotte*.

"Can't I go with you?" Zoé asked Freddie, hating the answer she knew was coming.

"No, *mon amour.*" He tapped her playfully on the nose. "For one thing, you are French and we will be boarding the flagship of the British commander of the Channel Fleet." Her gaze shifted to her uncle who was just descending the manrope to the skiff. If he could go, why can't—

As if reading her mind, Freddie said, "The only reason your uncle is invited to the *Queen Charlotte* is because Pitt requested he be consulted."

She pursed her lips. "And you?"

"It seems as I am a spy for England, Pitt allowed that I, too, might be of help."

She had always known he was working for England, but only after they'd returned from Paris did he tell her the accusations the republican soldiers hurled at him in the woods near Rennes were true. The coded message he had passed to her that was now in

Philippe d'Auvergne's hands would help England to meet the needs of the Chouans.

He was more gallant, more courageous than she had realized. And he was to be hers! The thought brought tears to her eyes and a tightness to her throat.

While she understood his refusal to take her aboard the *Queen Charlotte*, that did not diminish her disappointment. She had so wanted to see the ship her uncle had told her was the largest of the warships in the British Navy. "Oh very well," she said on a sigh, "I shall just have to watch her hundred guns from here."

"You'll not be as close as that, Pigeon. Bequel has orders to keep *la Reine Noire* far from any battle."

Aboard the Queen Charlotte in the North Atlantic west of Brittany

Freddie and Donet climbed aboard the admiral's flagship where Howe and his officers met them. His full head of silver hair rendered him very distinguished in his dark blue frock coat with large gold buttons, white waistcoat and breeches. Freddie was surprised at the age of the admiral; he had to be near seventy. For a man of the sea, his face bore few lines, but beneath his bicorne hat, his cheeks were red.

The admiral, made 1st Earl Howe by a grateful King George, carried himself with rigid British formality as he shook their hands, his accent crisp. "Pitt trusts you, Donet. So, it seems, must I. And you, West. I'm told you have already supplied the government with useful intelligence. Perhaps you can provide me with more." Gesturing them toward his great cabin, he said, "What can you tell me of Villaret's officers, his crews?"

They entered the well-appointed stateroom containing so many books it could have been a shop on Oxford Street. Howe removed his hat and bid them sit in the chairs set around the large mahogany table that matched his smaller desk. The admiral's forehead that had been protected by his bicorne hat remained the pale skin of an Englishman, unlike the rest of his sun-reddened face.

The steward, who'd been standing inside the door, poured coffee.

Taking a sip, Donet said, "Villaret's officers, like himself, have little training and little experience. As you probably know, sir, the French ships are built to a high standard but the French Navy is in a state of confusion. So many senior officers were executed in the purge of last year that junior officers had to be raised before they were ready. Even merchant captains, some I know, were among those made officers."

"Worse than I had imagined," said Howe with a chuckle and a small smile aimed at Donet. Freddie had heard the admiral was a man of dry humor.

"Indeed, sir," said Donet, "but I can assure you, given my loyalty to England in this war, I was not approached. Villaret himself was only a captain earlier this year when Mr. West and I engaged him in the Channel. Then, he commanded the *Trajan*."

"To your point about the high quality of the French ships," offered Howe in a more serious tone, "Villaret's flag now flies above the *Montagne* with her one hundred and twenty guns. Though I am reluctant to admit it, she is possibly the finest ship in the world."

"He may have a fine ship," offered Freddie, "but the supply crisis in France has contributed to the discontent that is rife among the French crews. From my observations of the French fleet off Brest for the past year, too often the crews are without pay and, at times, without food."

"I see," said the admiral staring out the stern windows.

"We were aware some battles have already occurred," Donet said, "and observed a few of Villaret's ships limping into Brest. How stands your fleet?"

"Twenty-five ships, though some have sustained damage. The

only good news is that Villaret's fleet has lost six ships. However, as of yesterday, I had a report four more have joined them, making our numbers nearly equal. Finish your coffee and we shall consult the master for the latest report."

The admiral rose, accepted his hat from his steward and strode from his cabin to emerge onto the quarterdeck.

"Sir," the master said, "the enemy fleet has been spotted six miles off the starboard bow steering in line of battle on the port tack."

Freddie had heard the rumor that "Black Dick" Howe, as his sailors had dubbed him, never smiled except when a battle drew near. He was smiling now.

"Signal the fleet to form in line abreast," ordered Howe. Then, addressing Freddie and Donet, "Too late for you to leave. It seems you are to have the privilege of witnessing our victory."

"Excuse me, sir," said Donet, "I must send a message to my ship."

"Why, of course. My signalmen are at your disposal to wave off your ship."

Which is exactly what happened. Freddie looked not at the British fleet forming into a line to converge upon the French fleet, but to the brig-sloop veering off from the battle to come. "Thank God," he said under his breath.

"Émile Bequel is a seasoned captain, West, more than capable of getting *la Reine Noire* free of the battle lines. Worry not for my niece and my ship. We are more in danger than they." But despite his words Donet's black eyes stared intently toward *la Reine Noire*.

Satisfied Donet's ship and Zoé were out of danger, Freddie turned his attention to the battle to come. Standing on the quarterdeck, he was awed by the twenty-five British ships moving in a line toward the French line of twenty-six. Pride welled in his chest as he realized that, in some small way, he'd served his country well in helping England fight a war she would surely win.

An hour later, the French opened fire, their mighty guns

sounding loud in Freddie's ears. But the shot was high. In turn, Howe ordered signal flags to be flown that called for his ships to turn into the French and engage in close action.

"An unusual move," said Freddie.

"Aye," said Donet. "The admiral has guts."

The British fire raked the French ships through the stern, Howe's fleet engaging them on the leeward side before the French guns could be brought to bear. The ocean exploded with the sound of guns firing, the white smoke shooting out from the gun ports. Soon the sky darkened with smoke from ships burning, the smell bitter in Freddie's nostrils.

The *Queen Charlotte* was not immune to the French guns. Shot fell on the quarterdeck near where Freddie and Donet were standing. Twice Freddie had to dodge a falling timber and torn pieces of shrouds. Flayed loose rigging fell to the deck, winding around men, causing injuries. Officers and sailors were picked off by French marksmen, making Freddie glad he and Donet did not wear the distinctive uniforms that would have made them prime targets.

As Howe headed for the ladder to join his senior officers on the poop deck, he urged his guests to go below.

Freddie declined. "Damn my eyes, sir, but I'd not miss this for anything."

At his side, Donet agreed, thanking the admiral. When the admiral had moved above them, Donet said, "We'll not be providing the details of what we experience to your sister, agreed?"

Freddie nodded. He'd not be providing the details to Zoé either.

Walking with his senior officers on the poop deck, Admiral Howe seemed unfazed by his crew falling around him and the spars and rigging rattling down on all sides.

Amazed at Howe's composure, Freddie heard Howe order no shot was to be fired. Instead, he ordered the pilot to lay the *Queen*

Charlotte alongside the *Montagne*.

After pleas from his officers to allow them to return fire, Howe agreed to fire from the main and quarter decks but insisted they hold back the rest of his guns.

"Now that's courage," muttered Donet. "He's reserving his broadside for the stern of the *Montagne*, a strategy I approve."

A minute later, Freddie witnessed the power of those guns trained on Villaret's flagship as the *Queen Charlotte* slowly passed through the French line between the huge three-decker *Montagne* and an eighty-gun French ship. So close did the ships pass that the tricolor flag, waving at *Montagne*'s flagstaff, brushed the *Queen Charlotte*'s mizzen rigging.

"Good God," Freddie gasped when the blast from the broadside tore into Villaret's ship, catching her unprepared.

"They didn't expect an assault from leeward," said Donet. "Inexperience and lack of foresight."

Surely Howe will take her now, Freddie thought. But just then, the fore-topmast of the *Queen Charlotte* came clattering down with a loud crash. In the confusion, the badly damaged *Montagne* sheered off, leaving Admiral Howe to engage with the two French ships astern of her.

A terrible battle ensued, in which the *Queen Charlotte* lost her main topmast. With one topmast gone and rigging and yards badly damaged, Howe's flagship had become practically unmanageable. One of his captains sent a lieutenant to ask if Howe wanted to transfer his flag.

The admiral vehemently refused.

At the end of the battle, the French *Vengeur*, having fought valiantly, began to sink. She displayed the British flag in submission and called for help. Three British ships sent boats into the water to pick up survivors. They were in time to save hundreds, though hundreds more went down with the ship.

The remaining French ships veered off in all directions. The British ships did not pursue but closed around the *Queen Charlotte* with their prizes. Except for four ships that had been disabled in the fighting, the British fleet was ready to renew battle.

"Shouldn't he take the French ships now?" Freddie asked Donet. "They are easy prey, shattered, dismasted and riddled with shot."

"*Oui*, I would have. But Howe seems content with his six prizes. And his victory. The republicans have lost thousands of sailors and the British, I would venture, have lost hundreds."

The firing stopped shortly after one in the afternoon. As the smoke began to clear, Freddie gazed about the deck of the great warship strewn with pieces of mast, torn rigging and shrouds and bodies of men who had served their last post. In the ocean beyond, debris from wounded ships bobbed in the waters. All around the *Queen Charlotte*, damaged ships like so many broken toys cast aside by a destructive giant child managed to stay afloat.

Freddie recalled Pitt's grave warning of an attack on England's southern coast. The Prime Minister would be pleased to learn of Howe's victory, accepting the price in men's lives as necessary. To the British people who had feared an invasion, the defeat of the French fleet would mean an end to that threat. Freddie had to wonder if he'd not accepted Nepean's challenge to become England's spy, would he have been here today serving on one of the ships in the Channel Fleet?

The admiral carefully took the ladder down to the quarter-deck and walked toward them. To Freddie, Howe looked as if he was near collapse, but his spirit remained undaunted. "Got more of a show than you expected, eh?"

"Indeed, sir," said Freddie. "Congratulations are in order. You successfully rendered half of the French fleet the passive spectator of the destruction of the other half."

"Your intelligence was spot on," said Howe, "and I took full advantage."

"We were happy to help," said Donet with a smile, offering his hand to Howe. "'Twas a job well done, Admiral."

Howe shook Donet's hand. "If you've a mind to depart, we can signal your ship and I'll have a boat row you out."

Donet thanked him.

As they looked toward the boat being lowered, Freddie paused and turned back to the admiral. "What news of the grain convoy?"

"None," said Howe with a frown.

It was then Freddie remembered Danny Barlow. "Sir, might I inquire how the HMS *Orion* came through the battle? A good friend's son, Lieutenant Barlow, serves aboard that ship."

An officer handed a list to the admiral, pointing to one entry.

"The HMS *Orion* sustained only minor damage to the masts and rigging," read Howe. "So, we can hope your young Lieutenant Barlow is well and happy to have been a part of so great a victory."

"Thank you, sir. I do hope that is the case."

As the admiral moved away to confer with one of his officers, Donet said, "Let's go home. Zoé will be anxious to know if you've managed to cheat death once more, and I, for one, miss my wife and the flowers of Guernsey."

Chapter 15

Zoé gripped the rail, her attention fixed on the longboat in the distance making steady progress cutting through the choppy waters toward *la Reine Noire*. A wave of relief washed over her at the first sight of Freddie's auburn hair blowing in the wind. All the men were sitting up. "Well, at least they're alive," she said to M'sieur Bequel, standing next to her.

"Aye, safest place would be the admiral's flagship."

As the boat drew closer, she said a small prayer of thanks when she saw no blood on either Freddie or her uncle. But that didn't stop her from being miffed at their being in the midst of what had sounded like a tremendous battle. And Freddie had the nerve to scold her for taking risks!

His smiling face emerged above the gunwale as he climbed aboard the ship.

She stood resolute with arms crossed under her bosom, refusing to welcome him with a smile, though she was fighting back tears she was so happy to see him.

He came to her and placed his hands on her shoulders. Except for the soot streaked across his face, no doubt from all those guns firing, he appeared well. More than well, he was excited. "Here I am, Pigeon, returned to you hale and hearty."

"So you are."

Her determination to stay angry withered away when he took

199

her in his arms and held her. "I couldn't wait to get back to you, *mon amour.*"

"Was it terrible?" she asked.

He held her away from him, meeting her inquiring gaze. "For the wounded and the dead, it was. Yet it left me wanting to live."

He bent his head and kissed her, right there in front of her uncle, M'sieur Bequel and the whole crew. Not a light welcome-me-home kiss, but a passionate taking of her mouth, a kiss like he'd given her in the garden only days before. His tongue invaded her mouth and his arms crushed her to his chest. Swept away with his masculine yet tender assault, she wrapped her arms around his neck and returned his kiss.

A cheer went up from the crew, reminding her they stood on the open deck. Red-faced, she broke off the kiss, dropped her arms and looked around her to see the crew's smiling faces.

"Aw, Pigeon, they're just showing how happy they are about our coming marriage."

M'sieur Bequel barked the order to prepare to set sail and the crew scurried to comply.

From amidships, her uncle grinned. "Back to work, Mr. West!"

The Isle of Guernsey

"They are calling it 'the Battle of the First of June'," Freddie said, reading the *Gazette* over a late breakfast of sausage and eggs accompanied by sweet oranges and coffee. "I must send a message to Zack Barlow on the next mail packet to let him know the *Orion* came through the battle with only minor damage."

"He and Polly will be much relieved," said Zoé, biting into an orange, the pleasing aroma filling the sunny room. She licked the juice from her bottom lip. Freddie tried to concentrate on what he had been reading but it was not easy. Returning his attention to the thin newspaper, he decided to tease her with news of England's victory.

"Just think, Pigeon, Howe's a celebrated hero in England. King George has presented him with a sword set with diamonds and a gold chain for a medal he's to receive."

"I suppose it helps to declare victory before the war is won," Zoé muttered, picking up her coffee, "but *Oncle* Jean told me France, too, claims victory because the grain convoy slipped into Brest while the battle raged. *That* was Admiral Villaret's objective was it not?"

"Yes, dictated by Robespierre himself."

"I wouldn't want people to starve, Freddie, even if it meant depriving England and her allies of an advantage. If they'd stopped the American corn, would it really have made a difference to ending the war?"

He set down the paper. "Of course, it would. A starving army cannot fight."

Soft morning sunlight from the window fell across her skin making her appear a golden goddess even with the look of frustration on her lovely face. Soon, very soon, she would be his in all ways. *Venus in my bed.* The very thought brought a bulge to his breeches he could do nothing about. *Patience.*

Forcing his eyes back to the newspaper, he took a drink of his coffee and read on. "It says here the prisons in France are full, so the Convention has decreed witnesses are no longer required at trials and there are to be no acquittals. Thousands have been sentenced to death."

"The situation grows worse," she said, lifting the cup of coffee to her lips. "I wonder how long it can go on."

He had the strongest desire to lead her into the garden for a morning kiss, to help them both forget about the situation in France and the war. Thinking about her work with the refugees, his protective instincts rose to the fore. Leaning across the table, he said, "Pigeon, since the flow of émigrés has slowed, I want you to leave the rescues to Erwan and his friends."

"But Freddie—"

"You can help the émigrés once they arrive on the coast, but I cannot let you enter the towns to meet them. 'Tis too dangerous. Besides, our mission is changing. I have spoken to your uncle and he is agreeable to helping us get the needed weapons and supplies to the Chouans. Now that we have Cadoudal's confidence, we can deliver supplies to him on the coast at the same time Erwan brings us any refugees he finds."

"This is hardly the conversation of two who are about to be wed!" He looked up to see his redheaded sister standing in the doorway, attired as if she were setting out for Oxford Street in London.

"You must admit these are unusual times, Jo." He couldn't help feeling a bit embarrassed she'd caught them discussing plans to return to France, albeit on the coast. She wouldn't be pleased they would take up even that limited role.

"That may be so, Freddie, but we've a wedding to plan and your excursion into the Atlantic has postponed that effort. I need to borrow Zoé for the day and Isabeau will be coming with us. The modiste is to do the final fitting for Zoé's gown and Isabeau's dress. Then there's the menu for the wedding breakfast to plan."

"I approve," he said with a smile. It would get Zoé's mind off her desire to venture into the streets of Granville and keep her busy till dinner. "What about the boys?" Since they'd returned to Guernsey, Jack and Pax had become inseparable.

"Jack has agreed to organize games for Pax and him, though I worry about the mischief those two will get into. He has promised there will be no lessons in how to use a knife. Hopefully, their governess will be able to keep an eye on them."

"What will you do, Freddie?" asked Zoé.

"Your uncle has released me from ship duties to take a look at some properties that might suffice for our new home. If there are any I think you might like, Pigeon, we can view them tomorrow."

Zoé's eyes lit up at the mention of their new home. They'd discussed where they might live and concluded Guernsey suited them well. An English Crown dependency where French was spoken in the streets and the food was as good as any capital in Europe. The brioches from the *pâtisserie* on High Street were a particular favorite of his. And, living on Guernsey, he could remain a part of her uncle's merchant shipping business.

"Are there many properties to see?" she asked excitedly.

"A few," he said in a droll manner. "One ramshackle farmhouse the agent told me about seems particularly interesting."

She threw her napkin at him and got to her feet.

He couldn't resist the laughter that bubbled up in his chest.

"You see what I'm up against, *Tante* Joanna."

"Indeed I do. Remember, I helped to raise him. Come, let us be off. Isabeau is waiting at the front door."

Zoé came around the table and kissed Freddie on the cheek, the fragrance of roses whetting his appetite for more. Before he could reach for her, she glided out of the room with his sister, leaving him with his coffee and a smile on his face.

He smiled a lot these days.

Shopping in St Peter Port with her aunt required decisions Zoé had not often made in the last several years. Choosing fabric, style, trim, stockings and shoes consumed hours and that was only the beginning. There were still underclothes to select, a chemise, stays and petticoats, not to mention a hat or a bonnet.

Having become used to the clothing of a peasant woman and lately that of a Chouan man, she had braced herself for her return to Society, which her earlier trip to West Sussex had required, and now she must do so again for her wedding.

The carriage moved along the town's cobbled streets toward the modiste's shop on High Street. "I'm determined to see you properly attired for this very important day in your life," said her aunt looking out the window. "We are nearly there."

Zoé's participation in the previous shopping jaunt on Jersey with her aunt and Madame de Montconseil had given her a new respect for her aunt's knowledge of a lady's frippery. Not that the princesse needed any instruction but Zoé surely had.

"Do you think our fittings will take very long?" Zoé wanted to visit the jeweler to buy Freddie's wedding ring, perhaps one easily seen from a distance.

"The fittings, no, but we have other stops to make." *Tante* Joanna looked across the carriage seat to where Isabeau sat next to Zoé. "What do you think of a straw hat with a wide blue ribbon, my dear?" she asked the girl.

Isabeau nodded. "'Tis not what Breton women wear, but I like ribbons."

"Very well, you shall have one to match your gown."

Isabeau had become fond of Zoé's aunt but, at times, the girl would stare off toward France. They'd not had word from Giles and Zoé worried for him.

The carriage stopped in front of the modiste's shop and her aunt accepted the footman's hand, stepping down to the street. Isabeau followed and Zoé trailed after her, sighing deeply.

"To my way of thinking," said her aunt, who hadn't failed to notice the sigh, "while it is important to understand the politics and issues of the day, a lady must also know how to dress to enhance her natural beauty. For your wedding, Zoé, you must look your very best."

The bell above the door jingled, alerting Mrs. Dobree they had arrived. The antechamber where she greeted her customers had a long counter on one side. Behind it, rising to the ceiling, were shelves filled with bolts of satins and silks and flowered, striped and sprigged muslin. On their first visit, her aunt had selected a beautiful Bremen blue for her gown of silk and a paler shade of the same blue for Isabeau's dress.

Zoé had chosen lavender silk. The color was her favorite but one she'd not worn since before the revolution began.

Mrs. Dobree came from behind the counter to meet them. *"Je pense* you will be pleased with the gowns," said the dark-haired woman, who had a pencil stored over her ear and a measuring tape around her neck. "The seamstress is my best. She just finished them yesterday. As you ordered, Madame Donet, the waists are higher, the style simpler. And for you, Mademoiselle Donet, only one petticoat will be required."

Zoé and Isabeau shared a smile. "Petticoats," she whispered to the girl, "can be such a nuisance."

By the time they had finished with the modiste, procured the needed underclothes and retrieved the shoes they'd ordered from Mr. Johnson on Queen Street, Zoé had just enough time to visit the jeweler.

"A wide gold band, please," she told the gray-haired man with spectacles perched on his thin nose.

He nodded and walked to another case a short distance away, saying over his shoulder, "I have just the one!"

Her aunt's auburn brows rose. "A wide band?"

"Oui. So other women will know Freddie is taken."

Her aunt rolled her eyes. "Time for tea, I think."

"Cover your eyes!" Freddie commanded as he slowed the buggy. He had told her he had found a house, one he thought might suit them. Though she was impatient to see it, she dutifully complied, shutting her eyes tight. Knowing his sense of humor, she expected a dilapidated shed or even a cave.

Some distance on, the buggy came to a stop and she heard him open the door. "Here we go," Freddie said, lifting her from the velvet seat and carrying her a ways to set her feet upon the ground. The cushiony feel of grass beneath her shoes told her she was standing on a lawn. She smelled salty sea air and, somewhere nearby, she could hear waves breaking onshore. The faint scent of jasmine blossoms wafted to her on the breeze, making her even more curious.

"Can I open them now?"

"Not yet." Zoé felt his arms encircle her waist from behind and he pulled her against his chest, making her snuggle against his warmth. Nuzzling her neck in the sensitive place just below her ear sent a shiver up her spine.

"Freddie, you are teasing me unmercifully."

"I know, but you like it."

"I suppose I do," she admitted. Freddie was wonderfully affectionate and, since they had returned from Paris, he filled her days with kisses and sweet words of love.

"All right, Pigeon, you can open your eyes."

What she saw robbed her of breath. The house Freddie had wanted her to see, the one about which he had been so secretive, was no ramshackle farmhouse, no dilapidated shed, no cave. It was her dream come true.

"Oh, Freddie. It's... it's perfect!"

Her gaze swept across the front of the two-story stone home, painted a pale yellow and trimmed in white to match the white front door. The roof was of a brown tile like the one atop the carriage house she could just glimpse through the trees in the distance. Not as large as her uncle's home in St Peter Port, it was perfect for the two of them. She could tell by the five large paned windows on the front of the house they would never lack for light. A wide green lawn flanked by star jasmine hedges stretched from the carriage drive to where she stood.

On Freddie's face was a pleased expression.

"I love it, Freddie, but can we afford it?"

"Oh, yes. Your dowry is more than adequate to pay for the house and the furnishings if we want them. The owner is willing to sell us those, as well. Before you see the inside, take a look at the view." Freddie turned her around.

"Oh, my." At the end of the green lawn, a beautiful beach of white sand gave way to turquoise waters that extended to the dark blue sea beyond. She had never been here before but she knew they were on Guernsey. "Where are we?"

"Perelle Bay in St Saviour's on the west coast of the island. It's country here, Pigeon, five miles from St Peter Port and very private. And nearby, there is a place where a ship could safely anchor." Taking her hand he led her toward the house. "Don't you want to see the inside?"

"You have the key?"

"Of course. A spy forgets no detail of importance. I told the agent we would want to see it by ourselves."

She laughed, happy for the house, but happier still for the man who would soon be her husband. Her very own English spy.

As she crossed the threshold, she had a sense of being at home, as if she had lived here before. The furnishings in the parlor were of good quality and elegant. The dark blue velvet sofas and wing chairs beckoned her to sit. In the center of the room an oval table would be perfect for tea. Under the furniture rested a large rectangular rug that, like Guernsey itself, was covered in flowers, gold ones woven between blue-gray leaves. In the carpet's corners were baskets spilling over with flowering bouquets of the same colors.

"That carpet looks like some I once saw in Versailles. Is it from the time of Louis XIV?"

"The agent told me it predates that Louis. They call it a 'Louis XIII' carpet because it was made between Louis XII and Louis XIV who succeeded him. Whether it was once in Versailles, the agent couldn't tell me. You can be sure I asked. Do you like it?"

"Very much," she said, nodding. "How nice to think some things from the palace might have been saved."

They went next to the dining room where a long oval table circled by eight chairs sat beneath a beautiful crystal chandelier.

"Large enough for a growing family, no?" Freddie asked.

Zoé felt her cheeks heat. They had yet to discuss children. "Well, and my uncle and your sister might visit, even your brother, Richard, and Annie."

Beside her, Freddie chuckled. "I was thinking of children, as you likely suspected. What would you say to raising Pax as our own? He's an orphan like both of us but more alone in the world than we were at his age." Pax had filled out since Freddie had brought him to Guernsey and no longer had that haunted look in his eyes.

"I would welcome Pax into our home, but what would Isabeau and Jack say? Would Pax want to leave them?"

"Isabeau will stay with my sister for the time being, until her brother comes for her, and if he does not, she can choose where to live. But you are right to ask about Jack. The boys might want to remain together. What say you to our asking Pax where he'd like to live?"

"A good idea," she said. "When both of us are away at sea, he would have to stay in St Peter Port with your sister anyway."

"Well, until he has siblings, yes?"

"I suppose." Freddie wanted children and so did she, but the thought of how one actually brought them into existence was still a bit vague in her mind. She had been raised mostly around men. Except for servants and other men's wives, *Tante* Joanna was the only woman in her life.

Freddie led her up the stairs. "There are four bedchambers."

The master bedchamber was well appointed with a huge oak half-tester bed, its cover in rich red velvet. "I don't think I've ever seen a bed so large," she remarked.

"Big enough for you and me and any children who might want to crawl into our bed on a cold morning. What do you think?"

"'Tis huge." Zoé was nervous staring at the bed knowing it would be here they would most likely consummate their marriage. But then she considered the man who'd be doing the consummating. Her Freddie. Facing him, she lifted her hands to lock her fingers behind his neck. "How is it I never realized I loved you until that kiss in the woods near Rennes?"

"People see what they expect, Pigeon. You expected to see only the friend you had known for years and I was your friend. Now, about that kiss—"

"Don't apologize for that kiss, Frederick West. Besides," she said, smiling up at him, "I love your kisses."

"Then you shall have many more." He took her waist in his hands and drew her close. When their gazes locked, he leaned down to plant tiny kisses all over her face.

She closed her eyes and smiled. He would be a gentle lover, her Freddie. Perhaps they need not wait to become one. If they had the option to accept the furnishings, then this was their bed. And they were alone with the warm ocean breeze blowing in through the open window.

When Freddie moved his kisses to her lips, she responded with all the love in her heart, opening her mouth to welcome his tongue and relishing the feel of it moving against hers as he slowly seduced her mouth. Her heart sped in her chest and her breasts became sensitive pressing against the buttons on his frock coat.

Deep in her woman's center she felt an ache, a need only he could satisfy.

He slid one hand from her waist to her breast, touching a part of her that had never been touched by a man before. With Freddie, it felt good. More, it felt right. "Freddie," she whispered, as he trailed kisses down her throat to the pulse beating wildly at the base of her neck, "we don't have to wait. We are betrothed and alone. And if this is to be our bed, you could make love to me now, *oui*?"

He lifted his lips from her throat and let out a sigh. "You have no idea how I want to, Pigeon. With your kiss-swollen lips and sleepy gray eyes, you are a temptress and I want you." He sighed again. "But I have not waited years, all the while wanting you more than you could know, to take you prematurely. 'Tis my fault we have come this close to the doing of it. Having waited so long, I can certainly wait a few weeks more."

"But Freddie—"

"No, *mon amour*, allow me this one thing, to do you the honor of holding back my desire until you are my bride. It won't be long."

She smiled at his determination to do the honorable thing, admiring him for denying his own wants, his own manly needs. "Do you mean you never went to a tavern or sought out a lady who would offer you her favors?"

"Not since you turned sixteen and I twenty-three."

Pleased his fevered dreams she'd listened to after he'd been wounded in Granville were not about tavern wenches, she smiled up at him. "It shall be as you say, Freddie." Taking his hand, she pulled him toward the door. "Perhaps we should see the kitchens?"

He laughed. "Aye, a stove and a sink would do much to cool my ardor."

They spent little time in the kitchens before moving on to the *potager*, the well-kept vegetable garden, and the small orchard of orange trees behind the house. When they'd seen that, they returned to the front lawn.

As they walked to the buggy, he said, "So, you are pleased with the house and its location?"

"*Oui*, I am. But Freddie, will you not regret acquiring a ship of your own instead?"

"Oh, do not worry, Pigeon. I shall have a ship."

She drew her brows together, puzzled. "But how?"

"From the years I worked with your uncle, I have my share of profits saved almost in their entirety. 'Tis enough for the schooner I want. And tomorrow, if you like, once I have acquired the house, I can show you the one I'm looking at in St Peter Port."

"You amaze me, Frederick West."

"I have only begun, Pigeon."

Chapter 16

When Freddie told Zoé he wanted to wait the few weeks until their wedding to bed her, he had no idea he would be waiting more than a month to meet her at the church. It was all due to his brother Richard, who being invited to the wedding had accepted but wrote them, "We must ask for a delay until after Parliament recesses in July." And then they'd needed time to return to West Sussex and prepare to sail to Guernsey.

While Zoé and her aunt planned the wedding, Freddie made several trips to Jersey to meet with d'Auvergne to arrange for the weapons and supplies needed by the Chouan army. He convinced the captain to have the materiel sent to Jersey where Freddie would assume control and see it arrived safely in Brittany.

Zoé had agreed to their new mission, allowing Erwan to lead the effort to rescue the French émigrés. "What better way to serve those who wear the sacred heart patch than to equip their army?" she had said.

The fourteenth of July came and went without fanfare in St Peter Port. In France, fireworks would have exploded into the night sky above the rivers in celebration of the revolution as they did each anniversary of the attack on the Bastille. Not so on Guernsey, where the day was viewed with disdain.

"The next time I expect to see fireworks," he told Zoé, "will be the day the war is over. That is, unless you were planning fireworks for our wedding."

She had laughed. "What? And have people believe we celebrate the Republic of France? Never." Thus, the subject of fireworks had been dropped.

Zoé stood on the quay, admiring the sleek schooner with the dark gray hull silhouetted against the waters of St Peter Port. Under the watchful eye of their new captain, the crew busied themselves getting ready to set sail.

"What do you think of the ship's name?" Freddie asked her.

Weeks ago, he had shown her the ship he intended to buy but that was before any name had been painted on the hull.

She walked to the stern and gazed at the transom, then returned to where Freddie waited, a smirk on his face. "The *Pigeon*?"

His smirk became a smile. "I have always known when the day came to name my own schooner, it would be named after you."

"That nickname you persist in calling me?"

He slipped his arm around her shoulder and led her toward the gangplank. "Did you never wonder how I arrived at the name?"

"Well, yes, but—"

"The first time I saw you the day you came to my family's estate, I thought your gray eyes were lovely, the color of a dove's wing. Even though you were a precocious child, trying my patience, your eyes held me captive. A pigeon, after all, is a dove."

"Well, I suppose I cannot be angry about that." She had to admit, if only to herself, that he had always said the name in a charming sort of way.

"'Sides, since pigeon is spelled the same in English and

French, the name will not alert the French Navy to a foreign vessel in their waters."

"Clever," she said. "And I assume she carries many flags?"

"Of course."

She followed Freddie aboard the ship just as Émile Bequel, standing at the top of the gangplank, inclined his head, "*Capitaine* West, mademoiselle."

"Give the orders to set sail, M'sieur Bequel," said Freddie.

"M'sieur Bequel is your quartermaster?" she asked, incredulous.

"Only for this trip, Pigeon." He led her to the wheel, as the ship got under way. "Bequel and Gabe asked to accompany us and your uncle thought that since it's our first voyage, they might help assess the crew. Though I handpicked the men for the missions we'll be running, I welcome the opinion of one who has sailed with Jean Donet for so many years. I suspect Gabe is along to help protect you."

This would be their first delivery of ammunition and muskets to the Chouans and Zoé was anxious to be about the task. Her uncle had suggested they use the port of St Malo instead of Lorient since it was only a few hours' sail south of Guernsey. More importantly, he had many friends in that port, privateers he called corsairs, who he had alerted to the schooner's pending arrival. "Protection from friends is to be prized," her uncle told her.

"How many corsairs have a schooner named the *Pigeon*, do you suppose?" asked Freddie with a twinkle in his eye. The wind whipped his auburn hair beneath his tricorne. In his captain's coat, he was very striking.

"Only this one," she said with certainty. "A privateer would hardly name his ship after a dove."

"My thought exactly. I am hoping Cadoudal received the message I sent him and will have no trouble spotting us."

Several hours later, Freddie ordered one of the crew to run up the corsair flag as they neared St Malo.

"'Tis a splendid flag," she said gazing up at the banner unfurled against the cloudless blue sky.

The sight of the blue flag quartered by a white cross with the upper left quadrant red with a white ermine brought back her uncle's words. "The corsairs are proud of their Catholic roots and many support the royalists. They also value their independence and fly their own flag, even during the revolution."

Not long after, they sailed into the ancient harbor with its imposing medieval ramparts. Zoé's spirits rose when she saw the harbor clogged with sailing vessels. Amid so many ships perhaps they could slip in, leaving the authorities unaware.

As soon as the *Pigeon* dropped anchor, M'sieur Bequel dispatched a skiff carrying gunpowder, shot and wadding packed in barrels like the ones used to transport cod. Zoé watched from the rail as a few members of the crew rowed Freddie and Gabe the short distance to shore. Before they had even pulled the boat over the sand, a group of four men met them, one very tall, whom she took to be Cadoudal. They did not dress as Chouans but as seamen wearing knit caps.

The barrels were hefted out of the boat and rolled to a waiting wagon over planks laid down as a pathway over the sand. Once that was accomplished, the skiff returned to the ship and Freddie climbed aboard. "Cadoudal sends his regards, Pigeon. Now we bring the muskets."

The crew stepped lively at Gabe's direction to lower two boxes of muskets to the skiff. As before, they rowed Freddie and Gabe ashore. "At this speed," she said under her breath, "it will take all day."

Just then, she noticed two republican soldiers had turned their attention to the men unloading the long boxes. The soldiers fixed their gazes on the activity at the shore's edge and headed toward Freddie and Cadoudal overseeing the delivery.

Zoé began to bite her knuckles. "Not again," she muttered.

M'sieur Bequel joined her at the rail. "Have no worries, little one. *Capitaine* Donet's colleagues are dependable. See?" he said, pointing to a group of sailors striding toward Freddie and the Chouans, "The corsairs arrive just on time, *n'est-ce pas?*"

A group of swarthy seamen placed themselves in front of Freddie, his crew and the Chouans and turned to face the republican soldiers.

The soldiers stopped, shrugged and turned away.

Mystified, she turned to M'sieur Bequel. "They leave at the sight of the corsairs?"

"*Oui*, little one. The privateers have commanded this port for generations and defend the coast against England. From a very old arrangement they had with the king, which they still honor, they bring much money to the government and food to the tables of the people. Even Robespierre would not be so foolish as to defy them."

When the final weapons were unloaded and carted away by the Chouans, Freddie returned to the ship and kissed her on the forehead. "'Tis a done thing, Pigeon."

"Will the corsairs help us again, do you think?

"Oh *oui*. They rather enjoyed reminding the republican soldiers who is really in charge of the port."

7 August

Finally, the day of their wedding dawned bright and clear. Freddie awakened early. While he dressed, he smiled to himself. The long wait was nearly at an end.

Warned not to see his bride before they met at the church, he sneaked downstairs while the women and the guests still slept. Before he was halfway down, the heavy scent of blossoms assaulted his nostrils. Glancing from side to side, he saw flowers everywhere. They were entwined in vines on the staircase, clustered with bows on the chandeliers and set in arrangements on tables. "My sister," he mumbled beneath his breath.

In the dining room, he found Donet sitting at the table staring into his coffee.

Fighting a sneeze, Freddie said, "It seems the ladies have been decorating."

"Since last night," Donet replied in droll fashion.

At the sideboard, Freddie found a veritable feast of pastries, fruit and eggs, enough to stave off his hunger until the wedding breakfast, which would really be a noon meal. Piling food onto his plate, he took his seat across from Donet. "At last the day has arrived," he said in a cheery voice.

Donet regarded his happy countenance. "You did not expect to be held at bay so long, *mon ami*, but your face tells me you do not doubt my niece is worth the wait."

"No, I have never doubted that. 'Sides, what could we do when Richard accepted the invitation but begged for a delay? It was good of you to send Bequel with *la Reine Noire* to transport them to Guernsey." In his letter, Richard expressed concern about meeting French warships on the Channel. "Your defeat of the *Trajan* impressed him."

"And you have kept busy?"

"Indeed. The selection of the crew for my new schooner occupied much of my time and then there was the first delivery of the promised weapons and ammunition to Brittany."

"I expect the Chouans are pleased."

"They seemed to be, though Cadoudal voiced some concern about whether there would be more."

"He will come to trust you."

After breakfast, Freddie returned to his room where he read a book until he was certain the ladies had left for the church. Retracing his steps to the first floor, he encountered Donet standing next to the front door, his pocket watch in hand.

"I have been wondering if the impatient groom intended to be late for his wedding."

"Not at all. I merely allowed the ladies time to depart. My sister was clear about that." Freddie thought of the list he'd been working from that morning. "Do you have the ring?"

Donet reached in the pocket of his ivory satin waistcoat and held the ring out, its lavender sapphire sparkling from the delicate gold band. "'Twas a good thing you let me know Zoé loves the color lavender, else I might have picked something she would have liked less well."

"I'm glad I remembered we had some loose stones in the warehouse from the trip to Ceylon last year."

Though Freddie had not been allowed to see Zoé's gown, he'd asked his sister for the color. When Jo advised him it was becoming fashionable for the bride and groom to match, Freddie had the tailor in St Peter Port make him a waistcoat of lavender silk. But when it came to his frock coat and breeches, like Donet, he chose black. Both of them wore a French small sword at their waists. To leave his sword behind would make him feel undressed.

"We'd best be off," Donet said, striding toward the door. "I grow old as we dally."

The footman handed them their tricornes and opened the door.

Once in the carriage, Freddie sank against the tufted velvet and gazed out the window, remembering the carriage ride that had taken him away from the Conciergerie more than a month before. "You didn't seem surprised when I asked for Zoé's hand that day in Paris."

A small smile played about Donet's mouth. "I've watched the two of you for years. Every time my niece set out on some wild adventure, you argued against it and, when she could not be dissuaded, went along to see she came to no harm. But it was Joanna who first remarked to me it would be a good match. Not many men would tolerate Zoé's independent spirit."

Freddie braced himself as the carriage took a sharp turn. "I rather like her tendency toward adventure. I expect we will have many."

"Doubtless," replied Donet.

The conveyance stopped in front of the Parish Church located on St Peter Port's seafront. The Gothic building was as old as the castle in Fougères and it would have fit well as a part of that town.

They stepped down and an anxious Émile Bequel, dressed like a gentleman of some import in fine apparel, approached. *"Vite!* We must make haste. I'm to lead ye through the side door to where ye will stand, Mr. West. Then I'll take ye, *Capitaine*, to where yer niece is waiting."

They nodded and followed.

When they arrived at the door, Bequel indicated Freddie should enter. As he reached for the handle, he heard Bequel say to Donet. "I should warn ye, *Capitaine*, Madame Donet is biting her knuckles."

Freddie turned. "What about Zoé?" It wouldn't do to anger his bride on their wedding day.

Bequel shrugged. "The mademoiselle just smiles at her bouquet."

"I hope that's a good sign," Freddie muttered.

He entered the church filled with people sitting expectantly in the pews and took his place to the right of the black-robed minister. The ceremony would be Anglican, but like his sister's wedding, a priest would conduct a second, more private service in a smaller chamber.

Moments later, his sister and Isabeau, wearing blue gowns, were escorted to the front of the church to stand opposite Freddie as Zoé's attendants.

Jo gave him a warm smile. He returned her smile, but he needed no encouragement. He'd waited years for Zoé to grow up, hoping she would one day come to love him. She was always the bright spot in the midst of his many disappointments. That she might one day choose another man had always been a possibility. If she had done so, he would have relinquished his unspoken claim and wished her happiness, no matter his heart would be breaking. But a miracle had happened and she had chosen him. He vowed to spend the rest of his life proving she'd made the right choice.

From the back of the church, the beautiful music of a violin sent a hush over the guests.

Not many people knew Zoé's uncle was a virtuoso with the violin, or that in his youth he'd considered becoming a concert violinist. A few weeks ago, she had asked if he might play for their guests just before he led her down the aisle. He'd agreed on the condition he could select the music. When the first strains of the piece came to her ears, she knew it was a reminder of the man she had chosen to wed.

The music was *The Guardian Angel* by the Austrian composer Heinrich Biber. An appropriate choice, she thought. Freddie had certainly been that, watching over her and protecting her from harm even at the cost of his own safety and, if need be, his own life.

Zoé listened to the ethereal music and peered around a pillar to see the enraptured looks on the faces of their guests. Gazing down at her bouquet of St Peter Port daisies, she was glad she had decided on the flowers that grew wild on Guernsey. A little like her, she acknowledged. That Freddie knew her wild tendencies and still wanted her warmed her heart. As much as it was within her power, she would fill their home with the children she knew he wanted and his life with love.

When the music stopped, all heads turned to the back of the church where Zoé entered on Donet's arm. As they began slowly walking toward Freddie, his gaze alighted on her glowing face and the lavender silk of her gown shimmering in the light from the stained glass windows. She wore no veil, not even a hat, but instead, a wreath of daisies crowned her long dark hair. She was beautiful, his Venus.

A wide smile crossed his face as their eyes met. When she drew near, her focus shifted to his lavender waistcoat and she smiled. Did she think a spy could not ascertain the shade of her gown?

Once she arrived in front of Freddie, Donet released her and stepped back. She handed her bouquet to Joanna and, together, they turned toward the minister.

The vows came easily to Freddie, so long had he waited to speak them. Zoé, too, spoke hers without hesitation.

When Freddie placed the ring on her finger, her eyes glistened with delight.

The minister pronounced them man and wife and Freddie leaned down to kiss his bride. The kiss he bestowed on his new wife was no perfunctory touching of lips. By the time he lifted his mouth from hers, the clergyman was coughing into his hand.

For a long moment, their gazes held each other's. Then they turned, hand in hand, to greet their family and guests as Mr. and Mrs. West.

Since the wedding breakfast was to be held at the Donets' home, Freddie's sister encouraged guests to meet them there, saying the bride and groom would follow. Émile Bequel assisted, ushering guests to the front of the church, save for those invited to witness the Catholic ceremony. Since the Vendéens and Chouans fought for the right to worship as Catholics, the ceremony conducted by the priest was especially meaningful. Freddie was an Anglican but his bride, like her uncle, was Catholic. Services in both faiths were held on the island, which was another reason for them to live on Guernsey.

Two carriages waited in front of the church to transport the eight of them to the Donets' home. Jack and Pax piled in with the Donets, and Isabeau and Émile Bequel stood waiting to ride with Freddie and Zoé.

The first vehicle departed and Freddie, Zoé, Isabeau and Bequel turned toward theirs. Before they could climb in, Isabeau shouted, "Giles!"

Zoé watched Isabeau run to the man who knelt with his arms outstretched. The girl had missed her brother terribly. Since none of them knew if Giles still lived, and Freddie had forgotten to ask Cadoudal in St Malo, it was a relief to see him here. Somewhere, he had obtained a set of clothes that blended well with the folks populating the streets of Guernsey.

Freddie offered Giles his hand as the Chouan got to his feet. "Giles, meet my new wife. You will remember her as Mademoiselle Donet; Zoé is now Mrs. West. We were just married."

With his arm around Isabeau, Giles said, "That is why I came to the church. The butler at Monsieur Donet's house told me where I could find you. My good wishes to you both."

Zoé thanked him. "We are very glad to see you, but why have you come? Is there bad news from Brittany?"

"*Non, pas du tout.* Cadoudal sent me to help arrange the promised shipments of weapons and supplies. Since Isabeau is here on Guernsey, he thought I should be the one to come. But I bring important news from Paris you will want to hear."

"As we are the last to leave for the wedding breakfast," said Freddie, "why not ride with us and you can tell us your news on the way."

Isabeau grasped her brother's arm. "You will stay?"

Giles smiled down at her. "*Oui,* as long as M'sieur Cadoudal wants me here."

They crowded into the carriage and, unable to wait any longer, Zoé said, "What news do you bring us, Giles?"

"At the end of July, Robespierre, his brother, Augustin, and twenty of his supporters were arrested and sent to the guillotine. They were given no trial as they had been declared outside the law by the Convention following a speech Robespierre gave calling for the arrest of traitors in the Committee of Public Safety."

"An unwise move on his part," said M'sieur Bequel.

Zoé's only emotion was one of relief. Sitting beside Freddie, she squeezed his hand.

"'Tis ironic he would meet his end in the same manner he dictated for so many others," said Freddie.

"*Oui* and *Oncle* Jean will be gratified to hear it," she said. "'Tis good news, indeed."

"Aye," agreed Giles. "Dozens more of his allies were guillotined the next day and, since then, we hear those who were imprisoned for suspected disloyalty, have been released."

Turning to face Freddie, Zoé asked, "Does this mean the Terror will end?"

"Doubtless things will change, Pigeon. There were many in the government who criticized Robespierre for the Terror he lauded as a virtue." To Giles, he said, "They must be celebrating in Brittany."

"Aye, they are, particularly because it is rumored General Rossignol will retire to his home in Orléans."

Zoé thought about the man who had helped them gain access to the Conciergerie. The one who had left early at someone's bidding. "Freddie, do you think François de Dordogne was one of those executed with Robespierre?"

"Very likely."

Chapter 17

Immediately upon their arrival at the Donet house, Freddie shared the news from Paris. In any other instance, to speak of death at a wedding breakfast would be bad ton, but Robespierre's execution and the possible end of the Terror were received with joy, buoying everyone's spirits.

Richard was elated at the pronouncement of Robespierre's demise. "I imagine Pitt is celebrating at this very moment."

Freddie's brother and his wife had made the crossing without incident and were delighted with Guernsey's more temperate weather. London, they said, had been especially cold this summer.

When the excitement settled, the adults took their places at the dining room table laden with a multitude of flowers. Filled with light, the room needed no candles.

In the center of the table beneath the crystal chandelier stood a fruited bride cake on a silver pedestal. Soaked in brandy, Freddie had witnessed the cook covering it with white sugar frosting. Surrounding the cake were platters of eggs, ham and asparagus served in the French style, set upon the table for the guests to partake as they would.

Ormer casserole, a specialty of Guernsey, was placed at both ends of the table. The shellfish, called abalone in the rest of Europe, was considered a delicacy.

Oranges, berries and brioches accompanied the meal as well

as chocolate and tea.

Richard got to his feet, looking every inch the British earl. "A toast to the bride and groom," he said, raising his glass of champagne.

The guests lifted their glasses into the air and drank of the sparkling wine.

Donet was next to rise from his seat. "The champagne is the drink of the Bourbons, appropriate for this celebration, I think. And this particular wine comes from my cellar in Saintonge, which my quartermaster and friend, M'sieur Bequel, retrieved at the outset of the revolution. I am glad I saved it for such an occasion as this." He lifted his glass. "Let us drink to the happy couple and to peace between England and France when champagne will again flow freely."

"Hear, hear!" said Philippe d'Auvergne. He had come from Jersey to be with them and had been engaged in an intense conversation with Giles about the situation in Brittany.

From across the table, Émile Bequel saluted Freddie. "Ye've done well, Mr. West. And now ye're well spliced to the very end."

"So we are," said Freddie. He turned to Zoé and, with champagne in hand, said in a quiet voice, "To my beautiful bride, my wife, my love."

"À mon héros," said Zoé, tapping her glass to his. "You will always be my hero."

She had given him a gold band for his wedding ring that he would proudly wear the rest of his life. "I'm glad you like the lavender stone of your ring, Pigeon."

"Oh, I do. How did you know I love that color? It's not as if I have worn it much since the revolution began."

"I have my sources," he said with a wry smile. "Not to be revealed."

In one corner of the room, the children had their own table but frequently jumped up to seek out an adult. Once they had chocolate, however, Jack began giving his own toasts. "To your new parents, Pax!"

"Well," whispered Freddie to Zoé, "since Pax is smiling and I hear no objection, perhaps he has decided."

"Possibly," she replied, "but Pax has grown close to Jack and Isabeau and he doesn't yet know we will be making our home on the other side of the island."

"Where are you to honeymoon?" asked Annie sitting on Freddie's other side.

He smiled at the thought of their destination. "Our own private oasis on the west side of Guernsey."

"You shall have to see our new home before you return to England," offered Zoé.

"I expect we'll be here for at least a week," Annie said, glancing at Richard, who was absorbed in a conversation with Donet.

"We might be ready for guests by then," Freddie said. He had told his sister of the home he'd acquired with Zoé's dowry but, as yet, he'd not invited anyone to see it, save for Zoé, of course. Even he had yet to sleep in the house. He wanted to share his first night there with his bride.

Once the food had been eaten and the cake cut, Freddie nudged his bride. "Are you ready to leave, Pigeon?"

At her nod, he stood and thanked the guests for coming. "We'll see you all in a week!"

Pax rushed forward to hug Freddie and, with wide eyes, looked up at him. "You promise to return?"

"Aye, I promise."

It took them nearly an hour to reach St Saviour's but they had not been in a hurry. Zoé was glad for the time with him away from everyone else. So often others surrounded them in France, on the ship and even in Guernsey.

Like the first time he had brought her to see the house, Freddie drove a one-horse chaise he called a cabriolet.

"The buggy is the only vehicle that fits these narrow country roads," he told her. "'Sides, I can drive the cabriolet myself so we can be alone."

Freddie had kept her entertained with stories of his smuggling days with Joanna that had ended when they'd encountered the fierce Captain Jean Donet one night off the West Sussex coast.

"Was it very frightening?"

"Zack Barlow and I thought so. I was seventeen and Donet was about to be attacked by a revenue cutter. My sister was still aboard his ship when he sailed away. I didn't see her for months and, by then, she had married him!"

It was afternoon when they arrived at Perelle Bay. The turquoise waters were as beautiful as she remembered them, the house equally as lovely.

Nothing had changed since the first time she'd been there except that now there were servants. First, Freddie introduced her to the stable boy who led the horse and buggy away. Inside the house, she met a young footman, who promptly carried their small pieces of luggage upstairs, a housemaid, and a couple in their middle years. Timothy and Martha O'Brien, Freddie explained, would act as housekeeper, cook and butler.

"If ye need anything, madame," said Mrs. O'Brien, "just let me know. Yer bed's been turned down and the chamber already attended to when we arrived a few hours ago."

Zoé wondered what the woman meant by that last comment but decided not to ask. She would see it soon enough. "Thank you, but I think we'll be fine for today."

The housekeeper curtsied and shuffled her husband and the maid out of the room. The footman remained by the door.

"We may need additional servants as we go along, Pigeon, but for now, with our voyages to France, a skeletal crew seemed best. The O'Briens live nearby, so only the footman, stable boy and maid will stay the night.

"In other words," she teased, "we're practically alone."

He returned her a sheepish look. "Well, yes, as much as is possible." He offered her his hand. "Shall we adjourn to our chamber, Mrs. West?"

The day had already been full of excitement and Zoé did not want to retire so late she would immediately fall asleep. Besides, Freddie was looking at her in that way that made her knees weak. She placed her hand in his. "*Oui*, Mr. West."

When he opened the door, Zoé paused on the threshold, surprised at what she saw. "Oh. Did you do all this?"

The red bedcover had been sprinkled with white rose petals, perfuming the air. On the pedestal table between the two wing chairs in front of one window looking out on the bay, a tray set with fruit, cheese and bread rested next to a bottle of wine and two glasses. In the fireplace, a fire had been laid, ready to light.

Freddie put his arms around her waist and leaned over her shoulder. "No, but I think I know who did."

"Your sister?"

"Aye, Jo's the only one who knew where our home is located."

"Now that I think of it, she may have enlisted Isabeau's help," suggested Zoé. "The girl has been giggling overmuch these last few days."

Zoé turned in Freddie's arms and placed her hands on his shoulders. "I think it was sweet of them to do that for us. It will make our wedding night that much more special."

He kissed her, taking up where he'd left off at the church. Raising his head, his brandy-colored eyes had turned dark. "If you say so, Pigeon, but as for me, all I need is you."

Why she should suddenly feel shy, Zoé had no idea. After all, she had been the one to suggest he make love to her the first time she had come to this room. But that was before *Tante* Joanna had told her what to expect. "Perhaps a glass of wine and some cheese?" she asked.

He chuckled and walked toward the small table. "Of course." He poured two glasses of wine and handed her one. She drank it down betraying her nerves then took a seat in one of the wing chairs. He sat in the other. "You have nothing to fear, Pigeon. I love you and I will be gentle."

"I know," she said, feeling like the biggest fool. "It's just that what your sister told me sounded... painful."

"Ah, so I have Jo to thank for this sudden reticence on your part."

"She was only trying to help."

He pushed out of the chair and came to stand in front of her. "Forget what she told you. I will teach you all you need to know, Pigeon." He reached for her arms and gently pulled her up. "Allow me to act the lady's maid, as I did in Rennes. Only this time, we'll be taking off our clothes."

She turned her back to him and kicked off her shoes. He loosened her laces. The stays she wore beneath her gown were not much of an obstacle and he adroitly removed them. "You seem to know what you're doing," she said, noticing he had draped her clothing on one of the chairs.

"Recall I grew up with two sisters, Joanna, who you know, and Matilda, whom you've not yet met as she lives in London. Growing up at The Harrows, it was impossible not to hear their conversations about a woman's frippery and all they wore underneath it. And then there were my youthful dalliances."

"Which we won't discuss," she said.

"Which we won't discuss," he repeated.

Once she was down to her shift, stockings and garters, she faced him, nibbling on her bottom lip. "Your turn."

He smiled and pulled off his boots. His frock coat followed to be tossed on a chair. Then he untied his cravat and began to unbutton his waistcoat.

"Allow me," she said, gaining confidence. "I am good with buttons."

He laughed. "I'll bet you are."

She took her time, teasing him with each button. His intense gaze told her he was not enjoying the pace. "Oh, very well," she said, finishing the last button. "Kiss me, Freddie, and make me forget everything but you."

"Gladly." He quickly unbuttoned his waistcoat, removed his shirt and drew her against his bare chest, slanting his mouth over hers. The kiss that followed awakened every fiber of her being and set her heart pounding. His warm skin under her palms heated her blood and his muscles flexing beneath her touch reminded her this man was now hers.

Eagerly, she opened her mouth to his probing tongue, experiencing the same ache in her woman's center she had the last time he'd kissed her in this room.

He pulled back and stared into her eyes. Apparently satisfied with what he saw, he lifted her into his arms and set her on the huge bed. "We've plenty of room." She opened her arms to him and he followed her down to sink into the soft feather bed, half of him covering her.

"I have dreamed of this day, Zoé, for a very long time. We still wear too many clothes. I want to see you naked."

"All right." She wouldn't have called what she felt just then fear but she did worry for what he would think of her body. With his eyes staring into hers, he lifted her shift over her head. She closed her eyes not wanting to see his disappointment.

"You are as beautiful as I imagined, Pigeon, even more so. Your breasts are perfect; your skin glows as if lit from within."

She opened her eyes and nearly drowned in the longing and the love she saw on his face. "Now will you make love to me?"

"As my lady desires," he said, grinning.

Her aunt had told her there might be little if any pain if her husband took time to prepare her. She had been right about that. By the time Freddie joined their bodies, she was half out of her mind with wanting him.

She awoke at dawn's light, hungry and a bit sore from their night of lovemaking. Nibbling on cheese and berries, she curled up in a chair and watched him sleep. His auburn hair caught the sun's first rays. She had always loved its color and imagined it threaded with gray. She would love him then at least as much as she did now, of that she was certain. How wonderful that she had married her best friend.

"Pigeon?" came his throaty voice from the bed as his hand reached out and found her gone.

"I'm just having a bit of food. Are you hungry?"

"For you. Come back to bed."

"Is that my husband's command?"

He rose on one elbow, trying to frown. "No, 'tis the wish of the man who loves you beyond reason."

She was certain he was teasing her but with his bare chest rising just above the sheet, he was quite irresistible. The thought of cuddling into his warm body, of hearing again how he'd waited for her for so long, was too enticing. Freddie made her feel precious.

"In that case, the woman who loves you is coming with breakfast." She picked up the tray and walked toward him and her destiny. Reaching the bed, she set the tray on the bedcover. "Did you want to eat now or later?"

"Later," he said, pulling her onto the bed. "Much later."

Epilogue

St Peter Port, 16 October 1802

Freddie lifted his gaze to the night sky where six rockets shrieked as they climbed upward only to burst with a loud boom, becoming fiery blossoms of blue, red and green. Cheers of delight rose up from their three boys jumping up and down on the Donets' front lawn. Pax stood nearby keeping a watchful eye on the boys who adored him.

"Oohs" and "ahhs" sounded from the guests invited to witness the spectacle celebrating the Treaty of Amiens ending the war between England and France.

Another rocket fired, this one exploding into the form of a willow tree, its golden branches sparkling in the dark canvas above them like glistening stars. The glorious sight was received by silent awe before exuberant applause erupted.

Their oldest boy, Willy, clapped his small hands together, shouting, "Do it again!"

His younger brother, Charlie, followed suit. "Pax, tell them to do it again!"

Their youngest, two-year-old Tommy, took Joanna's hand, his eyes glued to the sky.

Freddie tightened his arm around Zoé's shoulder and pulled her close to kiss her temple. "Like you, Pigeon, 'twas worth the wait to see fireworks exploding over Guernsey."

She turned into his kiss as she always did, as responsive now as when they were first wed. "I never thought the war with England would go on for so long, especially after Napoleon ended the battles in the Vendée two years ago."

"Pitt cannot like the peace he has bought," said Freddie. "Napoleon is not known for keeping his word. Nevertheless, I expect my fellow Britons will again be flocking to Paris. Perhaps your uncle will want to go and we might sail with him."

A series of fireworks launched into the sky and, with a great boom, broke into hundreds of small whirling stars.

"That reminds me," said Zoé, "I just received a letter from the princesse d'Hénin that I've not yet shared with you. She has already returned to Paris."

"Taking advantage of Napoleon's amnesty, I presume."

Zoé shook her head. "Actually, she arrived in Paris before he signed it."

Freddie thought of the woman Zoé had helped to flee to England years ago. "Perhaps we might visit her."

"She would like that."

More rockets were sent skyward in rapid succession, hissing, whistling and crackling as the night sky filled with light and bursts of vivid colors. "A fitting finale," said Zoé. "I do hope it doesn't give the boys nightmares."

"Come, *mon amour*, let us gather our chicks and put them to bed so we can indulge in some of that champagne your uncle and Émile Bequel have begun sampling."

Scooping up his two oldest boys to their disappointed groans, Freddie followed Zoé into the house. Young Tommy was already dozing in her arms.

The peace might not last but Freddie was a contented man.

Author's Note

The Reign of Terror

Maximilien de Robespierre was the mastermind of the Reign of Terror, which took place from September 1793 to the end of July 1794. He was the leader of the Committee of Public Safety, the executive committee of the National Convention and, in 1794, the most powerful man in France. In explaining how terror would lead to a "Republic of Virtue" in a speech to the National Convention, he said,

> *If the spring of popular government in time of peace is virtue, the springs of popular government in revolution are at once virtue and terror: virtue, without which terror is fatal; terror, without which virtue is powerless. Terror is nothing other than justice, prompt, severe, inflexible.*

In his haste to end all opposition to the revolution, he made sure laws were passed providing that anyone suspected of treason could be arrested and executed. He closed all provincial courts so that trials were held at the Revolutionary Tribunal in Paris. When Parisian jails overflowed with suspects, the process was speeded up, partly by ending the need for witnesses and any defense. The only punishment the tribunal could administer was death.

Thousands of people were executed, including not only Marie Antoinette, King Louis XVI and many of Robespierre's political rivals, but also nobles, clergy, bourgeoisie and peasants. Half a million Frenchmen were imprisoned or placed under house arrest during the Terror. Over forty percent of the death sentences carried out during the Terror took place in the Vendée.

Robespierre fell from power on July 27, 1794, a year to the day after entering the Committee of Public Safety. He and many of his close associates met the guillotine on the next day. With his demise, the Terror ended, though the blot on France's history remains.

Ironically, while the revolutionaries wanted no king, after having their fill of murder and bloodshed, they accepted Napoleon as emperor and eventually welcomed back the Bourbons to the French throne. If you'd like to read one of my stories set in England and France after the Bourbons return, you might like *Racing with the Wind*, book 1 in the Agents of the Crown series.

The Émigrés

With the storming of the Bastille on July 14, 1789, French émigrés began flowing into London and other parts of Europe in successive waves that became a tide of emigration. (The number is believed to be one hundred and sixty thousand.) In January 1792, the leaders of the revolution declared all of the émigrés to be traitors to France. Their property and titles were confiscated and the monarchy abolished.

The murders of September 1792, mentioned in my story, left an indelible impression. The victims of the slaughter included anyone the revolutionaries claimed might join an invading force. In reality, that was merely an excuse to get rid of those who disagreed with them. One of the most savagely treated victims was Princesse de Lamballe, the friend of Marie Antoinette who returned to France to be with the queen in her hour of need. Madame de Lamballe was stripped, raped, stabbed, her breasts cut off and the rest of her body mutilated. After she was dead, one of the assassins ripped out her heart and ate it while another stuck her head on a pike and paraded it under Marie Antoinette's window. Such was the evil of those times.

Before 1792, the émigrés were mostly of the nobility. Those who had ties to England were welcomed into London Society. After the horrors of the September Massacres, the wave of those fleeing France included clergy and refugees of the lower classes. (This is one reason why the family of Lady Mary Campbell in *Racing with the Wind* has a French pastry cook.)

With Britain's entry into the war with France in 1793, England opened her arms to the émigrés. London became an important destination for those seeking refuge. The comte de Provence spent twenty-three years in exile, some of them in England. In 1814, he returned to France to reign as Louis XVIII. The comte d'Artois, younger brother of Louis XVI, a character in *Echo in the Wind*, also spent many years in exile in England. Eventually, he returned to France to become King Charles X in 1824.

Anti-Catholic Persecution

During the Reign of Terror in 1794, the anti-Catholic persecution in France was fierce. Many nuns and priests were sent to the guillotine for refusing to repudiate their faith. In 1792, when the National Assembly called for the suppression of religious communities and the evacuation of pious houses, the Ursulines of Saint-Denis, who you will remember from *To Tame the Wind*, settled their debts and left the convent. Out of some 10,000 Ursulines living in France at the time, about 1,000 were jailed and thirty-eight guillotined.

The War in the Vendée

The War in the Vendée was, until recently, denied by the French government and not taught in French schools. Yet it was the first "total war" in modern history, in which men, women and children were involved. It was also the first modern war that saw regular troops beaten by mostly unarmed peasants. As I researched this part of the revolution, I kept thinking the Vendéens and their brothers, the Chouans, were like America's Minutemen who fought the British troops.

The Vendée was a poor rural region inhabited by peasants, impoverished aristocrats, petite bourgeoisie and poor priests. The social inequalities were less marked there than elsewhere in France. The people were loyal to their king and to the Church. Many of the priests came from Vendéen families. When both king and priests were denied them and a conscription of 300,000 demanded by Paris, they rose in rebellion.

The Vendéens fought on after their young general Henri de la Rochejaquelein was killed in January of 1794. But the revenge of the Committee of Public Safety on their defiance would be terrible. A quarter of a million royalists were slaughtered, including women and children in a campaign bordering on genocide.

Napoleon Bonaparte had great respect for the Vendéens. He called their war *"le combat des géants"*, the fight of the giants. He understood they fought for the preservation of their liberty and freedom of religion. In November 1799, when he seized power in a coup d'état, he immediately began talks with the Vendéen religious leader, the abbé Bernier, and set about repairing relations with the Church. Napoleon was no fool and realized if he was to be accepted as emperor one day, he must have the backing of the Church. By December, full rights of worship were restored, not only in the Vendée, but in the whole of France. Church bells rang once again.

The Isle of Guernsey

After Jean Donet's marriage to Lady Joanna West in *Echo in the Wind*, he built a home for them on Guernsey where, with excursions into Lorient and Saintonge, they raised his orphaned niece, *Zoé* Ariane Donet, and had a child of their own, Jean-Jacques Henri Donet, who insists on being called "Jack". Guernsey remained their home during the revolution. Donet's vineyards in Saintonge and his home in Lorient were being kept for him by others, much like his townhouse in Paris. Jack was heir to his father's title and lands, as you will see in *Rogue's Holiday*, book 5 of the Agents of the Crown series, set in England in 1820.

During the revolution, the Channel Islands, sometimes known as "the French Isles", took on a special role. Lying so close to France, they not only provided sanctuary to the fleeing French, but the islands were used by the British to monitor the movements of ships in and out of the Normandy's ports. Hence, it was not surprising that our hero Frederick West became a spy for the English while working with his brother-in-law to ferry émigrés to London. His superior in London would have been Evan Nepean, Undersecretary of the Home Office and, after 1794, Undersecretary of War. One of his chief interests during the revolution was intelligence and Philippe d'Auvergne on the Isle of Jersey was one of his contacts.

I hope you have enjoyed my story set in those perilous times. If you did, please post a review! And if you'd like to see my story in pictures, take a look at the Pinterest Storyboard for *A Fierce Wind*. www.pinterest.com/reganwalker123/a-fierce-wind-by-regan-walker-set-during-the-frenc

Author's Bio

Regan Walker is an award-winning, Amazon bestselling author of Regency, Georgian and Medieval romances. A lawyer turned full-time writer, she has six times been featured on USA TODAY's HEA blog and nominated six times for the prestigious RONE award. Her novels, *The Red Wolf's Prize* and *King's Knight* won Best Historical Novel in the Medieval category and many of her books have been finalists. *The Refuge: An Inspirational Novel of Scotland* won the Gold Medal in the Illumination Awards. *To Tame the Wind* won the International Book Award for Romance Fiction and Best Historical Romance in the San Diego Book Awards.

Years of serving clients in private practice and several stints in high levels of government have given Regan a feel for the demands of the "Crown". Hence her romance novels often involve a demanding sovereign who taps his subjects for special assignments. Each of her novels features real history and real historical figures. And, of course, adventure and love.

She lives in San Diego with her dog "Cody", a Wirehaired Pointing Griffon.

Follow Regan on Amazon and BookBub; keep in touch on Facebook, and join Regan Walker's Readers.
facebook.com/regan.walker.104
facebook.com/groups/ReganWalkersReaders

You can sign up for her newsletter on her website.
www.reganwalkerauthor.com

Keep reading for an excerpt from *To Tame the Wind*, book 1 in the Donet trilogy.

Excerpt from *To Tame the Wind* by Regan Walker

Claire stirred as the rays of the sun warmed her face, but instead of the gentle sound of the songbirds that woke her each morning, she heard raucous shrieking. *What was that noise? Was she late for Matins?* The cacophony of sound suddenly reminded her of her childhood in Lorient before she'd gone to live at the convent.

Gulls.

Eyes still closed, she frowned. *Non. It cannot be gulls.* She inhaled, deeply, cautiously, smelling fish, and the unforgettable briny smell of the sea.

She opened her eyes, and the memory of the night returned. *Mon Dieu!* Had all that really happened? She looked around the carriage, realizing she'd been left alone. Her captor had removed the blindfold and the cloth that had been stuffed in her mouth. *Dieu merci!* She swallowed and licked her dry lips, her dazed brain trying to make sense of her predicament. *Where am I?*

Realizing she was still wearing only her nightgown and wrapped in the blanket her captor had thrown over her the night before, a wave of shame rippled through her at the thought he and his men had seen her in such a state.

Not that she had been given any choice in the matter! Anger surged through her veins at the memory of her abduction. *English pirates!*

She drew the blanket more tightly around her and pushed herself into a sitting position. Through the open carriage window, she glimpsed the sun glinting off the ocean, so bright she winced. White, puffy clouds floated idly in the blue sky. A ship with sails furled was anchored just off shore. On the beach, men loaded crates into a small boat. It wasn't Lorient but it might still be France. The nearby cliffs looking out on *la Manche,* what these men would call the English Channel, told her it was.

Had she been left without a guard? Might she escape? A shout for help would only gain the attention of her kidnappers, but perhaps she could work loose the bindings on her hands and ankles and sneak away before they were aware. She reached toward the cloth around her ankles.

The door of the carriage swung open, a gown was tossed into her lap and a broad shouldered man filled the opening.

Claire's jaw went slack while her heart kicked into a gallop as if responding of its own accord to the first man to stir it from slumber.

"*Bonjour,* Mademoiselle Donet," he said in French. "Captain Simon Powell." He bowed in grand gesture. "Your humble servant with something for you to wear."

The golden one. It had been nearly two years since she had seen him, but she had never forgotten the night of the masquerade. She had never forgotten him. Though the linen shirt stretched tight across his broad chest and the leather breeches and boots he wore now were a far cry from the shimmering costume he'd worn then, his amber eyes were the same. Impossibly, he was even more handsome than in her faded memory. In the last two years, he had never been far from her thoughts, for the night she'd first seen him—and imagined a man's pleasure—was the night Claire's girlish dreams had ended forever.

And now he'd returned to France and abducted her.

He leaned into the carriage and untied her feet, then her wrists. The touch of his rough man's hands on her skin sent odd chills rippling through her. She bit her lip, shamed by her body's reaction to this stranger. Her living temptation turned away for a moment, then faced her, a cup in his outstretched hand. "'Tis only water," he said when she was reluctant to take it.

Too grateful to complain, she hastily brought the fresh water to her dry lips and drank her fill.

"I'll give you some time to dress," he said not unkindly. His eyes shifted to her blanket-covered nightclothes. "I wouldn't want my men to see you as you are."

Claire felt her cheeks burn at the thought.

"The gown is modest enough to please even your nuns," he said. "Call me if you need... ah, assistance. I will be just outside."

She fumed at his insolence, at his actions that had placed her at his mercy. Though she knew he was English and a privateer, she had no idea why he had taken her, and she would wait no longer to learn the truth of it. "Why did you bring me here? Why did you take me from the convent?"

Leaning one arm against the frame of the carriage, he regarded her intently, his eyes like chips of amber.

"You have your father to thank for that, mademoiselle. As soon as he returns what is mine you will have your freedom."

Claire blinked. "My father?" Her voice sounded to her like the pleading of a feeble schoolgirl. She would not be cowed! She lifted her chin, confident in his error. "What has he to do with this... this perfidy? Papa is a man of business and letters, a man of some wealth. He has no need to steal!"

His mouth twitched up in a grin, drawing Claire's gaze to his sensual lips, reminding her of a night when she had seen him use those lips to good effect. She scowled, angry with the rogue and with herself for finding him so attractive.

He shut the door of the carriage and peered in through the open window. "Your father, mademoiselle, is a *pirate*."

TO TAME THE WIND

Copyright © Regan Walker

Author's Books

The Agents of the Crown series:

To Tame the Wind (prequel)
Racing with the Wind
Against the Wind
Wind Raven
A Secret Scottish Christmas
Rogue's Holiday (coming soon)

The Donet Trilogy:

To Tame the Wind
Echo in the Wind
A Fierce Wind

Holiday Novellas (related to the Agents of the Crown):

The Shamrock & The Rose
The Twelfth Night Wager
The Holly & The Thistle

The Medieval Warriors series:

The Red Wolf's Prize
Rogue Knight
Rebel Warrior
King's Knight

www.ReganWalkerAuthor.com

Printed in Great Britain
by Amazon